Barry Phillips

Barry was born in Dundee in 1978. A third-generation Dundee supporter, he first visited Dens Park in 1985 and has since witnessed four relegations, two administrations and numerous false dawns. He lives in eternal hope of a return to better days.

He is the author of the cult *Real Leigh Griffiths Blog*.

The Tartan Special One is his first novel.

THE TARTAN
SPECIAL ONE

Barry Phillips

THE TARTAN SPECIAL ONE

ISBN: 978-0-9926859-0-4

Published by Teckle Books Ltd
c/o
10 Douglas Street
Dundee
DD1 5AJ

For more copies of this book, please email:
grant@tecklebooks.co.uk

Tel: 01382 523917

Designed and set by Chris Collins

Cover by The Brownlee Brothers

Printed in Great Britain by Bell & Bain Ltd, Glasgow

DISCLAIMER

The Tartan Special One is a satirical novel intended purely for entertainment purposes. Barry Phillips and Teckle Books accept no responsibility for the accuracy or otherwise of this information. The content is purely the product of the author's warped imagination and has no basis in reality.

This book is dedicated to
Poppy Hamilton

FIRST HALF

FIRST HALF

I lay gravely wounded in the cold, wet mud as battle raged on around me. My hands instinctively clamped upon the epicentre of agony but provided nothing in the way of soothing influence. My whole body convulsed in response to the blow that had befallen me and I cried out into the sky above, my eyes wide and bulging toward the blanket of dull, doom-laden clouds that responded with a lashing of hard rain. The wind howled and shrieked as moments from my short life flashed before my eyes: enthusiastically dribbling a ball round the communal back garden of our tenement from first light until dusk; my dad putting a bread knife through my ball in a fit of drunken pique, a blow so cruel the blade may as well have been plunged into my gut; the warm embrace of teammates celebrating my first goal for the school team. The memories, however, threatened to be snuffed out by a hurt so intolerable no man should be left to suffer it – few things in life are as ridiculously painful as a wet football driven hard against a cold thigh on a brutal winter's day.

"Lloyd! Get up, man! We need another goal to finish them off." The warning came from Jimmy Anderson, team captain and my best friend since the day he saw me lingering hopefully on the periphery of a 20-a-side game at the local park when I was barely old enough to tie my own boots.

I could only groan, "Jimmy, I think I'm dying."

"It's hardly fucking life-threatening, ya poofy bastard! Mon! Fucking up ye come!'"

He slipped my arm round his neck and dragged me back to my feet. My head lolled as I mumbled in protest, the pain refusing to subside. I felt sure I would never walk again.

"Walk it off, you'll be fine in a minute. The scouts winnae be impressed seeing you acting like a drama queen, will they?"

That got my attention, and I stiffened accordingly. The Midlothian Amateurs League was hardly the greatest place to showcase your talents but, every now and then, rumours would fly around that professional clubs had scouts out looking for young players with the potential to make the step up. At 17, and with more goals to my name than any player in the league this season or last, I was considered a prospect.

No longer feeling the pain of the near-fatal blow I'd been levelled with moments before, I burst into life as the ball was hoofed speculatively in my general direction. I brought it under control with one touch and pushed it into space, striding past my marker and gaining pace as I homed in on goal. The opposition goalkeeper looked startled at this sudden attacking development and I'd sent the ball looping over him and into the net before he'd been able to nip his cigarette out on the post.

I peeled away laughing, threw myself headlong into the mud and rolled over with arms spread wide in anticipation of my cheering teammates' arrival. Smiling brightly in the face of the undulating mass of grey above me I took a preparatory breath so that I could answer the delirious cries of joy fast approaching.

The call never made it past my lips. Air hissed out of me like a balloon freed from the grip of a breathless and frustrated parent preparing for their child's birthday party.

There was a figure hovering some way above me. My mind jammed as it tried to process this impossible vision. A man hung in the air as if held by strings dangling from the heavens. He was looking right at me. Before I could react my teammates blanketed me in a mass of cheering testosterone. I squirmed beneath them, struggling to breathe and desperate to regain my upward view. One by one they dragged themselves off, the last man hauling me up with him. I broke free of his grip and stood gawking at the sky, my eyes darting round sharply as they tried to trace the path of the now vanished flying figure. I saw nothing but clouds.

As I trudged back to our half of the field, thoughts like "trick of the light" and "minor concussion" beat a sensible path to my mind. But I saw it. I saw him. There was a man up there. A flying man had been watching the game from above.

* * *

What do you want to be when you grow up? It's a question asked every day of those still blessed with idealism untarnished by the grim reality of adulthood. The beliefs of the young are unshakable. Nothing is impossible, and the future holds whatever you dare to dream.

I had wanted to be a professional footballer, specifically one who played for Manchester United, since I'd watched them make the most dramatic and glorious of comebacks against Bayern Munich in the 1999 Champions League Final. Teddy Sheringham's equaliser, Ole Gunnar Solskjaer's winner, Peter Schmeichel's cartwheels, the ecstatic red mass of bouncing, cheering joy in the stands – images seared into my mind that left me in no doubt as to what I wanted to do with my life.

Scottish football had never been of particular interest to me, lacking as it did the excitement, breathtaking skill and big-name glamour of the English matches I watched avidly on television. I wasn't alone – it was far more common to see Scottish kids wearing Chelsea or Arsenal tops than ones belonging to local sides.

My ambition to carve out a career in the game was met with, at best, total apathy, and sneering ridicule at worst. The family business was long-term unemployment. The closest dad came to work was studying the form in the Racing Post, and mum had long since been worn down by a life on the breadline as viewed through a fog of prescription painkillers. Despite the absolute lack of encouragement from those who brought me into the world, my goals remained resolute.

"I'm impressed, Lloyd. You set your sights high – I like that in a man. So many of your generation fail to seek achievement beyond seeing how falling-down-drunk they can get on a weekend and collecting STDs."

Dundee Football Club Chief Executive Bob McCracken cut an impressive figure – the suit that looked fitted rather than borrowed, the tan that suggested he regularly enjoyed expensive holidays, and the general demeanour of a man who had attended a school where rugby was the predominant sporting concern. He spoke with the type of calm assurance only possessed by those of high social standing. Anyone who saw us conversing in the bar of the local hotel he'd chosen as a venue would think I was mixing in political circles. Or perhaps on work experience with a successful used-car salesman.

"The Glazers are businessmen I greatly admire, Lloyd," he said, as if reading my mind. "They bought and own one of the wealthiest football clubs in the world, a true global brand worth not just millions but billions of pounds. In a field that has long since stopped being a sport and is now a business, Manchester United are world leaders."

I nodded in vague agreement and shifted in my seat, uneasy in company I most definitely wasn't used to keeping and very much aware of the inquisitive eyes that looked our way from around the room.

"They've always been my favourites, sir."

He waved a hand dismissively. "No need for formalities, Lloyd. Call me Mr McCracken."

Swirling the hotel's second most expensive brandy skilfully round his glass, Mr McCracken got down to the business he was quite obviously good at.

"Dundee Football Club is going places, Lloyd. It was on the brink of financial disaster a few short months ago, a club teetering on the brink of doom until I swooped in and pulled it to safety." He turned to look wistfully into the middle distance and seemed to be speaking to himself more than me when he continued, "Many would no doubt call me a hero."

Dundee's troubles had been well documented in the recent past, but as the words "financial meltdown" had become as commonplace in the sports pages as a photo of a disgruntled Neil Lennon, I'd paid no real attention to the specifics of the situation and turned over in search of news of the Red Devils.

"So, eh, how come Dundee got themselves in a bit of bother then, Mr McCracken?"

A look of mild embarrassment briefly perforated the all-business exterior before he regained his composure. "The club was landed with an unexpected electricity bill. It sounds ridiculous, I know, but when you've had the stadium's floodlights surreptitiously wired up to the mains supply of your rival club down the street for a number of years, the bill that comes as a result of them finally catching on tends to be astronomical."

I tried to hide a snigger behind a swig of the orange squash I'd been sipping throughout the meeting. Mr McCracken decided to ignore it before resuming the patter that flowed as easily as water from a burst pipe.

"It's the kind of scenario I aim to resign to the past, Lloyd. Dundee FC, and indeed Scottish football, has long suffered at the hands of the 'old school' knuckle-draggers who see the game through rose-tinted spectacles, woodbine smoke and L.S. Lowry paintings. At the moment, Scotland just doesn't have enough bandwidth, but we – and by that I mean the new generation of dynamic, forward-thinking soccer entrepreneurs ready to unleash the game's commercial potential by securing new revenue streams and demographics – have been taking ideas showers together for some time. And do you know what Lloyd?"

Confused, I shook my head.

"Nothing short of a holistic, cradle-to-grave revolution is taking place in the game and I am at the vanguard." Mr McCracken paused to take a sip of his drink, raising one eyebrow at me, and gently pulled at the lapel of his suit before continuing, "I noticed you admiring my sartorial judgement, Lloyd. Would you care to guess where I bought the threads?"

"Errm... Savile Row?"

"No, Lloyd," he laughed. "I am a rich man, not a profligate one. No, this suit came from Burtons. Do you know how a High Street retailer can produce such high-quality tailoring at affordable prices?"

I confessed that I did not.

"Outsourcing. Siphoning off expensive, labour-intensive parts of the business for poor brown people to take care of at a fraction of the cost. Football is the next industry to be revolutionised by outsourcing."

I was at a loss to understand the relevance of this, but Mr McCracken seemed happy so I let him go on.

"Guys like you and I, Lloyd, are the type who will make the changes happen. I want to take Dundee beyond their status as a small-town provincial club and, in the process of doing so, perhaps you can take a step toward realising your dreams. It's a big leap from Dens Park to Old Trafford, but one that an ambitious and talented young man like you is capable of taking."

With that he delved into his leather attaché and invited me to sign on the dotted line for Dundee FC. I gave it only the most cursory of glances before putting pen to paper. We shook hands. The deal was done, and I was making inroads on my journey to the Theatre of Dreams.

As we left the hotel, a point of curiosity sprang to mind.

"Mr McCracken, I was wondering…how come I haven't met the club's manager so far? I kind of expected him to play a part in negotiations. At least, that's the impression I got from Sir Alex's memoirs."

"Jocky is…" he hesitated before regaining his composure, "very well thought of by players and fans alike. He gets results, although he is rather… *eccentric* in his methods, shall we say?"

Mr McCracken noted the look of concern on my face, and smiled as he patted me on the back.

"He is very much looking forward to your arrival though, Lloyd. I don't like to bother him about matters like this. He's a football man, not a business man."

We shook hands and McCracken made off for the kind of motor I'd only ever seen on Top Gear. After a few steps he spun round smiling.

"I almost forgot," he popped the attaché open, fished inside and pulled out a top-of-the-range, brand-spanking-new smartphone, "a welcoming gift to mark your signing for the club."

It was a fantastic piece of kit and I beamed at it.

"On the house, Lloyd. The club will take care of the bill. You can phone, text and access the World Wide Web as much as you like. A little present from your pal Bob McCracken."

"Thanks very much, Mr McCracken. That's dead nice of you, I'm well chuffed with that."

He gave me a wink that was marginally the right side of lecherous and made off again. As I stood transfixed by my new toy he turned and called back, "Oh, and Lloyd, one more thing – Jocky called me just before I got here to say he's found you accommodation. I don't know the full details yet but don't worry about it. I'll sort everything out in time."

I was so engrossed with the wonders of my phone that the last comment barely registered. By the time I looked up, he'd pulled out the car park and was disappearing into the distance.

* * *

A few days later, as I dodged a succession of inexpertly hit, dimpled projectiles while desperately trying to get a signal on my smartphone, I wondered if my dreams were more distant than ever. I wandered round the municipal golf course of Caird Park ducking whenever there was a cry of "fucking 'fore!" ya wee cunt!" as I sought confirmation that my "eccentric" manager did indeed plan to house me in a Native American tipi. A wigwam. Just off the 13th green. Jimmy Anderson had accompanied me to the train station and warned me that he'd heard Jocky was "a fucking mental case" and to "best be ready for anything, pal". At the time I'd been too busy trying not to let the lump in my throat get the better of me. The old man was too busy screaming at the telly as a three-legged Shetland pony cost him that week's dole money to notice I was leaving, while mum told me to have a good day at school. Jimmy's was the only warm farewell I received.

When I finally got through to Dens Park I was connected not to a helpful member of the club's staff, but a recorded message that offered a bizarre set of automated response options.

"Tae find oot wha's in cherge, press one; if yer a Jambo still seeking closure on the whole Albert Kidd in '86 thing, press twa; if it's some cunt fae the 'leccy company, wisnae me, aye."

By the time I'd stared at my phone in bewilderment long enough to decide I'd go with first option in the hope it might at least get me talking to someone who dealt with player accommodation, the line had gone dead.

"Alright Hiawatha?"

Two old guys in well-worn golf gear approached, pointing and laughing as they dragged their carts behind them. Much to the amusement of his companion, one of them started performing a loose interpretation of a rain dance, chanting, "Hey-how-are-ya, hey-how-are-ya, hey-how-are-ya," as he stooped and rose in a slow, deliberate rotation.

Already I wasn't particularly fond of the locals. The taxi driver who had picked me up at the station, bearing a small nameplate with the words "Lloyd George," had made me feel about as welcome as a Yorkshire policeman at a Hillsborough memorial fundraiser. He was well set in the same way an old stone wall is and was shaven of head. A neck as thick as my thigh was stamped with an unprofessionally administered tattoo declaring, 'FLEET RULE'.

Though intimidated I tried to make conversation from the back of his cab, asking if he was having a good day thus far. He blanked me, choosing instead to turn the volume up on the punk rock racket that screamed about it being "time for living" coming out of his stereo. Coldplay are my favourite band, but it didn't seem the appropriate time to ask for a bit of *Viva la Vida*.

With conversation clearly off the agenda, I gazed out of the window with interest at the new world around me. The busy city centre was full of handsome students, trendy artists and well-heeled office workers. As we proceeded up a hill so steep that climbing equipment would surely be required to make the ascent on foot, the population changed considerably. The elder members of this new group were dressed in drab clothing, their bodies withered and faces hardened by a lifetime of struggle. The equally tough-looking youngsters were clad in outfits more colourful and polyester, though probably not produced by the fashion houses the labels made claim to. Many were quite obviously under the influence of drink and the kind of drugs that blotted out life rather than enhanced it. One odd yet positive note was that the babysitting industry appeared to be booming here – never had I seen so many young girls pushing prams.

"Welcome to the Hulltoon, wee man." The driver spoke – growled – for the first time. Surprised by the sudden break in silence, my words stumbled out my mouth as I tried to win favour with the man.

"Oh, um, cheers mate. Is this, eh, where the Fleet rule the roost is it?"

My seatbelt's capability as a safety device was tested to the full as the vehicle screeched to a halt. The driver's head turned slowly to reveal a face so disgusted, so irate, it was as if I had just suggested a small naval cap might compliment the artwork on his neck beautifully. I cowered back in my seat, the sound of horns honked by angry motorists to our rear masking the slight whimper that escaped my throat.

"Are you fucking daft, ya wee cunt?"

I started nodding my head like the novelty toy dog guarding the rear window of the taxi, decided it was the wrong gesture and instantly switched to a shake that might have seen my head come loose from my neck had I kept it up for any length of time. His eyes bore holes in me as he sternly advised, "The Huns are fae the Hulltoon, the Fleet are fae Lochee. The only thing the Huns rule are the fuckin' bins. Lochee rule ya cunt."

I nodded meekly and wordlessly as he turned to look straight ahead again, engaged the cab in gear and angrily delivered me to my destination at breakneck speed. All this and I didn't even have any change to give the guy a tip when we arrived.

I was directed to the tipi by the amused staff at the starter's box and, after inspecting the surroundings, deduced that I must be the victim of an elaborate practical joke. I approached the only other person in the vicinity who didn't appear to be a golfer, a greasy, middle-aged man loitering by the nearby woodland, to ask whether he knew of any higher authority to put me right.

"Eh've nae idea," he replied looking puzzled. "Eh'm just here for the dogging." I looked down to see that an erection was indeed bulging through his tracksuit bottoms and sprinted in the direction of the tipi, deciding it wasn't the worst place in the world to be after all. I pushed through the thick hessian fabric and stepped inside to be greeted by a half-naked old man. I let out a terrified yelp, arms flapping as I jumped back toward safety. Just as I was about to run outside again and provide the golfers with further entertainment, the realisation that it wasn't really a man held me in place. I folded over to catch my breath, slumping down until I was anchored by hands gripping on to trembling thighs. I let my racing heart recover from the sprint it had been thrust into unawares.

It was not a semi-naked man that had greeted me. It was a life-sized cardboard cut-out of a semi-naked man. The man in question was Jocky.

* * *

I stared at him with unbelieving eyes, my mind jammed by the unblinking cardboard gaze of my new manager. I hadn't met the man yet but, as he was a fairly well known figure, even a non-Scottish aficionado like me recognised him easily enough. Looking a lot like Tom Selleck had Selleck been subjected to a brutal paper round, a nagging wife he never really liked in the first place and a posse of kids born of a need for an increase in benefit money rather than the love between two caring adults, he was one of those characters who had been around Scottish football forever. He was part of the furniture, a fixture of the game in one way, shape or form from time immemorial. I'd never seen him topless though; the cardboard cut-out was clad only in tracksuit bottoms. He was smiling brightly, and from his mouth a paper speech bubble declared, "Hiya Lloyd! Hiya pal!" As soon as I'd finished reading it the bubble somehow fell away on cue to reveal another beneath it. It asked, "WHA'S IN CHERGE HERE?" I must have stood gawking at it for a full five minutes before my basic motor functions started to make themselves available again.

I tentatively picked the cardboard up and moved it to one side. Almost reluctant to break the stare in case I missed a cardboard blink, I slowly looked away and took in the rest of my surroundings.

Without having the first clue how an authentic wigwam was approached in terms of interior decoration, I was none too impressed by the furnishings. There was an inflatable bed with a sleeping bag unrolled over it, a fridge connected to a small, petrol-driven generator outside, a two-bar fire unlikely to be sufficient in the circumstances, an old trunk I assumed would substitute for a wardrobe, and an empty bucket positioned in front of a carefully-stacked pyramid of toilet roll. A red, white and blue Dundee flag adorned the inner wall to my left side. Hanging on the wall to the right, and disturbing me more than I can articulate, was a poster of the crucifixion scene. Jocky's head was superimposed on Jesus, and mine on one of the weeping mourners kneeling by his cross. A soul-rattling shiver ran down my spine.

I switched the fire on and checked the fridge. It was filled to the brim with cans of Tartan Special. I wasn't a drinker. Having spent my formative years watching dad sink Kalashnikov Vodka and the cheapest, strongest lager money could buy, I'd made a point of avoiding the stuff. By the time my peers were whole-heartedly getting smashed in the park from the age of 12, I was smart enough to realise that downing cider best handled through protective gloves lest a spillage burn through several layers of skin was not the way forward for an aspiring sportsman.

As the fridge door swung shut my phone vibrated. The display screen lit up to announce Bob McCracken was the caller.

"Hi Mr McCracken. How's it going?"

"Lloyd my boy, I'm well thank you. I trust you've arrived safely and without incident." It was good to hear a friendly voice come down the line and he probably knew about the Fleet and the Huns already, so I decided not to bother him with all the details. "Yeah, that's me in the... house? I think it's called a tipi."

"I can only apologise for this tipi situation, Lloyd. This bizarre player accommodation ritual is an eccentricity of Jocky's that I'm attempting to put a stop to. But fear not, Lloyd. Your situation will be temporary, I promise you that. A signing I made a few weeks back had a similar issue. Jocky attempted to house poor Fong Du in the craw's nest of the RSS Discovery. I managed to intervene on that occasion; we couldn't possibly have a marquee signing, an internationalist and hero of his home nation living in a bloody barrel 50ft above deck of a tourist attraction."

I'd read about South Korean striker Fong Du's signing on the back pages. Though largely unknown in this part of the world, he apparently enjoyed a Beckham-esque status in his homeland. The press considered it an odd signing for a club like Dundee.

"Give me some time and I'll get a more appropriate homestead sorted, Lloyd. Hold tight until then, young man. Bob McCracken will see you right."

Catching the eye of the cardboard cut-out again, something occurred to me and I ventured a question.

"Here, Mr McCracken – what's the manager's surname? I just realised I don't know it. He's Jocky... what?"

The answer was unexpected. "I honestly have no idea, Lloyd. I've asked the same question of quite a few people and I've only ever been met with a shrug of the shoulders. I asked the man himself once and he told me he lost it whilst gambling on a dominoes match. He wandered off making allegations about stolen Tippex before I could enquire further."

It took me a good while to doze off that night. While my

body was exhausted, my mind was working overtime to process fear-laced thoughts of Jocky. After a staring match with my cardboard roommate that lasted several hours I decided enough was enough and turned him round to face the wall of the tipi. With his penetrating, unnerving gaze off me I fell into merciful sleep.

* * *

It wasn't the best night's kip I'd ever had. I was cold, restless and perturbed by strange dreams I couldn't quite remember. My eyes were only half open when they fell upon a sight that nearly launched me through the thick hessian wall behind me.

Cardboard Jocky had been moved from where I'd left him the previous night. He was facing me once again, this time from the bottom of the bed. The speech bubble that had previously offered words of greeting now read, "Rise and fuckin' shine, cunto."

He'd been here in the night. It could have been anyone working on his behalf but, instinctively, I knew it had been the man himself. Once again I found myself locked in a staring contest with a cardboard cut-out.

As a thin motorised buzz cut harshly through the dawn chorus, the speech bubble peeled off to reveal another underneath.

"Breakfast is fuckin' served."

The buzzing drew closer. It sounded like a hairdryer or a remote control plane, and yet... and yet it gave me a distinct sense that danger was approaching.

It came up directly behind the tipi and passed round it. Part of me wanted to rush out and see what on Earth it was, but another, less foolhardy, part told me I did not want to know. I pulled my knees up to my chest for protection as I watched the door flap, expecting it to burst open at any second. Although it lingered right by the entrance, whoever or whatever it was didn't come in. After a few seconds it moved off again, passing down the tipi's flank and disappearing the way it came. I was shaking, unable to work out why the experience had made me so nervous.

I finally mustered up the courage to tentatively peer out of the slightest gap in the flap. Nothing immediately molested me so I stepped out, kicking something as I went. A plastic carrier bag lay at my feet. As I reached down to inspect it, the smell wafting up let me know that breakfast had indeed been served in the form of two bacon rolls and a pint of milk.

My stomach rumbled in appreciation as I hooked my fingers into the handles of the bag. I took a few steps to gain a view beyond the tipi in the direction from where the buzz had come and gone. There was nothing to be seen. I looked around nervously, assuming Jocky or one of his cohorts to be hiding in a nearby copse of trees, trying not to burst into laughter at the fear and confusion his antics had left etched on my face. With no one to be seen I stepped back inside with as much nonchalance as I could manage.

I was just polishing off bacon roll number two when my phone vibrated. The number was unrecognised. I swallowed the food in my mouth a couple of chews too quickly and choked a little as it went down, which didn't make for the best welcome to my caller. I eventually managed to squeeze out a "Hello?"

Silence.

"He-llo?"

A cat meowed, and a male voice chastised it.

"Get the fuck aff the other line, wee aine! Fuckin' telt ye aboot trehin' tae phone they porno hotlines. They're no' advertisin' that kind o' pussy!"

The cat meowed again and I heard a click. The male voice muttered something about his phone bill before blaring out, "HIYA LLOYD! HIYA PAL!"

I pulled my phone away to arm's length and stared at it. It was him. My eyes were drawn upward to the cardboard cut-out of Jocky smiling down at me. The second speech bubble peeled away to reveal another below that read, "Ken aye." I put the phone back to my ear.

"Braw bacon rolls, eh Lloyd? That pig wiz hand-reared beh former St Johnstone supremo Geoff Broon himself. Boy's a fermer! The pig wiz meant tae tak' the helm at McDiarmid until it lost the plot in the 208 and hud tae be put doon. Fuckin' shame, like. Auld Geoff wiz pure devastated."

What in the name of Christ was he on about?

"Trainin' at Dens in one hour, cunto. Be there or be square. Beh square eh mean a bloody heap lyin' half-deid on Sandeman Street."

And with that he hung up. I got changed and ready to depart as quickly as possible. After a brief eyeballing session with the grinning cardboard representation of my new manager, I made haste for Dens Park and my first training session with Dundee.

* * *

A football team's dressing room is the inner sanctum in which players and coaching staff plan and prepare for the glory, a place of harsh words and hairdryer treatments. It's an environment where testosterone hangs as heavily in the air as the pungent deep heat rub used to soothe the aches and pains of both victory and defeat. It was all that and more at Dens Park.

I had arrived at the ground almost an hour ago and was immediately shocked by its proximity to that of Tannadice Park, home of the club's local rivals Dundee United. The two stadiums were only the length of a Schmeichel throw apart, although Dens was considerably more run-down looking, as was possibly to be expected given the relative levels of success the two clubs had enjoyed over the past few decades.

While the main entrance of Tannadice was a scene of great activity with numerous comings and goings, Dens appeared to be completely deserted. A sign on the locked main door informed me that the stadium was managed by McCracken Outsourcing Ltd and to call for service. I punched the numbers into the touchscreen and, after a lengthy wait, found myself speaking to a very nice Bangladeshi called Allan who told me that day-to-day operations were no longer managed from Dens but he would send someone out to unlock the door as soon as possible. Eventually

I made my way round the wooden-panelled corridors of the old ground and found myself facing a door that read "Hame Team".

As I popped my head round the home dressing room door for the first time, the reek of smoke, sex and booze hit me like Roy Keane extracting revenge on Alfe Inge Haaland. I swayed back on my heels, my eyes blinking hard to fight the sting in the thick air pouring out from the ajar door, before taking a deep breath and forcing myself all the way in the room at the second time of asking.

When I finally managed to waft the smoke away I laid eyes on a scene that was somewhere between a late-night, back-room drinking den and an episode of the Twilight Zone. What appeared to be some kind of Yeti was being shaved by three men dressed in traditional barber outfits. An old man lay bathing in a standalone bath filled with what looked and smelled like linseed oil. There were half-naked men clutching cans of Tartan Special as they whooped and cheered an aging buxom blonde who was cavorted in the middle of the room peeling off the remainder of what little clothes she had on. A sexual accomplice was across the room, completely naked and caught in the throes of passion as she bucked wildly on the lap of an excitable player whose drink spilled everywhere. Several players were capturing the moment for posterity on their mobile phones, and another was sucking hard on a homemade water pipe that produced an aroma unlike any tobacco I'd ever smelled before. All this to a loud hip hop soundtrack on which the rapper questioned, "So what 'cha, what 'cha, what 'cha want?" What did I want? I had absolutely no idea anymore. It appeared that I'd signed for Sodom & Gomorrah FC.

My presence was finally noted and I was greeted first by the team of barbers and the Abominable Footballer.

"Hello..."

"Hello!"

"HELLO!"

"HELLO!"

The final greeting was from the creature the other three were tending to, and as he stepped toward me with his paw outstretched I realised it was no mythical beast but an extremely hairy man.

"Alright Lloyd, how's it going? Welcome to Dens. I'm Harry Larkins."

As his team of barbers continued their clipper work, the Dundee team captain became more recognisable. Or at least more homosapien-like. When I'd used my new phone to do a little online research in advance of my arrival, I noted that Larkins had that rugged, unshaven, looks-nothing-like-an-athlete thing a lot of Scottish players had going on. I had no idea he was so hirsuit as to require three trained professionals to shave him from head to toe prior to training, though.

As the strippers gathered up their clothes and scuttled off with high heels clicking, the rest of the team stood to greet me as I moved round the room shaking hands. Davie "Davo" Milne was the illegal smoker in the room and greeted me through a fog of bong smoke with a fist-bump and a lazy, stoner smile. Eddie McGlone was quick to offer me discounted prices on three packets of bacon he'd procured from Lidl earlier in the morning. While most seemed friendly enough, one man was completely disinterested in my arrival, and let my hand hang alone in the air for a few seconds before I awkwardly lowered it to my side again; South Korean striker Fong Du. He was too busy babbling away on his phone at breakneck speed in his native tongue to pay the slightest bit of attention to me. The young boy who sat attentively by his side wearing nothing but a thong beamed at me, however, and introduced himself as Dong Chu.

"C'mere, young man."

I turned to find the old man in the bath of linseed oil summoning me with a goalie-gloved finger. I hadn't recognised him at first, but at close quarters I realised it was former Celtic and Scotland goalkeeper Doug Roberts. I'd seen him on the TV quite a few times over the years, mainly old black-and-white footage, but I had presumed him long retired. The wrinkles across his forehead were deep and plentiful, and his skin was covered by liver spots and Indian ink tattoos that had long since faded beyond recognition. His voice was so thin and choked I wasn't sure he'd still be alive by the time I took the couple of paces across the room to take the hand he was offering me.

"When I was a lad this was all fields! You boys dinnae ken you're born."

And with that he fell asleep. The floatation device that doubled as a pillow prevented him from slipping under the linseed.

A large flat screen TV positioned on the dressing room wall burst into a crackle of static. The babble of noise bouncing around the room was immediately hushed as the players fell silent, took a seat on their respective sections of bench and looked up to the screen in anticipation. Unaware of what was going on, but left in no doubt something was about to happen, I followed suit. The black screen turned to light and was filled with the face of Dundee FC's manager, Jocky.

"Mornin' a'body."

As one the entire room replied, "Morning gaffer." Having missed my cue I found myself muttering it meekly as a late, lone voice. Jocky's big, dark eyes fell on me and I felt my cheeks redden and my balls shrink back up into my stomach. He held his gaze for a deeply uncomfortable moment before looking away and continuing.

"Right lads, bit o' shopliftin' up Tesco on the Kingsway the day. Ye ken the drill: in, oot, shake it a' aboot. Nane o' that Hokey-Cokey shite though, that's for fuckin' bairns, aye."

It wasn't just his thick Dundonian accent that made what he was saying unintelligible to me.

"Doug Roberts! A'right, auld aine? Eh want three punds o' corned beef aff you the day. The good stuff, no' the shite that's crushed up cat nipples and stoor."

Doug's head tipped back as a mighty snore was offered as a response.

"Eddie McGlone! Hiya pal! Three big bags o' tatties, cunto. Maris Pipers tae, nane o' they King Edward pricks. Send they cunts homeward tae think again, aye. You ken the score, pal."

The gaffer went round the room running through what was sounding increasingly like his weekly shopping list. His diet was fairly basic, consisting of little but "ingins" and "broon sauce" as well as the aforementioned meat and potatoes. Three guys had each to pick up a case of Tartan Special. I wondered if any would end up in the tipi fridge after a secret visit in the dead of night, and shuddered.

"Fong fuckin' Du." He ran the palm of his hand over his face, shaking his head slightly, before turning his attention to his compatriot. "Hiya Dong Chu! Hiya pal! Tell that dipped-in-cheese-cunt tae check oot thon machine that cashes yer copper collection in for proper money. The machine never accepts a' the coins 'cause some are a wee bitty fucked, and maist cunts just leave the shite aines in the tray. Big Fong the Mong might find enough for a 10p mixture or somethin'. It'll keep the daft prick oot o' trouble while the lads get put through their paces."

Dong Chu started relaying the message. The two jabbered away in their native tongue, with Fong gesticulating toward the screen and getting rather wound up as Dong tried to calmly interpret the instructions. The gaffer looked on with an ear cocked toward the camera, baffled as he tried to make sense of a language he clearly didn't understand a word of. He let it go on for a few more seconds before ordering Dong to "get him telt" and waved a hand to signal he'd had enough of them.

He turned and laid those wild black eyes on me. A sheen of sweat glazed my forehead.

"Hiya Lloyd! Hiya pal! Check you, ya new cunt. Has a'body met Lloyd? Boy lives in a fuckin' tipi! Unusual choice for a hoose but each to their own."

I started mumbling nervously about there potentially being some kind of misunderstanding regarding my accommodation, but he cut me off and continued, "Lloyd, ya Hiawatha-didnae-bather-too-much cunt, ken what eh want you tae get?"

He waited for an answer, so I stuttered, "Um... eh... more Tartan Special?"

He gave it a considered shrug and spoke quietly to himself

a moment. "Gie the boy his due, it's a no' bad answer," before bursting back into life. "Fuck up ya cunt! Big Jock's got plenty fuckin' Special!" He calmed down again almost instantly, and with a measured tone told me, "Lloyd, ken the wummin wha works behind the deli counter? The wee aines wi' the teckle hats wha ken their coleslaw fae their corn doag? Get me aine o' them. Pity yer stealing her, she's probably worth hunners o' Clubcard points."

I sat in stunned silence with my mouth hanging wide open. A few snorts of laughter and disguise-coughs came from the rest of the lads. The gaffer was already on to the next man.

"Right, Kev Rafferty, mind eh asked ye tae get bog roll last time? Mind that, pal?" He started talking to someone behind the camera that was filming him from his end, "Back up a bit, wee aine. That's the gemme," before readdressing Kevin, "eh meant FUCKIN' TWO-PLY, YA CUNT!"

The camera panned back, moving away from the full-face shot that had filled the screen up until that point. The gaffer was sitting on the toilet, topless, with the same tracksuit bottoms he wore in the cardboard cut out from my tipi wrapped round his ankles.

"Big Jock cannae wipe his dunger wi' this, ya cunt! Meh fuckin' finger went right through the paper and up ma hole for fuck sake!" He held his chin in his hand and mused, "And while that wisnae entirely unpleasant, IT WID NEVER HAVE HAPPENED WI' TWO-PLY FUCKIN' BOG ROLL! YOU'LL NEVER PULL ON A DARK BLUE JERSEY AGAIN YA DIN-GHY-BOG-ROLL-BUYING CUNT!"

The screen turned itself off again. The transmission was over. Training was about to begin.

* * *

Another hour into my career as a professional footballer and I was sitting in a cell at Bell Street police headquarters. I'd been arrested and charged with assault, attempted kidnapping and breach of the peace. I'd been in town for little more than a day and could scarcely believe how badly wrong things were going.

The "training" exercise had been an abject disaster for me, which was pretty much to be expected given the jaw-dropping impossibility of the task.

My teammates applied themselves with studied professionalism, stuffing their ill-gotten gains into concealed areas of their training kit and executing well-practised and rather cunning diversionary tactics that allowed them to make good their escape. I, on the other hand, stood staring vacantly at Ethel, the delicatessen attendant whose customers were guaranteed a cheery smile and pleasant word. Inspired by signage in the bakery aisle promising big prizes for competition winners, I steeled myself and hoped somehow to smooth-talk the woman into going along with the morally questionable plan I had hatched.

Unfortunately, the wiliest of foxes would be hard-pushed to outwit a working class Dundonian grandmother and Ethel looked at me with deep distrust from the start. Adopting my best game show host impression, I made the faux-gleeful announcement that she'd won an all-expenses-paid day out to Dens Park. In the face of her suspicion, my forced smile faltered and Ethel began looking round for a supervisor who would deal with the possibly demented boy holding up the increasingly impatient queue forming behind him. Then, when it became apparent I was failing in my task and the presumably terrifying wrath of Jocky would have to be faced, I lost the plot entirely.

In a move born of pure desperation, I leapt over the counter and threw Ethel over my shoulder in an attempt to spirit her out the store forcibly. I made it as far as the frozen peas before a store detective came to her aid and unceremoniously wrestled me to the ground where I offered no resistance as we waited for the police to arrive.

As I sat in the cold 8 x 12ft cell contemplating an extended period behind bars, realising I was in no way mentally or physically tough enough to cope with a jail sentence, my guardian angel swooped low to save me.

The cell door swung open and a stern-looking police officer announced, "You're free to go, Mr George." My heart nearly leapt out my chest, and I sprung to my feet and waited for a second to confirm he wasn't kidding. The officer offered an impatient shrug that jumpstarted me into life and out of the cell before he changed his mind.

I was led out to the main reception area, where I found Bob McCracken and a senior-looking police officer chatting amiably. Mr McCracken broke off conversation when he saw me, smiling sympathetically.

"Apologies for taking so long to get here, Lloyd. I came as soon as I heard."

He was the last person who needed to apologise. Grateful didn't come close to how I was feeling at that moment.

"Mr McCracken holds considerable influence around these parts, Mr George," explained the senior officer. "He is a keen supporter of the local force's charity foundation. Had it not been for his insistence that this was a regrettable one-off incident I'd have thrown the book at you."

Mr McCracken gave me a sly wink.

"I... I don't know what to say. I'm really sorry, officer. I don't know what came over me. It definitely won't happen again. Sorry."

We departed the station, my head hung low and Mr McCracken's arm draped over my shoulder. I went to speak, to apologise as best as I possibly could, but he cut me short.

"No need to apologise or thank me, Lloyd. When times of trouble arrive old Bob McCracken is here to help."

I smiled weakly.

"As you will now be all too aware, you won't find any of Jocky's methods in any training manual. I don't think Sir Alex has the Manchester United lads running round the local Waitrose shoplifting, do you?"

I snorted out a laugh, wiping away the mess it made with the sleeve of my training top. Mr McCracken patted me on the back.

We got in his car, which he skilfully reversed out its parking space and out of the car park. Beethoven's Fifth accompanied the purr of the vehicle's high-powered engine.

The driver shook his head and picked up the thread of conversation once again, "Lloyd. I don't blame you for what happened today; I know it was entirely Jocky's doing. The man's mind has, in my opinion, come loose from its moorings. Quite how he's managed to put the team in a position to challenge for the league title is beyond me." He paused as if to weigh up the words that would follow. "This is a dilemma for me, Lloyd. Despite the fact he does get results, he's not the kind of man I want at the helm. His media profile is entirely at odds with the core values of the brand. But the future is yet to pass. I'd hate for you to think you'll always have to suffer as you did today. Only when the likes of Jocky are put out to pasture can us visionaries take the game forward in this country. Bandwidth, Lloyd, bandwidth."

I turned to meet his gaze and found another wink waiting for me. He let his words hang in the air for some time, allowing me to mull them over and saying nothing more than farewell as we pulled up outside the ground. I thanked him once again for his assistance and watched as he sped off into the distance.

There were no signs of life when I entered Dens Park following a brief, cursory chat with Allan and the inevitable wait for a security guard to come and unlock the door. The dressing room looked as if it had hosted an all-night party in hell. Every surface was strewn with empty and crushed cans of Tartan Special. Cigarette butts littered the floor and a discarded shocking-pink thong acted as a centrepiece for what could pass as a Tate Modern installation by Tracey Emin called "Boorish". I was relieved that no one, particularly Jocky, was around to welcome my inglorious return.

Stripping off and tip-toeing around the debris on the floor, I entered the shower room adjacent to the main dressing room hoping to wash my troubles away. Within seconds the fog of steam was so thick I could barely see in front of me.

As I leaned against the cool tiled wall and let the hot water run over me, I heard the dressing room door creak open. I stood up straight, wiped water from my eyes and heard a familiar sound from the room next door – the whirring engine that had delivered breakfast that morning.

The fear it induced was much stronger this time around, naked, vulnerable and without the sanctuary of the tipi as I was. I found myself sliding along the wall into the corner, focusing on not breathing or making the slightest noise that might alert whatever it was to my presence.

Mercifully it left almost as soon as it had arrived. The buzzing seemed to sweep slowly across the room, turn, then head back the way it came. When the water pouring from the showerhead and gurgling down the drain were once more the only sounds to be heard I let out a long, slow sigh of relief.

I turned the shower off and tentatively made my way out. With the steam still hanging in the air I moved with caution, but it evaporated into a fine mist within a few feet of me entering the empty dressing room. There were no signs that anyone or anything had been there.

And then, just as I was once more questioning my sanity, I spotted something that left me frozen to the spot.

A "Get Out of Jail Free" card had been left perched on my training kit. I picked it up and looked at it for a while, and became very aware of the sound of my heartbeat thumping up in my temples. When I flipped the card over I saw that the message, "HIYA LLOYD! HIYA PAL!" had been scrawled in black marker.

I tugged my clothes on with lightning speed, almost tripping over my own feet as I stumbled out of the door into the corridor and then into the street, dodging pile after pile of dog shit as I began the trek "home". My first day of training was over.

* * *

There isn't much in the way of entertainment to be found in a tipi situated just off the 13th green at Caird Park. Had I been a golfer it would have been a dream location, but my knowledge and experience of the game centred around how well I handled a PS3 controller. I hoped to make friends with whom I could enjoy what free time I had away from the madness but, in the meantime, it was just me and nothing but my new phone to keep me amused.

In an attempt to stave off the inevitable masturbation session at least for a little while I decided to see what search engines could teach me about the two key figures in my new life.

It didn't take much digging to find out that Bob McCracken's past had seen its fair share of dubious business dealings and allusions of wrongdoing. His involvement in companies often seemed to end in disharmony, and he appeared to have a knack for either walking away unscathed from smoking ruins, or abandoning ships just before they started to list. In one particularly revealing interview just after he'd taken up the reins at Dens, he talked about Dundee being a transformational city, billion-pound waterfront developments and reimagining the post-industrial landscape. The interviewer asked him if he lived in Dundee himself. "God no! I'm a St Andrews man. Uuurgh, can you imagine it?" was his response.

While there didn't seem to be any trace of the mononymous Jocky's surname, or indeed the fateful dominoes match in which he somehow managed to lose it, there was ample proof that he was indeed some kind of mental case.

"DUNDEE BOSS CLAIMS NAZI GOLD BURIED UNDER TANNADICE"

"'PAUL STURROCK A CYBORG ASSASSIN FROM THE FUTURE,' CLAIMS JOCKY"

"ELECTRICITY SCANDAL ROCKS DENS – 'I THOUGHT THE FLOODLIGHTS RAN ON THE POWER OF POSITIVE THOUGHT,' CLAIMS 'DEE BOSS JOCKY"

If he was half as good a manager as he was an outrageous headline generator then I'd come to the right place. Unfortunately it wasn't a thought that eased my growing worry about meeting him face-to-face.

As I switched the safe-search function off and started typing altogether more explicit terms into the search engine, I took a moment to appreciate the masturbation-aiding technological advancements that had been made in recent times. Though I'd been born in what had to be considered a golden age of pornography in terms of choice and availability, it wasn't so long ago that getting hold of the stuff was an entirely more difficult proposition. My cousin Kenny, a connoisseur of all things filthy, regaled me with tales of top-shelf raids engineered with surgical precision so that no member of the public would witness him feeding his craving for naked ladies in the 50-plus age bracket. He also told me how a daring adventure into the farthest reaches of my Uncle Tam's sock once yielded a battered VHS copy of a Niddrie woman strategically placing Pedigree Chum on her person to ensure both she and her Labrador could enjoy meal time.

Times had changed. While women, and men, were still carrying out depraved sex acts with all manner of members of the animal kingdom, you didn't have to battle through a protective barrier of Donnay socks in the hope you might find videos of them doing so; it was all there and more at the touch of a button on the Internet.

I summoned up a couple of sites that had taken my fancy over the years. The first was a Scottish adult chatroom where sex-minded people could log on under an alias username and talk dirty to each other. Conversation with the only other user in the room, *Black_as_fuck_ken?* was unlikely to be to my taste, so I switched tabs and made for my favourite digital filth repository, www.schemiehoors.com.

I'd first been alerted to this site by Jimmy Anderson who, being a few years older than I, was something of an authority on the subject of women.

"Lloyd man, it's got burds just like ones we know fae the scheme and that! None of yer septic tanks with giant fake tits and a shitey accents, this is proper lassies getting shagged here!"

And 'proper' lassies they were. The site was a collection of distinctly amateur footage, warts-and-all videos taken from makeshift porn sets located in council estate homes around the nation. It wasn't so much 'the girl next door' but 'the wee mink with the tits from the next closie.' While it often got a little too authentic at times – Staffordshire Terriers wandering into shot, hungry bairns crying in the background, debt collectors shouting through the letterbox – there was a definite appeal in seeing the kind of girls who hung around the local chippy doing the type of things your sex-crazed mind wanted them to do to you.

Knowing I'd be visiting the site regularly I bookmarked it in my browser favourites and loosened the ties of my tracksuit bottoms. Just as HMS Wank Spanner approached dock at the South Pole an unwelcome pop-up box appeared.

Black_as_fuck_ken? has started a private conversation.

Jeez-oh. I flicked back to the chatroom with the intention to close the browser, but decided to have a quick look at the message first.

"Alright doll? Ever sooked a black toby before?"

I should have just closed it down, but I always felt compelled to be polite despite the anonymous nature of online conversation.

"Hello m8. Sorry, I'm not a girl lol"

The response was instantaneous.

"Answer the question ya wee ride."

Fuck sake. I closed the chatbox and browser down so I could concentrate on the matter in my hand. Deftly navigating the site with one hand I found an old favourite, a video of a buxom blonde with an Aberdeen accent doing unseemly things with what appeared to be a Stornaway black pudding as Rod Stewart's *Do Ya Think I'm Sexy?* played in the background. It was Scottish as fuck. And hot, too – the girl was bottle-blonde, bottle- tanned and had tits you'd punch your Gran in the throat just to play with for five minutes. She also looked a lot like Joanne Martin, a girl from school who every guy in the place had a wank over at some point. Including the teachers. Mr Graham from Geography certainly did but, as he didn't have the good sense not to do it in front of her, lost his job and ended up on the Sex Offenders' Register as a result.

Ten minutes later I was mopping gunk off my stomach with a dirty football sock, and my mind was returning to reality. I had training again in the morning. The very thought of it made my heart sink and my stomach turn to a churning bag of nerves. Would I be forced to attempt another kidnapping? Would I end up in jail? Most terrifyingly of all, would I meet Jocky for the first time?

* * *

He descended from the heavens like a moustachioed fallen angel.

We were being put through a series of sprint drills by Jocky's second-in-command, former Dundee star Wally Gordon. I took an instant liking to Wally, who seemed remarkably pleasant and downright normal compared to the man he acted as assistant to. I'd taken a real ribbing about the previous day's disaster from the lads, more than a few of whom seemed genuinely pissed off at me. Perhaps the group as a whole would suffer for my failure.

I was mightily relieved when the TV screen in the dressing room didn't turn on as we got changed and, when Wally told us to get out onto the pitch, I was thankful the day's training would take place in a more conventional environment than the local supermarket. There was no mention of the gaffer. Thinking – hoping – that perhaps he only showed face on match days, I threw myself into the training exercises with gusto in an attempt to impress Wally and my teammates, who I hoped would appreciate a hard worker despite his inability to purloin delicatessen assistants.

As I tried to catch my breath after running the length of the pitch in a series of bursts of pace, my attention was taken by what sounded like a single engine drawing ever closer. It appeared to be coming from the air, yet didn't seem loud enough to be a plane or helicopter. I looked skyward, turning slowly in a full circle as I failed to make visual contact with anything that would explain the noise. It was coming from the east side of the ground, growing louder with every passing second.

"What the fuck is that?" I asked Eddie McGlone, who was catching his breath closest to me.

"You'll find out soon enough," he said, smiling as he looked up in the direction of whatever was approaching.

My eyes followed him as he darted off up the pitch again and a cold chill fell upon me. I looked back up over the stand, and the source of the noise finally became visible.

"Holy... fucking... shit..."

It came out in a whisper that even I could barely hear. It was the flying man. The flying man I had seen hanging in the sky that day.

"Lloyd!" The call came from Wally Gordon, "Get yer arse in gear!" He glanced at the airborne newcomer then back at me with a look that suggested it was for my own good.

Trembling and mumbling incoherently to myself I started jogging back up the pitch. Just before I reached the marker that signalled I should break into a full sprint, I glanced back over my shoulder to see the flying man had dropped into the stadium and appeared to be headed right for me.

"What the fuck..."

I sprinted faster than I had ever managed before, and would have kept going for quite some distance had the next marker not forced me back down to a jog. I looked over my shoulder again to find the flying man about 20 feet behind me at a height of about half that distance.

He was wearing trackie bottoms and football boots. He was topless.

I turned round and tried my damnedest to focus. Another marker, another burst of pace. I ran like the wind itself, and felt like bursting into tears when the next marker slowed me down.

I tried to ignore the fact a semi-naked man was now flying alongside me. It was just my brain fucking with me. None of this was real. I must have taken a knock on the head playing wrestling with my pals in the park or something. I'd wake up in a minute and tell them all about the mental dream I had whilst unconscious.

I looked left to find Jocky looking back at me. His moustachioed face was stern and unflinching. He was flying a fucking jetpack.

I looked straight ahead again. Focus, Lloyd. Another marker came and I sprinted hard toward the next. He kept up with me and, out of the corner of my eye, I could see that he continued to stare. When I slowed down again I met his gaze. I didn't want to, but it was like he had my head attached to a piece of string he was tugging at.

"Hiya Lloyd! Hiya pal! Whaur's meh auld wummin fae Tesco ya hopeless cunt? Big Jock wants some insight on the mysteries o' Gala Peh."

He was talking to me through a megaphone. I had no idea how to respond. No words were forthcoming.

"How wiz the jail, Lloyd?"

I had reached the end of the pitch, so I turned and jogged back the way I came, unable to talk but equally unable to break his stare.

"Eh wiz in the jail once. Eh yased tae be aine o' they cunts wha wiz easily influenced beh music, and took thon NWA song 'Fuck the Police' a wee bit too literally. The copper didnae appreciate it. Mibbe he would o' been up for it if he wisnae on duty at Fir Park at the time."

I instinctively burst into a sprint despite not looking to see if I'd passed a marker. It was as if his black eyes were a hypnotist's watch; I was powerless to do anything but gaze directly back into the dark pools trained upon me.

"That wisnae the worst o' it either. There wiz a' kinds o' bather that time 'Bring Your Daughter to the Slaughter' beh Iron Maiden hit the charts."

Good grief.

"Anyway, eh'm awa' tae see auld Walzo." His eyes narrowed as a mean grimace formed. "Eh'll see you again soon, cunto."

And with that he gained a little height and veered to the left, flying over the players running up and down the pitch and headed toward Wally, over by the dugouts. I'd never seen anything like it in my life.

As the running drills were brought to a halt, the three barbers who had once again worked their magic to transform Harry into something vaguely resembling a footballer dragged out a giant sack filled with what looked like...

"Plastic carrier bags filled with human hair," interjected mid-fielder Chrissy Reilly as he clocked me looking puzzled by this latest development. "The gaffer reckons if we can play with bags of hair, using actual balls will be a piece of piss." Cutting my next question off before I could form the words out loud he explained, "It is Harry's hair, aye."

As we began a series of passing exercises with "balls" that made it much like playing with a Mitre Delta a dog had gotten its teeth into, Jocky circled us from just above head height, his instructions spliced with lines from hip hop songs.

"One touch tae control, one tae pass... would the real Ivo Den Biemen please stand up... kerpit fuckin' futba, that's the gemme... check yo'sel befo' yo wreck yo'sel ya cunts..."

The day's session ended with a bounce game. Determined though I was to impress well, my attempts were repeatedly thwarted by Jocky, who had taken up a position cross-legged atop the home dugout and kept bellowing at me through his megaphone.

"Lloyd ya cunt! Wha's in fucking cherge here?"

I stood looking up at him, nervously hopping from foot to foot as if I was there to ask permission to take a piss.

"Eh, you are, gaffer."

"WHA'S IN FUCKIN' CHERGE HERE?"

"You are!"

"EH?"

"You are, gaffer!"

"Fuckin' right, aye. Big Jock's in cherge here. A'body kens that. Get back in the gemme, mongchops."

I got no farther than 10 yards away before he called me back.

"Lloyd! Get back here!"

I jogged back over.

"Question fur ye, ya tipi-dwelling cunt: Wha's in cherge here?"

I was totally flummoxed. This was insane.

"You are, gaffer. You're in charge here."

"Eh?"

"You're in charge here!"

"Fuckin' right! Get back in the gemme, let's see what yer made o'."

Again I was only a few paces away when he called me back.

It was a routine that ran on a perpetual loop. It went on so long the rest of the team eventually left and went home. Yet he kept calling me over, asking who was in charge, sending me back into a bounce game that had long since finished, then calling me back for more questioning and creatively profane verbal abuse.

Hours later, as darkness fell, he finally let me be. He stood on the dugout, hit the ignition on his jetpack and bid me farewell.

"Right Lloyd, eh'm awa' hame tae get showered and cheenged before headin' tae the Rep. Walzo's got the lead role in 'Jesus Christ Superstar', should be fuckin' teckle. See ye the moarn."

With that he ascended, taking off over the Main Stand. As he vanished out of sight I dropped to my hands and knees and let the tears I'd been fighting for hours run free. What in the name of fuck had I let myself in for?

* * *

"It's a long way from the Theatre of Dreams, eh Lloyd?"

Bob McCracken wasn't wrong. The metaphorical distance between ramshackle Dens Park and Old Trafford was so great you'd have to ask a Wookie co-pilot to initiate the jump to light-speed to travel it in any reasonable time.

The Main Stand I sat beside the CEO in was the kind of place where you had to turn your watch back 40 years to get the right time. The enclosure opposite looked as if it might collapse at any given moment and kill the thousand or so people sat in it. The stands behind each goal were much more modern, albeit in a Barratt Homes-generic-looking way, and they clashed heavily with the rest of the ground. Dens Park was, in short, a bit of a dump.

"It's far from my cup of tea either, Lloyd," he said in response to the frown I had surveyed the ground with. "The old timers around the place make claim of it having atmosphere and something they call "soul", but I find tangible factors such as comfortable seating, exemplary corporate hospitality facilities and ample car parking to be far more agreeable. Soul indeed. It's a sporting arena, not Motown!"

He laughed heartily at his own rapier wit, elbowing me a little too sharply in an attempt to elicit the same reaction. I managed a half-hearted chuckle and fixed grin, and was thankful for the emergence of the teams from the tunnel relieving the awkwardness. I stood to join the rest of the ground in welcoming Dundee and their opponents for the day. In spite of a training regime seemingly concocted by someone certifiable, self-destruction being an accepted – nay, integral – part of the club culture, and a manager who quite literally flew over the cuckoo's nest, Dundee were sitting top of the league with more than half the season played. I couldn't begin to fathom how, but by some miracle of the footballing gods, what went on here seemed to be working.

Mr McCracken hadn't bothered to rise or applaud the team when they came out, but when some men in suits shuffled along the row in front of us to take their seats he was up like a shot to shake hands, slap backs and enquire whether they'd enjoyed the pre-match hospitality. When he nestled back into his seat he leaned over to whisper, "Sponsors, Lloyd. The lifeblood of the club and a hugely important source of revenue."

I looked towards the four or five thousand paying customers sat around the ground and asked, "The supporters must play a big part in that too though? Money coming in, I mean. I thought they would be the most important part of the set up."

He looked at me with a forgiving smile.

"Ah, the naivety of youth. Supporters being the lifeblood of the club is a myth, Lloyd. If these troglodytes want to hand over their dole money then who are we to say no? But the future is corporate hospitality, innovative sponsorship packages and lucrative television deals, tapping fresh markets and looking far beyond what happens on the pitch to create not a great team, but a great brand. The real game goes on in the boardroom, Lloyd, not out there on the pitch."

His spiel was drowned out by the crowd giving a rousing cheer to mark kick off.

As things got under way my attention was drawn to the trackside area. Jocky was making his way toward the dugout. Well, not quite. He had stopped to turn and goad the small band of Dumbarton fans in the far corner of the Main Stand. He stood with arms outstretched in the classic "come ahead" pose, an action which had the desired effect. The 100-strong travelling support were out of their seats screaming blue murder at him. As they did so a stream of stewards made their way out from the concourse below and formed a yellow-jacketed ring around them.

"Here he comes, the court jester himself."

Mr McCracken wasn't doing a great deal to conceal his distaste for the manager. His eyes narrowed into the kind of glower I imagine he usually reserved for those who asked whether his tan was spray or bottle.

I watched as Wally guided the gaffer along the track. While he'd removed the jetpack, he wore no vest or shirt beneath the kind of coat sported by managers and coaches the world over. He paused briefly at the away team dugout to strike the same arm-outstretched pose in an attempt to antagonise their manager and once again had to be hauled away by Wally. I noticed he'd had the words 'FUTBA JAIKIT' stitched on the back to avoid any confusion.

The amusement his entrance gave the sponsors sitting in front of us didn't please Mr McCracken much. He leaned forward to mutter apologies and vague, faux-jovial explanations as to why the manager of the club was acting in such a manner. While they didn't seem put out in the slightest, the man next to me was incandescent with rage. He was even more pissed off moments later when Jocky produced his megaphone from a pocket of the "futba jaiket" and started talking to him from the side of the dugout.

"BOOOOAAAAAAAABY McCRACKEN."

The sponsors turned to see what Mr McCracken would say. With his jaw clamped so hard that his tongue was probably bitten in half, the crimson-headed CEO mustered a friendly wave. His other hand had such a grip on the arm of his luxury director's box chair that his knuckles turned white.

"WHAUR'S MEH TIPPEX, BOABY?"

Every head around us turned to Mr McCracken, who was now shaking with anger.

"SOME CUNT'S GOT IT, AYE BOABY."

As he lowered the megaphone he raised his opposite hand to point up at the man who stood accused. Once again it was the calming influence of Wally Gordon that prevented the situation from deteriorating further.

Whether he actually did have the Tippex or not, Mr McCracken was utterly seething. He made his excuses and stomped off down the stairs into the stand, quite possibly to hide in a confined space and scream the rage out of his system.

The game turned out to be a fairly straightforward victory for my new club. Despite poor lifestyle choices, the onset of senility, freakish follicular activity and other obstacles, they could certainly play. Tough, industrious, and clearly willing to bust a gut for their teammates, fans and manager, I began to understand how they'd reached the summit of the league.

When my attention wasn't taken by Jocky howling insults at all and sundry through his megaphone, or encouraging the opposition bench to join him breakdancing on a piece of linoleum he laid out between the dugouts, I focused on the man I presumed I'd been brought in to form a partnership with. Unlike the rest of the team, Fong Du wasn't a hard worker. The steady flow of abuse from the manager didn't seem to phase him, and he paid little attention to Dong Chu when he was told to relay the insults in his own language via the megaphone. Maybe his delivery wasn't quite so vitriol-packed, or maybe "Eh'll be wearin' your heid as a hat at Tam McGinty's birthday perty if ye dinnae start running the fuck about ya lazy cunt" doesn't translate well into Korean.

Lazy as he was, Fong Du knew where the goal was. He powered home a header on the stroke of halftime to send Dundee, and his instincts had him in the right place to finish off a neat passing move and effectively kill the game just after 70 minutes. Dumbarton were done, and Dundee had another three points in the bag.

But the action didn't end there.

Events on the pitch hadn't dulled the away support's enthusiasm any. They had sang throughout the game and added some atmosphere to an otherwise lifeless Main Stand but, as the game entered the last 10 minutes, something triggered a full-on response from the ring of stewards who had surrounded them the entire game. They waded in among the boisterous but in no way troublesome supporters and began unceremoniously ejecting them from their seats. One by one, the Dumbarton fans were led out, quite rightly complaining bitterly about their treatment as they went.

To my horror, one young guy who had been particularly vocal in his protests was given a jab in the ribs by an instrument that, judging by the shocked-then-instantly-placated reaction of the recipient, was some kind of cattle prod. I'd seen plenty football in my time, but it had always been on television. Although this was the first game I'd attended in person, I was pretty sure that cattle-prodding supporters wasn't normal.

"Hooligans, Lloyd. A plague on this fine business we call football. Disgraceful scenes in the away end there."

McCracken had finally returned, tutting, to my side.

"You're not kidding, Mr McCracken. I think I just saw a guy being cattle prodded by a steward! What the hell's going on over there?"

He sat back in his seat, crossed his legs and paid no more attention to the confrontational scene taking place to our left.

"Quite clearly the away supporters were being overly loud and aggressive. The stewards are merely defenders of the peace. The kind of behaviour they were forced to act on has no place here, and must be stamped out. Supporters of visiting clubs must learn that this is no place for drunken tomfoolery."

I followed his gaze to the enclosure opposite us. The Dundee fans housed in it were on their feet, twirling their scarves above their heads and singing their own rendition of Hey Jude.

"If our own fans don't learn the same lesson they'll put off the high-spending guests, and we can't have that, can we?"

I was fumbling about in my pocket for my phone.

"Sorry, Mr McCracken? I didn't catch that last bit."

I flicked on the camera function and aimed it toward the activity on the other side of the ground. All those twirling scarves made for an impressive sight that I wanted to capture for posterity.

"Nothing, Lloyd. I'm pleased to see you're making use of the new phone. How's it working out for you?"

I kept my arm stretched out to film as I turned to answer, "Oh aye, brilliant, Mr McCracken. Dead chuffed with it like. Thanks again."

"No problem, Lloyd. No problem at all."

There was something about the sleazy grin that accompanied his words that I didn't like one little bit. I stopped filming and watched the final minutes of the game play out in uncomfortable silence.

* * *

My second week at Dens got off to a bad start thanks to Dundee's new, Bob McCracken-sanctioned away kit.

"Sponsorship, Lloyd. The paving stones which form Dundee FC's path to national and global recognition."

The path was heavily paved. As a new signing I'd been selected as the player to wear the new kit for its unveiling in front of local press. It was the most hideous item of clothing that I'd ever laid eyes on. Every inch of the top, shorts and even socks were covered in corporate logos. It was a Formula 1 car in football strip form.

"It's a wee bit... different, Mr McCracken."

He tucked his thumbs under the lapels of his official club blazer and crowed, "It is indeed, Lloyd. There's tens of thousands of pounds worth of sponsorship on that strip, vital revenue that will help finance some of the big plans I have for the future. In time..."

He drifted into a now-familiar refrain about outsourcing, bandwidth and synergy when he was cut short by Jocky flying out of the tunnel like a bullet from a gun, sending the small group on the track sprawling as we ducked for cover.

"In the name of Christ!"

Mr McCracken thumped a fist on the red blaize and hauled himself up, dusting himself down as he went. The blazer was probably going to need a dry clean.

Having roared up round the enclosure in a quick lap, Jocky was now landing directly in front of me.

"Hiya Lloyd, hiya pal." The greeting lacked its usual enthusiastic delivery and his eyes darted around the strip I felt increasingly embarrassed to be wearing. Man United might be the "world's most sponsor-friendly sporting brand" in the words of Bob McCracken, but Rio or Rooney would never be seen dead whoring the badge like this. Looking over Jocky's shoulder I saw that McCracken's mouth had twisted into a self-satisfied smile.

"Like the new away strip, Jocky?"

The gaffer straightened up, gave his moustache a good massage then turned to face the CEO.

"Boaby, what in the name o' Mark McGee's teeth is this shite? That's no' oor fuckin' away strip."

Mr McCracken was clearly delighted he'd managed to wind up Jocky with new kit.

"Oh but it is, Jocky. A week on Saturday in Greenock, Dundee will be proudly wearing this new strip as they step out onto the pitch at Cappielow. Save your breath arguing about it – it's a done deal."

The gaffer was perplexed.

"Ye cannae hae the lads wearin' this in Greenock, fur fuck

sake. Eh dinnae even wear meh good trainers tae Greenock in case some cunt takes exception tae them. If we turn up wearin' this monstrosity we'll end up gettin' dooked in the Clyde in a witchcraft trial."

McCracken started heading toward the tunnel with a sneering, "I'm sure you'll manage," and chuckled to himself as he went. The gaffer kept his eyes fixed on him until he disappeared out of sight.

"Fucking Boaby McCracken," he muttered. "That cunt better no' hae meh Tippex..."

With that he hit the switch on his jetpack and shot directly upward into the sky at pace. I watched him vanish into the clouds before lowering my head and smiling for the flashing cameras.

* * *

He reappeared from the clouds for training the next day. We'd entered the dressing room to find an array of camouflage gear and paintball guns waiting for us. Once we'd changed and filtered back out again five minutes later, Wally was on hand to streak our cheeks with a couple of fingers of black grease. I was more than a little apprehensive about where this was going. We marched across the pitch into the dilapidated, corrugated iron-and-crumbling-concrete enclosure where all the scarf-twirling had taken place on Saturday past.

As we climbed the stairs past rows of red, white and blue benches, Davo Milne bellowed, "D! E! DOUBLE-R! DOUBLE-R! Y!" and everyone else joined him to shout, "DERRY!" in unison. I had no idea what they were on about, but it sounded good amplified by the low, pitched roof that hung over us.

We passed through the back of the stand and found ourselves atop a steep slope that ran down onto Dens Road. The slope was so thick with overgrown bushes and vegetation it almost looked like a jungle. The gist of the day's training exercise was starting to become clear.

The gaffer descended from above just as Wally had finished dividing us into two teams.

"Hiya a'body. Sorry eh'm late. The cat wiz at the Vu last night and got in a right state. There wiz spew a' ower the loabby. A'body ready fur paintball?"

A collective cheer went up.

"Teckle! Right, same rules as ayewiz: if ye get hit in the chest or back yer oot and hae tae run up the Hulltoon wi' the nearest available mink on yer back. If ye get hit on the arm or leg ye hae tae tuck it back intae yer tap or troosers and pretend there's only a stump left; if ye get hit in the pus ye hae tae reenact the scene fae 'Byker Grove' whaur PJ got blinded. Eh'll be on hand tae play the role ay Geoff pet. You ken score, lads – get in aboot it."

The teams separated and moved to starting positions at either side of the forest.

"Stick with me, Lloyd, I'll show you the ropes."

I was grateful for Davo's offer. The vegetation was higher and thicker than it appeared from the top of the slope. It had caves, trails running through it, little bolt-holes dug into the mud and vines hanging from tree to tree. It was as if a little piece of Vietnamese jungle had been grown in Dundee, and was surely the oddest thing to grace any football ground the world over.

"Welcome to the Derry Jungle, man. Fancy a blast on a bifter?"

He offered me a large, conical joint.

"No thanks, Davo. I'm not much of a smoker."

He took a long, deep drag of the joint, and with a croak, replied, "Neither was I, man. Neither was I," before releasing a huge plume of thick grey smoke and moving off with a signal for me to follow.

Davo was fleet footed for a stoned man. We moved swiftly and silently into a forward position until he motioned for us to halt and take stock in a small trench dug in a previous training exercise. We lay with our guns poised as we awaited the enemy and I took the opportunity to pick Davo's addled brain.

"Davo, what was it you were shouting earlier? What's this Derry thing?"

He relit the joint he'd started earlier, sucking hard on it and exhaling before responding.

"This," he waved the joint around around. "is the Derry, well the bit that faces the pitch is. It's the spiritual home of the Dundee support." I must have looked confused so he explained it in terms I would understand. "Liverpool have their Kop, Man U had their old Stretford End and Dundee has its Derry."

There was a rustling in the undergrowth to our right. As we tensed up and readied our trigger fingers he whispered, "You have to get Derry'd oot yer nut here, Lloyd. Gaffer won't have it any other way."

Jocky came bursting through the trees swinging a machete as big as my leg. He'd painted every inch of his naked top half green, and was wearing a tin helmet bearing the legend "MEAT IS TECKLE." He was speaking into a plastic Fisher Price walkie-talkie.

"10-4, cunto, VC on the perimeter. Wha's in cherge here? Repeat, wha's in cherge here? Over."

He sat himself down next to us.

"Hiya lads! Right, there's an enemy position aboot 20 yards ahead. Lloyd, eh want you tae take it oot. Sneak up on the fuckers and take nae prisoners. Over."

Davo gave me a firm nod. The look in his eyes told me this was my chance to impress.

"10-4, gaffer. Over."

I moved forward in a crouching run. Suddenly I heard the whizz of paintballs flying past me. There was no time to lose. I burst into a sprint, dipping left, then right, zig-zagging through the trees at full pace. The enemy didn't expect me to come at them with such velocity. Doug Roberts, in full World War I regalia, floundered as I charged in on him with my finger on the trigger. Seconds later his chest was splattered with green paint.

War is hell.

But it gave me the opportunity I needed. Though the gaffer said nothing, the thumbs up Davo gave me told me all I needed to know. At the end of the week, my efforts running around bushes shooting goalkeepers of pensionable age and doing passable impressions of a deeply upset Spuggy as Eddie McGlone took a head shot were rewarded. When the team sheet was posted next to the prostitutes' business cards and anti-Dundee United propaganda on the dressing room wall, I found myself listed amongst the substitutes.

I was all set to make my debut appearance as a professional footballer.

SECOND HALF

SECOND HALF

The first team squad gathered late morning for our pre-match meal ahead of Raith Rovers' visit. It's a ritual you might assume consists of carbohydrates consumed with precision timing to maximise energy levels during the game. I'd be interested to hear what a nutritionist has to say about professional sportsmen munching their way through complimentary pies in a pub near the ground as a means of preparing for a top-of-the-table clash.

"Eat up ya cunts. If ye dinnae finish yer peh there'll be nae Scampi Frehs for puddin'."

Jocky was holding court, topless, wearing the usual jogging bottoms and a pair of muddy football boots. His very presence continued to shake me to the core.

The pre-match warm-up was unorthodox to say the least. An hour before kick-off, the team and coaching staff were called through to the pub's function suite. Everyone bar me was drinking, albeit with the degree of professionalism that comes with a three-pint-maximum, no-spirits rule.

"Right lads, youse ken the score. Fuckin' pre-match dance aff. Twa crews on either side o' the room, a'body takes a turn in the middle and nae moves that featured in the video fur thon Jason Nevins vs Run DMC tune. Shitey remix. Fuckin' Pat Nevin would o' done a better joab than that."

The squad split into two and formed lines facing each other.

When everyone adopted a cross-armed stance and scowled mockingly at the man opposite, I did the same. The gaffer had moved behind the DJ booth and was now sporting a pair of gold-plated headphones. A hip-hop beat kicked in and he showed off some hugely impressive turntable skills before picking up a microphone and guiding the proceedings.

"Dark Blue killer bees, we're on the swarm! Ain't no thang but a Dee thang. Ken aye!"

Chrissy Reilly sauntered into the middle of the room and started body-popping.

"Eh've shagged Jason, eh've shagged Kylie, check oot Chrissy muthafuckin' Reilly," came the rhyme from MC Mental Bastard behind the decks. He continued, offering words of instruction for the game ahead.

"Get right through that Grant Anderson in the first fehve minutes, Chrissy. Boy said you've got the lyrics tae 'It's Raining Men' tattooed on yer back! You gonnae tak' that? Are ye fuck."

A hyped-up Chrissy finished his routine and slipped back into place in the line. With the exception of Doug, who was loudly demanding that the gaffer play "somehin' wi' a tune", the entire squad took a turn dancing to the hip-hop and electro soundtrack Jocky was, quite brilliantly it must be said, throwing down. The unquestioning way they went about the task and the practised nature of their moves suggested this was no one-off. Each player's instructions amounted to little more than an order to "get right through" someone in the first five minutes for some odd, non-footballing reason. Jason Thomson was apparently telling people Davo Milne had sold him inferior quality marijuana, and a pornographic film featuring half the Rovers team and Eddie McGlone's mother called *Bone After Bone For Mrs McGlone* was allegedly doing the rounds.

After Fong Du's *Gangnam Style* dance saw his time in the spotlight end under a barrage of abuse that Dong Chu didn't even try and interpret, it was my turn. With it came a distinct change in musical direction. As 10CC's *I'm Not In Love* made for a somewhat incongruous finale to an otherwise upfront, well-executed old skool set, Jocky announced that everyone else should start making their way toward Dens. As they filed out looking very much ready to get stuck right into Rovers, the blinds fell down, the lights dimmed and a mirrorball's reflections shimmered across the dancefloor.

I went to follow them, but the gaffer bounced out from behind the decks to intercept me, shouting, "Hiya Lloyd! Hiya pal! Ye dancin'?"

Involuntarily stepping back as he approached, I managed to stutter, "Are... are you asking?"

His features softened ever so slightly as his chest puffed out.

"Eh'm askin' if you're dancin'."

He lifted his chin, maintaining a stern look as he stroked his moustache.

"I'm dancing if you're asking."

He pulled me tight to his half-naked body and pushed my head down so I was nuzzling his right shoulder. We swayed gently in unison to the music.

"Lloyd, Big Jock couldnae help but notice you wurnae drinkin' Special like a' cunt else in the bar there. What's the dae wi' ye?"

I tried lifting my face off his shoulder to reply but he pushed it back in place. My response that I was teetotal was therefore rather muffled, though clearly understood. Taking me by a handful of short hair, he yanked my neck back and looked at me with wide, shocked eyes.

"Ye dinnae drink? A futba player? Meh Goad, that's like bein' a priest and no' raping bairns! Jesus fuck, laddie, ye'll never mak' a futba player if ye dinnae drink."

He shoved my head back to his shoulder.

"We'll hae tae get this sorted oot, Lloyd. Me and you. The Fairmuir. On the Special. Yer career pretty much depends on it, aye."

I was in no position to argue. We swayed as one until the music faded to silence.

"That's what eh'm talkin' aboot!"

And with that he dragged me by the hand out on to the street. We caught up with the rest of the lads at the top of Provost Road and Jocky immediately burst into song.

"Walking down the Provie Road, tae kick fuck out United! Away the lads..."

The whole team joined in with him, as did the Dundee fans making their way to the ground. As we turned into Sandeman Street and made our way toward the players' entrance we passed a small band of Rovers fans in their team's colours. They were also in the mood for song, and were belting out a number about people in Dundee living in slums. This did not go down well with our manager.

"Ow! You ya Fife cunts, you gettin' fuckin' wide? Dundee's fuckin' teckle!"

He stopped right in front of the Rovers supporters with his arms outstretched in challenge. Boisterous and well-oiled as they no doubt were, the Fifers knew a proper nutter when they saw one, especially as they recognised him as the manager of the opposition. As they quietened down and adopted a look of submission, Jocky took advantage of his dominant position.

"Train station, six o'clock. A' you cunts plus whaever else is in yer mob against me, a couple o' lads fae the Utility and as many Lochee Fleet boys that can be bathered hoppin' on the 28 doon toon. Fleet rule!" he said, making an L shape with his arms. While the gaffer didn't resist as a few of the lads guided him away, he continued to shout abuse over his shoulder as he made his way into the ground.

"These colours dinnae run! Fuck runnin', eh just walk up and kick fuck oot every cunt. Casuals, scarfers, wummin, bairns, doags, fuckin' abody. Wha's in fuckin' cherge here, Rovers?"

I realised I was about to share a dugout with this certifiable lunatic and felt the colour drain from my face. Reflecting once again that this wasn't how I'd always imagined professional football to be, I meekly followed the pack into the main entrance for my first game as a Dundee player.

* * *

As I walked to the dugout and looked around the ground I felt a little awestruck. Dens Park was perhaps only half-full, but the five or six thousand people who were here made for a crowd far greater than any match I'd been involved in before. As the teams ran out on to the field, both the nearly full Derry and the sizeable away support behind the goal to my left broke out into song in support of their respective tribes. The PA's trebly transmission of song, an old Scots number that referred to "the brave boys who wear the dark blue of Dundee", cut out and elicited a roar from the home support, and the hairs on my arms rose involuntarily. How must it feel to walk out at Old Trafford before a crowd of 75,000? Mind-boggling? Nerve-wracking? Arse-dropping?

I took a seat in the home dugout next to Wally and my fellow substitutes. The gaffer, resplendent in his "futba jaikit", came out last and paused only briefly at the away dugout to inform Raith's physio there was a square-go at the station after the match if he fancied it.

"Right Lloyd, eh've got a special joab for ye the day, son. Pay attention."

Great stuff, I thought. Although I was starting on the bench, the gaffer obviously had an important role in mind for me as the game wore on and wanted to discuss the nuances of his strategy.

He pulled out what at first appeared to be a lengthy roll of toilet paper, but turned out to be a coupon the gaffer had put on at the bookies. It was thrust it into my hand, along with a miniature red pen, and I was instructed to keep an eye on his bets. When unravelled, it buried my feet in paper, suggesting the accumulator was a tad speculative. This notion was confirmed when I saw that Jocky's 10p bet would land him a cool £76.9 million should it come up.

"77 mill, Lloyd! Imagine a' the corned doag ye could buy wi' that!"

To allow me to keep up with results, he provided a small, ancient transistor radio. This, however, was unlikely to prove much use given that games from the Honduran women's lower leagues were among the less obscure components of the gamble.

The game got under way and I made a valiant but fruitless attempt at trying to tune in to a signal for even a local radio station. The gaffer patrolled the dugout area, using his megaphone to hurl vicious abuse at the referee, linesman, Rovers players, their bench and supporters. On numerous occasions the fourth official attempted to subdue him only for Jocky to protest his innocence, claiming not to "speakee the Eengleesh." As had been the case the previous week his vitriol wasn't just reserved for anyone dressed in black or the colours of the opposition either.

"Get yer fuckin' arse in gear, Fong! Chase every fuckin' ba' ya useless cunt!"

Whether coming from the gaffer himself or Dong Chu, Fong dismissed instructions with a shrug that made Jocky turn to the stand, shake his head and mutter about, "Fuckin' Boaby McCracken."

The game was keenly fought and reached half time still goalless. Back in the dressing room the physio's table had been used to lay out bowls of one of the few non-deep-fried staples of the Scottish diet. With an extra large bowl marked 'BIG JOCK' in hand and a look of happiness on his face, the gaffer was waxing lyrical about the contents.

"Fuck aye. The auld Jon Bon Jovies. Pure, undiluted YAAAAAAAS! for yer taste buds. The snowy peak o' Mount Teckle! And the stuff that was glowing in thon suitcase in Pulp Fiction, if Tarantino's memoirs are tae be believed."

Unlikely claim and questionable nutritional value aside, they really were delicious.

With the half-time snack devoured and team talk delivered ("It's punch in the fuckin' pus time if you cunts dinnae fuckin' win here aye.") we headed back out into the arena. No sooner had I taken my seat on the bench than Wally Gordon gave me a nudge and told me to get warmed up. I leapt up like a jack-in-the-box and began jogging and stretching my way down the track. To my surprise, this was greeted with a hearty round of applause from the fans and club mascot Deewok the bear as I passed them. I responded with a wave before turning away quickly to hide the fact my face was beaming brighter than the floodlights that were illuminating the second-half proceedings.

The atmosphere became more tense as the game, a scrappy affair with few chances and little flair to speak of, wore on. The noise coming from the home end of the ground took on an increasingly frustrated tone while the Raith fans, delighted by the prospect of a point away to the league leaders, generated an altogether more positive racket. Their vocal support increased as the minutes ticked by, both spurring their side on and bringing them to the attention of the authorities. As the players in the white away kit threw themselves into tackles, a stream of stewards were lining up along the bottom of the stand.

Wally Gordon's signal for me to return to the dugout came as a Rovers player received treatment in his own 18-yard box. I removed my training top and prepared to make my entrance, but the attention of the whole ground was drawn to the chaos behind the goal as the stewards turned a mobile water cannon on the away support.

"What in the name o' fuck is goin' on there?" the gaffer screamed. "A water cannon? They're no Old Firm fans fur fuck sake, there's nae need tae treat them like animals."

With 10 minutes left to play and with hundreds of soaked Fifers being dragged out the stadium I made my debut for Dundee. Davo was looking somewhat worse for wear – possibly as a result of the bong he'd smoked at half time – so the gaffer took his borderline whitie as an excuse to throw on an extra striker.

"Eh've got us on the coupon tae win 1-0 here, Lloyd – if you mak' that happen eh'll hae every junkie prostitute on the Arbroath Road in that tipi tae reenact the Battle o' Little Big Horny wi' ye. It'll be sexier than that time eh bumped intae Stuart Cosgrove on Chatroulette. Hiya Stuart! Hiya pal! Dinnae worry, eh'll no' tell Tam yer a webcam masturbator. It's no' even cheatin', really."

The fourth official raised his electronic board to reveal the shirt numbers of the players leaving and entering the field, the PA announcer told the crowd what was happening and I ran on to the pitch with cheers ringing out from three sides of the stadium and the beat of a throbbing heart pounding in my temples.

In the name of Sir Alex, please let this go right.

* * *

It went spectacularly wrong. After chasing long balls in vain, taking a sly dig in the ribs that made the accompanying "welcome to the first division" seem somewhat insincere, and receiving an earful of what I could only assume was abuse from Fong Du, I finally got a chance to shine.

A hopeful punt forward was poorly dealt with by a defender whose attempted clearance was sliced directly in front of me on the edge of the six-yard box. My poise and balance were perfect as I stepped into the ball and swung my foot at it with the intention of driving it into the prominent gap between the goalkeeper and his left-hand post. My mind's eye saw the net bulging; my actual eyes watched in horror as the ball flew high and wide into an away support that now looked as if it had swum the Tay to get here. Howls of frustration gave way to loud jeers as the final whistle sounded. My chance to be an instant hero was gone.

The handshakes I offered to opponents were weak and I trudged, slumped-shouldered, off the pitch, desperately trying to avoid the malevolent glare of Jocky, who remained frozen to the spot by the dugout as everyone else drifted toward the tunnel.

My teammates weren't in a forgiving mood. "You bad player. Fong Du would have won game if presented that opportunity," was how Dong Chu jovially translated my new strike partner's unkind words, while even Doug Roberts chipped in to say it was the worst miss he'd seen since 1951.

The dressing room door burst open and Jocky stormed in, radio to his ear, eyes ready to leap out their sockets, body tense and enormous coupon trailing behind him. The transistor spoke a language foreign to my ear, but familiar to his.

"Choluteca Chicas fuckin' won at Santa Lucia." He took the

radio from his ear, twisted the dial and instantly tuned into a station where the language appeared to originate from Eastern Europe. "Auschwitz and Belsen finished nothings-up in the Holocaust Memorial Cup." As he turned the dial once again his eyes fell on me with a look so charged with energy I half expected lightning bolts to shoot out and strike me down. "THE BAYVIEW BEAT UNITED SOCIAL AT LOCHEE PARK!"

Sweet mother of fuck. Surely not. There was no possible way that coupon could have come up.

"LLOYD YA HOPELESS FUCKIN' CUNT! THAT MISS AT THE END COST ME ENOUGH TAE BUY UNITED, RENAME TANNADICE 'THE CUNTODOME' AND BUILD WILLO FLOOD A SPACESHIP TAE TAK' HIM BACK TAE WHICHEVER DISTANT GALAXY HE CAME FAE!"

Seething to the point that steam actually appeared to shoot out of his ears, he dropped the radio. The impact of its fall changed the station once more and the crackling Scottish voice within declared, "Heart of Midlothian 1, Dundee United 4."

With a roar that shook the century-old stand to its foundations, Jocky lunged at me, hauled me to the ground and roughly manoeuvred me into a figure-four leg-lock. I was too stunned to offer any resistance and quickly found myself screaming in agony, but Jocky just sat up and stroked his 'tache thoughtfully without releasing his grip.

"Huv ye seen ET, Lloyd? Ken the bit whaur a'body's BMX starts flyin'? Willo Flood cannae dae that. Mind wrappin' the boy in a blanket and launching him doon the Hulltoon in a Lidl trolley. Eh thought he'd tak' aff!"

The pleas for mercy that I screamed were finally answered when the rest of the team took pity and hauled him off me. As I lay weeping in the foetal position, he cracked open a can of Special, announced he was off to the Fairmuir and sauntered out. As the rest of the players filtered into the shower without a word of consolation or sympathy, I pulled myself off the floor up on to the bench.

* * *

"I can't do this," was the thought ricocheting around my head. I repeated the words out loud, knowing them to be true. I wasn't cut out for life at Dundee. I wanted to go home, to give up and sit in front of the telly shouting at horses with my old man. Suddenly exhausted, I used my last reserves of energy to pull my clothes on and meekly creep out of Dens without another word.

I walked out into Sandeman Street with the slouched posture and tortured gait of the drug addicts who never seemed too far away. Across the road I spotted Bob McCracken deep in conversation with two Asian gentlemen he was ushering into a waiting limousine. He looked across at me awkwardly, waved and, after a moment's indecision, walked swiftly over the road toward me.

"Lloyd, well played today. Unfortunate that the ball bobbled at the end there, eh?"

I half-heartedly agreed, slightly embarrassed by his face-saving false reasoning.

"Watch and learn from Fong Du, Lloyd. You can learn a lot from how he plays the game. A couple of his compatriots are my guests for the weekend and, despite the less-than-salubrious surroundings, they were thrilled to see a national hero in action."

I considered the gaffer's attitude to Fong Du and very much doubted he'd agree.

"I'd love to stay and chat, Lloyd, but I mustn't neglect my hosting duties."

"No bother, Mr McCracken. What are your plans for this evening then?"

Adjusting his cufflinks and glancing briefly toward his car before returning his attention to me, he continued, "St Andrews, Lloyd. The Home of Golf, a town steeped in history and prestige, and the jewel in the crown of an otherwise culturally bereft region of the country. My kind of town, Lloyd."

With a pat on the shoulder and a wink he bid me farewell and departed. When I reached the end of street and paused to cross Provost Road the limousine passed by. I waved at the blacked-out window of the back seat, felt like a dick and left my hand hanging awkwardly in mid-air as the car vanished out of sight.

That night was the loneliest of my life – quite an achievement given that parental neglect was the abiding feature of my child-hood. I'd been hoping one of the lads might invite me to join them for whatever they got up to on a Saturday night, but I was a long way from flavour of the month after that miss. I consoled myself with a visit to schemiehoors.com and pulled the head off it watch-ing a buxom blonde dole claimant getting shagged up the arse in the back green as her mum shouted out the window to tell her tea was ready. The familiar post-orgasm self-loathing compounded my misery and I eventually cried myself to a restless sleep.

I burst back into consciousness with a start, my body snap-ping into an upright position so fast the beads of sweat coursing down my brow were sent flying on to the cardboard gaffer that stood at the foot of the bed. The speech bubble greeted me with, "Hiya Lloyd! Hiya pal!"

Without moving its lips the cardboard cut-out repeated the words out loud.

I jumped so hard and fast I believe I felt my skin stretch as my skeleton came close to bursting through it.

"Were ye haein' a nice wee dream Lloyd?"

Jocky stepped out from behind the cardboard likeness of himself. My scream must have been heard halfway down the Hilltown.

"Eh hae them masel sometimes. Does Jocky dream o' electric sheep? They're maistly aboot tits, tae be honest. Sometimes cocks tae!"

Convinced I was still dreaming, I retreated under the duvet and curled into the foetal position. This isn't happening. This is not happening. I closed my eyes as tightly as possible, scrunching them shut in an attempt to flee the terrifying vision my mind had cast up. When I felt the duvet lifting and someone crawl into bed to "spoon" into my back, I whimpered and realised the nightmare was far from over.

"Comfy Lloyd? Auld Jock's a good big spoon, eh? Be thankful eh'm no' feelin' fruity, else ye might've ended up gettin' forked. Yaaasssss! Eh'm just kiddin' pal, it's nae bather."

He draped an arm over me to hold me tight and I wondered just how it was anatomically possible for his other arm to be in a position where it was nestling against my buttocks and the back of my thighs.

"Rest yer weary mince pehs, Lloyd, we'll get a half-hour kip before gettin' up and in aboot Sunday. Eh'm fuckin' knackered here, huvnae even been hame fae the Fairmuir yet. Fuckin' Tam McGinty hud a perty, the decks got hauled oot and they tenner ectos are the fuckin' damage."

He yawned, muttered, "that's the gemme," contentedly and fell silent. After a few seconds his breathing grew heavier and he was soon snoring lightly.

I dared not move a muscle. I hardly dared breathe. I wondered how much the extensive therapy I would unquestionably need in due course would cost me and concentrated all my energy on staying completely silent and still so as not to disturb him.

It was an inertia that lasted only as long as it took me to realise that wasn't his arm down there. As he talked in his sleep, a quite disgusting monologue that featured television personality Lorraine Kelly and someone called Gentle Ben, I felt his arousal growing rapidly and made my break. As I scrambled out of the bed, he awoke with a cry, "Lorraine ya manky Arab cow, get a hud o' yersel'! Boy's a bear for fuck sake!"

He looked mightily confused for a few seconds, asked what the fuck I was doing on the ground and casually extended his limbs to stretch out the little sleep he'd had. Sitting up, he took stock for a moment and finally got around to explaining why he'd broken in to my tipi.

"Lloyd, there's a word in Dundee for your brief appearance at the gemme yesterday. Ken what it is?"

He answered his own question before I could form a response. "That word, Lloyd, is 'shite'. Ken what eh mean?"

I cast my eyes downward, ashamed yet fully aware he was right.

"But we'll work on that, cunto. Eh dinnae sign shite players. Eh've seen you play mair than ye think, son, and although yer a bit rough around the edges ye do hae potential."

The faint praise allowed me to look him in the eye again. Although his demeanour remained stern, I wasn't detecting the usual level of stomach-churning malevolence in his dark eyes.

"What we need tae dae, Lloyd, is tae get you up tae speed wi' some additional practice. Big Jock's organised a wee gemme o' fehve-n'-a-boot. Once we're done there we'll head tae the Fairmuir and get this "eh dinnae drink" shite sorted oot. There'll be futba on the tele, and eh'll mibbe show ye how tae fling a few arrows while we're at it."

I hadn't the slightest clue what "fehve-'n-a-boot" was, and I was apprehensive about the prospect of breaking my vow of abstinence, but I was in no position to argue and it wasn't every day your manager invites you for a drink at his local.

He left me to get changed. When I got outside a few minutes later I asked if the training was to take place at Dens. His jetpack was back on and he was hooking some kind of harness over his shoulders and making adjustments to various buckles and seatbelt-like straps.

"No' Dens, no, but close enough. We're meeting the lads at the sweeng park at the tap o' Dens Road, aye. There's plenty space for a kickaboot, and the sweengs huv just been taken doon again efter big boys wrapped them roond the tap poley. Shite when that happens, eh?"

I agreed despite being none-the-wiser to what he was talking about and made a mental note to purchase a Dundonian phrasebook so that I might try and learn the lingo.

He fired up his jetpack and motioned for me to come to him. Over the roar of the engine coming to life, he shouted, "Right you, 'mon get strapped in and we'll get going."

I remained motionless, hoping he didn't mean what I thought

he meant. Slightly exasperated, he sighed and made a come-hither motion with his index finger.

"Gaffer, there's no danger I'm..."

He started nodding slowly with a look that suggested further protest wouldn't go down well. I walked toward him as if expecting the ground below me to fall away and send me plunging into the abyss. When I got to within arm's length he rolled his eyes, grabbed me by the shoulders and spun me round so we were facing in the same direction. He quickly manipulated my limbs into the harness and in seconds I was trussed up like a man about to take part in a tandem skydive.

"Ever flown Air Jocky, Lloyd?"

The thought of what was about to happen had rendered me dumbstruck, so a shake of the head was all I could muster.

"Maist cunts huvnae, and only a few that did lived tae tell the tale. This harness falls laughably short o' any kind o' safety regulation, ken?"

And with that we left terra firma. As we rose vertically my stomach dropped, my heart jumped into my mouth and I started whispering prayers to a God I didn't believe existed.

"This is yer captain speakin', welcome aboard Flight Wha's in Fuckin' Cherge Here fae Cairdie tae the Hulltoon sweeng park. There's nae refreshments, nae toilets and nae chance o' survival if there's even the slightest hint o' technical difficulties. Bit like Ryanair, only eh'll fly ye directly tae the destination instead o' drappin' ye aff a three-hour bus journey away. Enjoy yer flight!"

I kept my eyes firmly shut as he whistled Elton John's *Rocket Man* in my ear, felt sure it would be the last song I ever heard and cursed the fact I never became famous enough for him to play at my funeral.

* * *

"Ladies and gentleman, welcome tae the Hulltoon sweeng park. The local time is ten-past-fuck-knows-eh've-no'-got-a-watch-on, the temperature a wee bit chilly, and the climbing frame free tae scale and admire the view fae the tap o'. Thank you for flyin' Air Jocky, it's nae fuckin' bather."

I opened my eyes and breathed a gargantuan sigh of relief. When the gaffer unbuckled the last of the straps that had mercifully held firm, my legs gave way and I found myself crumpled in a heap on the spongey rubber surface that would soften the fall of anyone daring enough to jump off the swings.

"Away and collect yer luggage aff the roondaboot, Lloyd. I'll go and get the lads ready."

Swallowing hard and unable to stand, I dragged myself toward the roundabout in question, mentally kicked myself for somehow expecting to see my bags revolving on it and stretched flat out to look up to the sky I'd been flying through via jetpack mere moments ago. Breathe, Lloyd. If you can get through that you can get through anything.

My moment of peace was broken by a football rolling past and coming to rest by my side. It was the impetus I needed to pull myself up and find my feet. With legs still trembling, I took the ball under control and moved toward the gaffer and the lads, who weren't my teammates, as I'd been expecting. My colleagues for the day were the kind of lads you see in gritty Channel 4 dramas about modern first-world poverty. Clad to a man in white sportswear and baseball caps they observed my approach with disdain and distrust.

"Lads, this is Lloyd. Boy bides in a tipi up Cairdie!"

They snorted with laughter and shook their heads with derision. I nodded, smiled weakly and offered a hello that was barely audible to myself, never mind them.

"Lloyd? Fuckin' mongo-Lloyd mair like," said the tallest and most assertive of the young teens before leading the appreciation of his own rapier wit. Jocky remained silent and straight-faced until the rest of them fell silent. Then, he finally got the "joke" and folded with laughter.

"Mongo-Lloyd! Mikey, that's a peach. Gutted eh didnae think o' that aine! Mongo-Lloyd. Fucking yaassss!"

My temporary training buddies were representatives of the

Young Hulltoon Huns. I was introduced to them in turn, starting with the joker of the pack, Mikey. Like him, his cohorts had each been subjected to a complex nomenclature that involved adding either 'O' or 'Y' to all or part of their first or surname.

Though I hadn't recognised the local terminology for the game, I understood the concept of Headers & Volleys. One man in a goal formed by empty cider bottles and an invisible, roughly head-height crossbar faced a team who could only score via a header or volley. If such an attempt went high or wide of the target, or if the goalkeeper made a clean catch, then the player who made the failed attempt switched places with the present 'keeper. The Dundonian version saw a goalkeeper who let "fehve" (five) goals past him receive a "boot" (kick up the arse) from each outfield player. It was simple in design, conducive to the odd flourish of skill and certain to end in violence. It was Scottish football incarnate.

To my complete lack of surprise I was nominated to be first in goal. Jocky and his hoodlum associates formed a rough arc around the goal, with wingers on each side providing crosses for the four central players, who acted as main forwards. They knocked the ball around for a while, getting in the swing of passing at a height suitable for a legitimate shot or header on target. The gaffer continued to compliment Mikey on his "Mongo-Lloyd" comment, a tactic that distracted me as he smashed the ball beyond my reach.

"ONE!" they shouted in unison.

I wasn't much of a goalkeeper, and the gaffer and his young team were much more talented than I had given them credit for. They knocked the ball around gracefully, deftly flicking it between themselves before blasting past me on the volley, or swiftly removing their baseball caps to head home.

"TWO!", "THREE!" and "FOUR!" came all too quickly. Before I knew it, I was facing a kick up the rear-end from a group who, in all likelihood, weren't unfamiliar with practising violence for leisure.

"Fuckin' focus, Lloyd! Fehve n' a boot ya cunt."

The gaffer fell back and barked at me as he let the Huns play among themselves.

"These boys will kick ye harder than any defender in the league son. What ye gonnae dae aboot it?"

A volley came in from Hendo. I dived low to push it back out and sprung back to my feet before they could prepare a rebound effort.

"Good save. Ignore the pressure o' the worst that could happen and play yer aine gemme."

Steve-o set up Marko and I got both hands to his thundering strike but couldn't quite hold it. I jogged on the spot and cursed an opportunity lost.

"Close but no cigar, and there ain't no smoke in here... apert fae that joint Mikey just sparked."

The reek of marijuana permeated the air around us and a siren in the distance made me, for the briefest moment, think we were about to get busted. I took my eye off the ball and Mikey showed remarkable dexterity for a man smoking a reefer the size of a wombat's tail to control and slot it past my flailing arms.

"FEHVE!"

Grinning maniacally, they danced around me knowing they had carte blanche to administer my punishment as and when they saw fit. As Jocky took a long draw from the joint that had been passed his way he shrugged and confirmed I was for it. "Fehve n' a boot, cunto."

I was told to turn to face the goal and stand still. Before I had time to consider how hard I might be kicked the first blow was delivered with enough force to make me yelp and stumble forward. They all laughed. The pain had barely registered when it was multiplied by the second kick, this one a little harder than the first. Both the laughter and my humiliation increased, sending water to my tear ducts to prepare for deployment.

"Lloyd!"

I looked over my shoulder to see the gaffer holding me tight in his gaze, his chin raised and chest puffed out as if preparing to take the blows for me.

"Tak' yer kickin' like a man, son. That's the gemme."

The third blow landed. Then the fourth. I bit my lip and tried desperately not to succumb to the tears that filled my eyes. The fifth sent a solitary drop running down my cheek and I quickly wiped it away.

"Last aine, Lloyd. Ready?"

Jocky stepped up and dragged his right foot over the ground like a bull preparing to charge.

"Assuming Walter Kidd disnae come oot o' retirement this is the worst hit ye'll take in yer entire career."

I steeled myself, closing my eyes and tensed every muscle in my body. The foot that connected with my arse sent me flying to the ground. As a mocking cheer filled my ears I grimaced, growled under my breath and stood right back up. I did not cry. I turned and faced them, and found Jocky staring me down. When I remained unflinching under the full beam of his stare, he smiled slightly and nodded his approval.

"Job done. Right, Mongchops, you get tae nominate the next goalie."

I spat my response back at him instantly. "You!"

He looked genuinely taken aback. "Whit?! Fuck up ya wee cunt." Jocky looked around for support only to find the YHH roaring their approval, grudgingly accepted his fate and shoulder-barged me as we swapped places.

This put me at ease in the company for the first time. I began to play a pivotal role in proceedings, knocking the ball around, commanding teammates to cross, lay-on and shoot, and commending their efforts. The abuse stopped as I took control to fire headers and volleys relentlessly towards goal.

The gaffer might have been skilled as an attacker but lacked the ability to be a goalkeeper. Despite desperately blocking a few efforts, the strikes against him soon amounted to four.

"Fuck sake, man, this is worse than that time eh fell in Eddie Thompson's grave when eh wiz helping lower him six feet under. Hiya Eddie! Hiya pal! Love ye, big aine, but eh wiz a terrible choice tae be a coffin bearer."

Mikey played keepy-up, grinned and asked if I was ready. I refused the joint he offered me and the ball was flicked into my path. It fell at a perfect height and I crashed a left foot volley past the gaffer.

"Fehve!"

He did not look amused.

One by one the lads took their turn kicking him. None of them, not even Mikey, applied anywhere near the level of force they'd used on me. They were scared to give Jocky anything more than a cursory tap and, although somewhat annoyed at their lack of consistency, I understood their reluctance.

"You're up, cunto. Let's see what yer made o'..."

The expectant 'I dare you' look he gave me from over his shoulder confirmed I was being challenged to prove my mettle. The fire in his eyes suggested my next flight with Air Jocky would prove to be fatal if I wasn't careful here, yet I knew he would think less of me if I didn't follow through with this. More than anything, I was pumped up on adrenaline and felt in control of my own destiny for the first time in weeks. Deciding to trust my instincts, I ran up and booted him full force in the arse.

He went flying, just as I had. The Hulltoon boys gasped as he collapsed face-down in a heap. I froze and immediately regretted my actions. What the fuck had I been thinking?

He pulled himself back up and stood facing away from us, fists clenched and head popping out to each side in turn. Hendo whispered, "Lloyd ya daft cunt, what the fuck did ye dae that for?" He looked scared half to death. Seeing him look it made me feel it.

The gaffer turned slowly to reveal a surprisingly expression-less face. He walked slowly and deliberately toward me, stopping inches from my face. As I closed my eyes in anticipation of being beaten to within an inch of my life he calmly announced, "Right lads, cheers for the gemme, aye. Me and Lloyd are awa' up the Fairmuir fur a pint. See yiz efter!"

I opened my eyes and he was shaking each of his young pals'

hands in turn. As he walked off, motioning for me to follow him, they offered their hands to me with respectful farewells such as, "Good game, mate," and, "Nice to meet ye, Lloyd." I returned their grips and walked taller than I had since arriving in the city as I strode away to join my gaffer for a pint at his local.

* * *

"Rule number one, Lloyd: Nae cunt gets in unless ye get signed in by a member."

Clubbie rules. He'd spoken solemnly of them on the short walk to the Fairmuir, giving me the distinct impression they were to be broken at your peril. I had asked if there was a dress code and been told that patrons were generally expected to wear smart evening attire. Confusing words from a man about to enter the place naked but for jogging bottoms and a jetpack.

There was no question of his unconventional sartorial choice preventing entry, however. He was greeted like a returning hero by the elderly gentleman who manned the signing-in book while each and every person we met on the way to the main function suite had a warm welcome for him. He was certainly popular.

My knowledge of working men's' clubs stretched no further than the odd episode of *Phoenix Nights*. I expected well-worn faces and furniture, stoic expressions and decor long since out of fashion. I expected it might be grim.

The very last thing I expected was an explosion of sound and light the moment Jocky pushed open the swinging double doors.

"Looks like Tam McGinty brought the perty back here at openin' time!"

He was screaming in my ear and yet I still barely heard him. The sound system was cranking out a piano riff over a symphonic passage that had dozens of people on the dance floor – none of whom were younger than 60 – cheering with their hands in the air. When the DJ – an old man with headphones looped over his tartan bonnet and false teeth floating in a pint glass by one the turntables – flicked a dial and introduced a thumping drum beat,

I felt it vibrate into the very centre of my chest. The dancers went wild. A woman so frail she might float away in a strong wind lifted her zimmer frame and punched the air with it in time to the beat.

"G'on yersel' Beryl!" The gaffer was pumping his fist in the air along with her. He grinned to me and shouted, "Strings o' Life! Fuckin' tune and a half, eh? Derrick May's a sound cunt, yased tae play fir oor dominoes team," before showing great fleet of foot to glide into the throng with a "Yaaaaassssssssssssss!" I stood motionless with my mouth hanging open until a new song segued into the first and he danced his way back to my side again.

"Every cunt's still melted," he explained. "They a' went and took anither o' they tenner ectos efter eh left the perty. Crazy eh? Just as well pension day falls on Suicide Tuesday, they'll be able tae get right back on it before the heid-fuck kicks in. Pint?"

I nodded vacantly and followed him to the bar.

There was no queue and the barmaid was dancing. She reached over the bar and embraced the gaffer in a tight hug before grabbing two glasses and reaching for the pump marked 'Tartan Special'. As the gaffer dug around his wallet for enough change to prevent him having to break a note, I picked the first of the freshly poured pints up off the bar and turned to look around the place. An old photo on the wall caught my attention and I wandered off to get a better look.

The music stopped with a thump and the room fell silent. I looked to the DJ booth to see what had interrupted proceedings and realised every single person in the room was staring utterly aghast at me, some openly weeping. I turned back to the bar to see the gaffer look equally horrified and the barmaid, who appeared ready to rip my guts out and serve them as bar snacks, pointing to a sign above the bar that clearly stated "DO NOT LEAVE THE BAR WITHOUT PLACING DRINKS ON A TRAY". I hadn't noticed it. I returned to the bar as if walking on eggshells and whispered my apologies. Jocky spoke softly but firmly, the barely-restrained rage dancing in his eyes once again.

"Clubbie fuckin' rules, Lloyd. Abide beh them, or go the same way auld Davie Morrison did."

My curiosity about what had become of this Davie Morrison character obviously showed in my face so he added, "Boy got banned for a week," and just as I thought that didn't seem so bad, he elaborated further. "Once he was allowed back he hud tae dae three months manning the gloryhole in the gents bog. The auld cunt's probably in there the now. Tell ye what though, Lloyd, eh've hud worse blowjobs."

He smiled at the memory of a geriatric administering oral pleasure through a hole in a cubicle wall, waved a hand of apology toward the dance floor, and led me through to a side room. The music kicked back in at the very point it had been halted and I made a mental note to be very careful about the drinks tray rule in future. And to use the disabled toilet if nature should happen to call.

Under the watchful gaze of the gaffer and a silver-haired, pendulum-jawed Ecstasy-head called Jeanie McKay, I took my first sip of Tartan Special. I held it in my mouth a moment, allowing it to register fully on my palate before swallowing and licking a frothy moustache from my upper lip. The gaffer leaned in like a chef awaiting the verdict of a VIP diner on his signature dish.

"Well?"

I lightly smacked my lips together as I let the aftertaste do its work and considered my response.

"FUCKIN'... fuck, man... huv any o' you twa got weed on ye? Fuckin' dyin' fur a wee puff tae level iz oot a bit here, eh." Jeanie was worse for wear and struggling to see straight out of the one eye she was managing to keep open.

"Jeanie, shut yer fuckin' pus fur fuck sake. The boy's tastin' the Special fur the first time here! Eh've no' been this keen tae hear a verdict since Davie Narey wiz up in court fur stealin' wummin's clathes aff washin' lines. Couldnae believe he got 'not guilty', cunt wiz wearin' a dress that wiz three sizes too big for him in the fuckin' dock fur fuck sake."

Jeanie continued talking to herself and Jocky turned his attention back to my verdict.

"It's nice and smooth…"

"Oh fuck aye, smoother than Wullie Miller at the Logie Club's singles night."

"Really malty, nutty even…"

"Nuttier than Gazza fishin' for chicken in the KP factory."

"And really quite tasty. Not the kind of thing I'd have thought I'd like, but it is a decent tipple. Cheers."

I raised my glass for him to clink and, although his tough guy mask didn't slip, he did so with a barely concealed look of joy in his eyes. We took a good, long sup together. As we gasped in unison and returned our glasses to their beer mats I wondered how much I'd have to drink, because I wasn't enjoying it half as much as I was making out and felt sure my tolerance for alcohol would be low.

I looked up to the giant screen above Jeanie's head showing the build up to the afternoon's live Scottish game. Jocky produced a remote control from nowhere and adjusted the volume so the sound came pouring through the speakers. This prompted a terrified and confused reaction from Jeanie, who looked to the sky as if her maker was calling her name and clamped her hands to her ears as she slid off the leather upholstery to curl up in a ball under her table. The gaffer gave her a cursory glance but seemed entirely nonplussed by behaviour polite society would have deemed worthy of a sectioning.

"There's Wullie Dawes," he said, waving at the televised face of the retired footballer-turned-pundit. "Hiya Wullie! Hiya pal!"

"Do you know him, gaffer?"

"Oh eh, eh ken Wullie. Good cunt. Loves futba. LOVES it." He looked off into the middle distance with a smirk. "He's ayewiz sayin' that, aye. Fucking yaasss!"

I remarked that he was a good pundit, one who seemed very tactically astute and had a great television manner. The gaffer began giggling but said no more than, "He's somethin' fuckin' else like."

I took another gulp of the pint and fought my facial muscles as they instinctively attempted to grimace.

Feeling that the positive review of the gaffer's favourite tipple had helped me recover from the near-disaster of Traygate, I decided to attempt some regular conversation.

"Any chance of putting the English game on gaffer? Manchester derby. Should be a cracker." He shot me a look that made clear his bewilderment that anyone would choose to watch a top-of-the-table clash in the best league in the world when Inverness were about to take on Kilmarnock on the other channel. After what seemed like an eternity he silently passed me the remote control.

Nervous at this latest setback for our fledgling relationship and feeling the effects of alcohol for the first time, I began babbling away, "The Manchester derby. Two of the biggest and best teams on the planet going head-to-head. This is what it's all about, eh? Should be a brilliant game."

His snort of derision suggested he disagreed. He elucidated, "Is it fuck what it's a' aboot. Twa teams wha sold their fucking soul for TV money run by foreign cunts wha think futba's a commodity to float on the fuckin' stock market." He took a triple-gulp-swig of his pint before continuing, "The boy wha runs Man U's a fuckin' glazier fur fuck sake. Fuck off back tae the replacement windae business ya gless-sellin' cunt."

I wasn't sure if he was being serious but he looked it.

"Time is it, Lloyd?"

I checked my watch. "12:30, gaffer."

"Futba at half 12 on a Sunday. Near on 24 hours since real futba gets kicked-aff. Why?" He made the tongue-pushed-into-cheek and accompanying hand movement universally recognised as 'blowjob' then the finger-and-thumb-rub of 'money'.

"It's a piece o' nonsense. Sunday's fur gettin' on the Special and hidin' under tables 'cause yer still fucked aff yer pus on tenner ectos. You a'right there, Jeanie? Rave safe, pal."

The gaffer ranted on about how things were changing for the worse and delivered a lengthy diatribe on the "Coldplayfication" of the game he so obviously held dear. I daren't mention my record collection and found my beer to be a welcome means of occupying myself. It provided a good shield during moments of awkwardness, although I was probably drinking too quickly for a novice.

The game began. Despite his lack of appreciation for aspects of high-level modern football, the gaffer enjoyed a good match as much as anyone and discussed the game's talking points with a surprising degree of insight. The Special continued to flow, courtesy of a skilled barmaid who knew exactly when the gaffer was about to finish his pint and would be delivering fresh supplies on the compulsory tray just as he wiped the last mouthful's foam from his moustache.

With the game approaching full time, Man United took the lead. As Wayne Rooney broke free of his marker and bore down on goal I stood in anticipation and shouted, "Finish it Wayne!" When he duly obliged I jumped around the room like Jeanie had presumably been before her comedown kicked in.

The gaffer seemed confused by this, and when I settled back down he asked, "Lloyd, huv you got Man U on the coupon here?" I told him I didn't gamble and, with narrowing eyes, he asked why I was getting so excited.

"Because I support Man United," I answered proudly. Jocky laughed a little, shaking his head.

"You support Man United?"

I nodded emphatically. "Best team in the world, gaffer."

He seemed to accept that as a reasonable answer.

"Mibbe they are, like, there's no' many better than Man U. But tell me this, Lloyd. Why do you support them?"

I got a little nervous as my reasons suddenly sounded a trifle weak while I listed them in my head. My explanation amounted to little but verbal stumbles and drawn out silences.

"Yer no' fae Manchester."

I shook my head.

"Yer old man or any o' yer family arenae Mancunians or Man U fans."

I shook my head again.

"You huvnae been within a hundred miles o' Old Trafford."

I didn't bother with a third shake. He knew the answer. Up to that point I'd never had cause to feel embarrassed about my love of Manchester United, yet I suddenly felt my cheeks redden to match their home kit.

"Dinnae get iz wrang, son, they're a brilliant team tae watch. Great futba team, nae question. And Fergie's a good cunt. Shitey dominoes player, but a helluva nice man and a world-class manager. Still, admirin' a team's hardly the same as supportin' a team. That's like claiming Cheryl Cole's yer burd 'cos ye had a wank over the video for 'Love Machine'."

He took a drink. I took a bigger one, downing the remaining reddish-brown liquid in the glass.

He excused himself, announcing he was "awa' fur a pish, and mibbe a swift BJ if auld Davie's on duty." As he walked off, a thought appeared in my mind and seemed to jump out of my mouth before I had the chance to censor myself.

"Gaffer! Who do you support?"

He looked at me as if I'd asked a question so blindingly obvious it was equivalent to "Does Fabian Barthez's morning routine involve use of hair straightners?"

"Eh wiz born in Dundee, raised in Dundee, played fur Dundee and manage Dundee. Wha dae ye think eh support?"

With my mouth now operating completely independently of my brain I blurted out, "United?"

He smiled broadly with genuine amusement before a hearty laugh broke through. Feeling bleary-eyed and as bold as brass I laughed along with him.

"Funny cunt. Very good, Lloyd."

As he disappeared out the door I could offer no resistance as my body suddenly and involuntarily slipped off the seat and came to rest in a heap under the table. My head was spinning. I could barely muster a thumbs-up to mirror the one Jeanie was offering her new floor buddy from under her own table. I felt nauseous, and so decided the best plan of action was to close my e...

* * *

The beeping penetrated the darkness and would not give up until it woke me from the near-coma I'd fallen into. My eyes opened and the light they let in felt like it was crushing my head. Using both hands to shield myself from the brutal brightness, I summoned up every available ounce of energy to pull myself into an upright position. I shivered, whimpered, groaned and would have uttered the drinker's remorseful pledge to forego future intoxication had my mouth not been glued shut by dehydration. The steady, never-ending beep smashed my temples like a series of blows from a toffee hammer and only a massive defensive effort from my gag reflex prevented the contents of my stomach making a break for freedom. The wreckage of a once-functional mind sent out the emergency signal "find the noise – stop the noise" on repeat until I began to hone in on the sound that pained me.

My phone. It was close by. It was on the floor. I reached down, fumbled it into my hand and pulled it towards me. The increase in volume that came as it grew closer threatened to overwhelm me, and I managed to deactivate the sonic assault of the alarm just before my head split in two. I breathed a huge sigh of relief and fell back into a horizontal position. The phone buzzed and vibrated, sending shockwaves up the length of my arm. I lifted my head to see what news it brought forth.

1 NEW MESSAGE

I pushed the screen and tried hard to focus on its contents. The words appeared jumbled and unintelligible at first, but my vision eventually centred and allowed me to make sense of them.

MONGO-LLOYD (YAAAAASSS!). EH'M LETTING YOU AFF WITH MISSING TRAINING BECAUSE YER FUCKING GUBBED JUST THIS ONCE. GET IT TOGETHER, CUNTO. SEE YA THE MORRA. LOL. JOCKY.

Training? I was missing training? What day was it? What the hell happened? And where in the name of fuck was I? This wasn't my tipi...

Another buzz from the phone.

1 NEW MESSAGE
PS – SAY HIYA PAL! TAE JEANIE FUR IZ.

Jeanie? Who the fuck was Je...

A boney hand snaked under the duvet and rested on my naked, exposed crotch.

"Mornin' Lloyd. Thanks for last night, that wiz braw. Last time eh got a ride like that the Discovery was seaworthy and Dougie Roberts wiz in the youth team."

And with that the contents of my stomach gained the liberation they desired.

* * *

It isn't uncommon for football to be described as an uncivilised affair. The players are reckoned to cheat and act their way through Saturday afternoons and drink, fight and philander the rest of the time. And those who follow the game enjoy an even less enviable reputation – marauding hordes of savages hell-bent on unleashing merry hell on whichever town or city they happen to be visiting.

Away supporters are wilder, more vocal and unquestionably drunker than the home crowd. Having congregated at their local, still bleary-eyed from Friday night's excesses, they load up on breakfast pints before piling on to barely roadworthy coaches only kept in use for animals likely to inflict further damage on it. Armed with soft drink bottles topped up with cheap spirits, they attempt to circumvent the "no alcohol" rules that drivers and police officers periodically attempt to enforce. Inevitably, any group of drinkers travelling cross-country on a vehicle with no toilet will have to make numerous pit-stops along the way. Should you happen to be travelling along a motorway in the hours prior to kick-off there's every chance you'll encounter one of footballing culture's less edifying sights – dozens of men lined up by the side of the road like a giant defensive wall. Give your horn a toot and pay homage to the inebriated,weak-bladdered, piss-anywhere lifeblood of the game. They'll probably wave back, though not necessarily with their hands.

For all their faults, the players might be expected to act with a degree more civility as they journey to the match. And for the most part I'm sure they do. Dundee FC, however, was not most teams.

"Got a bit of stage fright there, Lloyd?"

Eddie McGlone was to my immediate left in the long line formed by the first team squad in a layby just outside Perth.

"Better get thinking of Niagara Falls and flushing toilets, we'll probably not stop again until Stirling services."

"Aye, the gaffer reckons the Aberdeen casuals will be there and a square-go's on the cards," chipped in old Doug as he managed to balance on a zimmer frame and take a piss at the same time. They weren't helping as I tried to release the pint I'd had in the Centenary Bar and the can of Special I'd drank on the bus.

Having already made use of his jetpack to relieve himself against the side of a Celtic supporters bus we passed at 60mph outside Longforgan, the man himself hadn't joined our number for the group urination. Instead he spent the duration of the comfort break standing under the Dundee flag he'd hung across the back window, arms outstretched and eyes keen to seek out anyone in passing traffic who might fancy the kind of trouble he was all-too-ready to get involved in.

The line-up dissipated and left me as the solitary figure quite unable to piss in the wind. The beeping horns and jeers that swept by only added to my frustration. I looked over my shoulder to gauge whether we were about to get on the move again and was pleased to see Davo Milne still taking short, sharp blasts of the joint he'd lit as soon as we had stepped off the bus. I had a few moments yet to try and do the business.

"Davo ya Boab Marley cunt, eh've fuckin' telt you aboot that afore. The baccy in that joint's bad fur ye, aye! Straight ganja only; bong on, cunto."

Davo coughed an apology as the gaffer grabbed the joint off him and proceeded to help himself to the last few draws. Seeing that I was the only man yet to board the bus, Jocky checked his watch, tutted loudly then strolled up the embankment to stand by my side. Without saying a word he stood there blatantly staring at my penis. After a few deeply uncomfortable seconds he held his arms out in front of him, wiggled all his fingers and began the ever-increasing-in-volume 'Ooooooooooohhhhhh' that supporters use to break the concentration of 'keepers winding up to take a goal kick. When he reached the climax and shouted, "YOU'RE SHITE AHHHHH!" I quite miraculously began pissing.

"That's what eh'm talkin' aboot!"

He patted me on the back and left me to do my business. I chuckled to myself as the stream flowed with enough pressure to put out a small fire. He was mental. Absolutely mental. But actually quite likable once you accepted him for what he was. He wasn't a bad...

The sound of the bus engine revving back to life forced a sharp look over my right shoulder. With my piss still in full flow, the coach began pulling away. My manager and teammates were banging on the windows in derision, deeply amused by their sudden exit. Hopping from one foot to the other I pushed what was left in my bladder out as fast as I could and, without taking the obligatory shake to finish, sprinted after the bus, which was now back on the motorway and gaining momentum. As the vehicle moved into second gear I hit my fifth, my feet moving faster than they had ever done before. I drew alongside the open door, reached out and grabbed the aluminium handrail inside, hauling myself in just as the bus accelerated to a speed I'd have been unable to match.

"Yaaaaasssssssss! That wiz funny as fuck!"

Jocky led the chorus of laughter, then offered some applause.

"Good stuff, Lloyd. Ye were movin' faster than Usain Bolt that time he got chased oot the Fairmuir for cheatin' at bones. Fuckin' Jamaican dominoes meh erse. Eh'm impressed."

He patted me on the back as I breathlessly made my way down the aisle, receiving congratulations and good-natured ribbings as I did so. By the time I was back in my seat I had a smile on my face as wide as the Aberdeen casual willing to meet the gaffer's challenge at Stirling services would need to be.

* * *

"Lloyd – get stripped. Dong Chu – hiya wee man! Tell Fong Du eh'm gonna strangle him wi' meh toby."

The gaffer did not share the jubilant mood of the Dundee support behind the goal to our left who were celebrating Fong Du's second goal of the afternoon at Cappielow. As he passed Dong the megaphone, Wally tugged the gaffer's futba jaikit and leaned in close to talk quietly in his ear.

"You're taking Fong Du off? McCracken winna be happy, especially now that his boy's scored the goals that should see us win this one."

Wally was economical in words and delivered them calmly. But he was a wise head, respected by the whole dressing room, and Jocky paid attention to him. Strong-willed though he was I saw him pause to reconsider the substitution he was about to make.

Fong Du had not covered himself in glory during the course of the game, at least not as far as his manager was concerned. The South Korean internationalist didn't put in the graft the gaffer demanded of his players, and spent as much time rolling around the turf in faux-agony as he did on his feet. His first goal was a penalty he'd clearly dived to win, and the gaffer had been almost as apoplectic as the Morton players who surrounded the ref to protest. He'd been equally irate when another innocuous-looking clash in the box saw Fong Du collapse like he'd been shot and convince the ref not only to point to the spot again but also dish out a second yellow card to the "guilty" defender. Regardless of the advantages it brought his team, the gaffer clearly did not condone such behaviour.

"Ye ken the score, Walzo. Eh'd rather we didnae score than get the goals the way that cunt gets them. Boot fuck out o' yer opponents, that's nae bather, but divin' is wrang. Cheatin' bastard so he is."

"I agree wi' ye, Jock, but McCracken will want answers come Monday morning."

He gave it a few seconds more thought then came to his decision.

"Fuck it, and fuck Boab McCracken."

Pointing to his chest, he justified his choice with an "Eh'm in cherge here" that was full of conviction.

Wally shrugged and gave him a pat on the shoulder before picking up the electronic board. I was going on.

The change was announced as I bent and stretched on the touchline. Fong Du stood gesticulating toward the bench. He was not happy. Neither were the away support and, as Fong Du trudged off, a chorus of boos went up that left no one in any doubt what they thought of the substitution. I gulped at the prospect of being thrown to the proverbial lions.

"Never mind they lads, Lloyd. Sound cunts one and all, but right oot their nut on drink and tenner ectos. Maist o' them winnae even mind being here the day."

He offered the disgruntled clump of travelling supporters a cheery wave and a thumbs-up.

"Let's turn the boos intae coos. No' bovine coos ya daft cunt. Unless they start squirting Special instead o' milk when you wank them aff they'll be fuck all use. Eh mean coos o' admiration. Coos o' admiration fur the bold Lloyd George. Get them telt, son."

He winked and gave me a pat on the arse before turning to loudly berate the approaching Fong Du, who gave as much abuse back and didn't return my offer of a handshake as I took his place on the park.

I was thrust into action almost immediately. Chrissy Reilly was on song and, not for the first time that afternoon, burst down the left flank and whipped in a cross. I broke free of my marker and controlled it with one touch, pushing the ball into space on the left hand side of the box. As the defender rushed in with a sliding tackle I knocked the ball past him and darted round the opposite side. I looked up to see Harry Larkins storming into the box screaming for me to feed him the ball, the resulting testosterone surge causing his stubble to explode into a full beard within a few yards. I gave him what he wanted. His left foot drive would've killed a ballboy had the net not stopped it going any further. 3-0.

I was thrilled to make my first positive contribution to the team, and even more so when my captain chose to forego any elaborate celebration and instead jogged straight toward me with a pointed finger of approval.

"Great ba', mate. Well played."

I hoped my blush wasn't burning as brightly as I feared and congratulated him on a fine finish. The rest of the players who joined us offered further plaudits and, as we jogged back to the centre circle for the restart, Eddie offered me a right bargain on a pair of Diesel jeans that he assured me would fit perfectly.

Keen to build on my successful start, I threw myself into what little time was left to play. I chased down every ball even if they looked like a lost cause, tried to get involved whenever possible and hoped a goalscoring opportunity would come my way.

When it did, I completely fluffed it.

After some neat interplay in midfield, Davo threaded a through ball past two defenders for me to run on to. I collected it 25 yards out and looked up to see the Morton 'keeper rushing out at me.

Go round him? Slide it past him? Lob him? I was yet to decide by the time a nippy full back swooped to thump the ball off my toe and into touch. As I stood with my hands on my hips looking to the sky the full-time whistle ensured there would be no chance to redeem myself. We won, and I'd played reasonably well, but I left the pitch bitterly disappointed for passing up that glorious opportunity.

The gaffer seemed pleased enough though. There were no death stares or figure-four leg-locks this time, partly as a result of our convincing victory, and, perhaps most importantly, due to a treble that included Dundee coming up.

"Fucking should o' put mair than 25p on the cunt. Could o' got a sassij supper at the chippy in Auchterarder instead o' a fritter roll," he rued wistfully as we stripped off and hit the shower.

I'd barely gotten wet when what I considered a surprise addition to the steam-and-banter-filled room sauntered in. With swimming goggles over his eyes and floatation aid armbands round his biceps Jocky joined his winning team for the post-match shower. He was sans jogging bottoms for the first time since I'd joined the club and, although it's bad form to make anything more than accidental or fleeting eye contact with another man's penis in such situations, his cock was so big it made me drop my shampoo bottle and stare as if it were pissing rainbows.

"Some banger, eh Lloyd? Ye dinnae get many o' these to the metric tonne."

Horrified that he'd caught me gawking at it I looked away sharply and coughed an embarrassed apology.

"It's nae bather, pal. A'cunt gets a good peek the first time. It's £3 a minute to look at it fae here on in though."

The rest of the lads chortled, and submitted to full-blown laughter when he continued, "You're still due me 15 quid by the way, McGlone."

Eddie looked none too amused, but even he couldn't help but smile when the gaffer body-popped his way into the centre of the shower room and started breakdancing by way of celebrating a first class "telt". For all the deeply unprofessional and wildly unconventional things that went on at Dundee, there was certainly a conviviality among the staff.

"Right Dong Chu, get in here, laddie," he called toward the dressing room. With Fong Du apparently not interested in the post-match frivolities and already out getting changed, his young interpreter was summoned to join the rest of the team. He entered in a pair of trunks, his slight body bony and hairless, carrying a large wooden scrubbing brush.

"Naebody works up a lather on the auld ball-bag like Dong Chu, eh pal? Get tore in ya wee ride."

And with that the young South Korean boy got to work scrubbing a naked and freakishly well-hung old man. My teammates began rapidly rinsing soap off themselves so they could flee the scene and I attempted to follow suit but the gaffer told me to hold on a minute so he could have a word. I let the hot water run over my face as a means of keeping my eyes off the deeply weird and possibly illegal picture playing just feet away from me. Once the last of the other players had filtered out he addressed me again.

"Ye did better the day, Lloyd. Set up that goal well and worked hard."

He was holding his cock upright with both hands like a snake handler might grip a python so that Dong Chu could build up the lather he was apparently famed for producing on his scrotum.

"But ye should o' scored tae – that was a great chance ye missed at the end there."

I agreed, and apologised.

"Dinnae be sorry; ye'll get the next aine. Eh've got an idea that'll help ye through the next gemme ye play."

He made sure Dong Chu was sufficiently distracted with his duties before whispering, "And ye'll be playin' mair often soon enough, aye."

He gave me a conspiratorial wink and indicated I was free to depart.

* * *

The day's training had consisted of "backie-trooping" the streets around Dens. In simpler terms, the exercise involved charging through gardens and leaping fences and walls as if participating in a demented version of the Grand National while the gaffer hovered above us shouting "Somebody's in yer gairden" through his megaphone. Numerous brushes with devil dugs and angry residents threatening us with the police proved surprisingly enjoyable. In a good mood, I decided to spend my afternoon more productively than abusing myself in the tipi, which had been my main leisure activity since I arrived in Dundee. I decided to explore the city a little and took a walk downtown.

The city centre was a heaving mass of Dundonian humanity. Students lounged around, office workers went about their lunch-break business, blazer-wearing pupils of the private school in the heart of town clogged up sandwich and fast food joints, junkies lost in their own inner space meandered aimlessly, and shameless chancers requested spare change for buses I very much doubted they had any intention of catching.

There were all sorts to be seen here. My favourite ingredient of the bustling human brew was the girls. Dundee was chock-full of lassies who could be considered Playboy models in scheme-based relative terms. Sitting outside a coffee shop nursing a can of juice was like being on the sidelines of a council-grade catwalk as they passed by modelling the finest scheme couture. Although some favoured the methadone chic look a little too much for my tastes, by and large they were girls plucked straight from my fantasies. I'd do a week in Bell Street to see some of them on schemiehoors.com.

With my wank bank bursting at the seams, I left town and made my way back up the road. I had no idea which bus would take me toward Caird Park, so decided to scale the urban Everest that is the Hilltown. I was somewhere around base camp (a shop where bags of clothing could be exchanged for cash, which to my mind only encouraged washing line pilfering) when I spotted a couple of billboards announcing the local news headlines on the other side of the street. Today's Dundee Courier celebrated some local girl who'd landed a role in the Scottish soap opera River City, while the Evening Telegraph announced "DEE BOSS HAPPY WITH AWAY WIN, LESS SO WITH NEW STRIPS – UGLIER THAN JIM McLEAN'S MOOD AFTER ANOTHER PUMPING AT HAMPDEN". I chuckled to myself and cast my mind back to the post-match press conference at Cappielow.

As the players had started making their way back on board the team bus, the gaffer had asked me to join him in speaking to the assembled journalists.

"It'll just be Tam fae the Tully and mibbe that boy fae the Sunday Post, Hen Broon. It's nae bather, they're good cunts, aye."

They seemed pleasant enough. Conscious that my words would end up in print I politely talked about my part in the third goal, my intention to work hard and earn a regular first-team place, and my belief that we had a great chance of winning the league if we kept up the good run of form we were enjoying. Tam asked if a regular starting place would serve as a good present for my upcoming 18th birthday and I enthusiastically agreed that it would.

The gaffer was less concerned about what came out his mouth ending up in the sports pages.

"Did ye see they fuckin' strips, Hen? What in the name o' fuck are they a' aboot?" He had the boy from the Post in a headlock as he spoke into the dictaphone he'd grabbed off him the minute he'd entered the room. "They're uglier than that baldy-heided cunt McLean's mood efter United took a pumpin' at Hampden in an '80s Cup Final. Hiya Wee Jum! Hiya pal!"

Curious as to whether the paper had printed his claims that Morton manager Allan Moore knew more about Tupac Shakur's untimely death than he was letting on, I crossed the road to go and buy a copy. A beeping horn caught my attention just as I went to enter the shop. Bob McCracken had pulled up.

"Mingling with the local wildlife I see, Lloyd."

He was looking even shiftier than usual as he spoke through the rolled down driver-side window, his eyes darting up and down the street as if expecting to come under attack at any given moment.

"Be very careful around these parts, son. It's a jungle out here. The natives are savages and are often restless. Quite understandable given the downtrodden nature of their futile existence, I suppose."

Regarding myself as a man of the people and growing to like my adopted city, I felt compelled to defend the local residents.

"I haven't had any trouble, Mr McCracken. Everyone seems sound enough. Just normal people going about their business."

He went to reply but stopped short when a passing pensioner nearly coughed up a lung and spat a giant globule of brown phlegm on the pavement. As the old man carried on his way, McCracken whispered, "Mandatory euthanasia for the elderly, Lloyd. Britain could be Great once again if it would only stop pandering to those beyond help and concentrated on tax breaks for the super-rich wealth creators."

The lecture didn't last long as his attention was caught by the same billboard I had noticed minutes earlier.

"In the name of Saint Fred, what has that fool been saying this time?"

He rubbed what appeared to be a sudden headache before letting his hands fall down his despondent face.

"That man shouldn't be let out in public, never mind allowed to talk to the press. He's the very definition of a PR disaster. He just won't accept the links between a strong brand profile and results on the park. What I wouldn't give to get a man with good media training at the helm."

I smirked a little, pleased that karma had offered some retribution for McCracken's contempt for decent old guys, whose only ostensible character flaw was a lack of consideration for where they deposited their lung contents.

McCracken's eyes narrowed a little as he continued reading the headlines before suddenly becoming a whole lot friendlier again.

"So, Lloyd! How are things with you? Are you well?"

"Och, not bad, Mr McCracken. Settling in, I suppose. A wee bit bored when I'm not at the football, if I'm being honest."

"Perfectly understandable, Lloyd. The city's a slum, for the most part, and essentially devoid of culture and means of entertainment. Not like St Andrews, wonderful town." He grinned and give me a matey wink as he suggested, "I dare say some female company might not go amiss, eh?"

It sounded weird coming from his mouth, and I didn't feel particularly comfortable discussing such matters with him. I could feel a hint of a blush in my cheeks as I looked down at my shuffling feet.

"Aye, maybe, Mr McCracken."

He laughed and revved his engine.

"Well Lloyd, time is money. I better make haste. If I sit here much longer I'll find myself propped up on bricks. Bye for now."

He pulled out, gunned his engine and roared off as ostentatiously as possible. I was almost home before I realised I forgot to pick up a copy of the Tully.

* * *

Match day came around again and the visit of Partick Thistle began in typically unorthodox fashion. The team gathered in Frews, a traditional pub full of character at the top of Dens Road, for our pre-match pints and a buffet of steak bakes and sausage rolls Eddie had procured from the Hilltown branch of Greggs. We mingled with both home and away fans while the gaffer held court among the pub's ladies' darts team, showing off his impressive abilities with "the arrows" and constantly referring to them as "lads". I took the opportunity to browse the numerous football photos that graced the walls, looking deep into faces from the city's sporting past and wondering if one day my image would come under such scrutiny from an unknown stranger.

"Good photaes, eh Lloyd?"

Wally Gordon was by my side, his eyes a little misty as they drifted over faces he was obviously familiar with.

"There's a lot of good memories up on the wall here, son. This town's seen some teams over the years. Lot of great players played down the road at Dens there. Tannadice, too."

Nostalgia filled the air like the meaty aroma wafting from the buffet. Smiling, Wally gave me a gentle nudge with his elbow and directed my attention to a team photo positioned up high. "Recognise anyone?"

I scanned each player's face in turn and spotted a younger version of the man stood beside me.

"There's you! You haven't changed much, Wally."

Flattered, he thanked me and told me to keep looking. Within seconds I was in fits of giggles. The gaffer, sporting an afro so immense that the players to each side of had to lean out its way and a handlebar moustache so bushy it could have been described as Larkins-esque, was stood back-centre. His chest puffed out and his handsome young face beamed with pride.

"Auld Jock there was some player in his day, let me tell you. Fast, skilful and twice as hard as any nails I've ever come across. Had the heart of a lion. Still does."

The pair of us stood admiring him for a moment.

"He's daft as a brush, but you'll never meet a man more proud to play for his club as Jocky was to play for us. Or as proud to manage a club as he is now."

I looked over to watch him as he struggled to gain an advantage in an arm wrestling contest with the captain of the darts team. Bicep bulging and face turning red, he asked if his opponent had started yet, and I couldn't help but grin. He sensed me watching him, looked up and smiled back. The split second of relaxation saw his arm slam down hard against the table, and a cheer went up from the ladies' darts team. He wasn't best pleased.

"Fuck sake, Lloyd!" He shouted across the room. "What you smiling at ye cunt? The boy fuckin' beat iz 'cause o' you!"

Wally was quick to defend me.

"Suck it up, you old goat. The lassie won fair and square. We better watch our time anyway."

He checked a watch-less wrist, nodded in agreement and bellowed, "Right lads! Drink up, we're oot o' here. D! E! DOU-BLE-R! DOUBLE-R! Y! DERRY!"

As the Dundee fans took up the song he shook hands with the victor and made for the exit. He turned to us and cried, "Let's get right intae these weegie cunts!" as he held the door open for a Thistle fan and gave him a friendly pat on the back as they crossed paths. The players downed what was left of their pints and we followed our leader to Dens Park.

* * *

"Substitution for Dundee: Number 9, Fong Du, to be replaced by number 15, Lloyd George."

The stadium's squeaky, eardrum-shattering public address system announced my unexpectedly premature introduction to the game. We were only minutes into the second half of a keenly fought yet scoreless encounter when Fong Du went down heavily under a challenge from an over-zealous Thistle defender. Instead of performing his usual theatrics, he lay motionless clutching his right knee. The physio who attended him was quick in signalling that he was unable to continue.

"Awww, poor Fong Du. Wee shame, aye."

The gaffer was uncharacteristically sympathetic. When the offending defender gave a discreet thumbs up in the direction of our dugout, he pulled the top of a brown paper bag out his futba jaikit pocket and gave his nose a tap with his finger.

"Gaffer, please tell me you didn't..."

"Shut yer pus, Lloyd. Right, cunto, gie me exactly the kind o' performace ye gied iz at Morton and eh'll be happier than Arthur Scargil at Thatcher's funeral on a tenner ecto."

He put a reassuring arm around my shoulder and squeezed me closer to him.

"Also, stick this in yer lug," he said, handing me a tiny earpiece.

"What's this for, gaffer?"

"That, Lloyd, will let Big Jocky talk ye through the match. Look, there's a wee microphone attached to meh nipple!'

He opened up his futba jaikit and tweaked his nipple, nodded his head and smiled at me long enough without breaking eye contact for it to be quite disturbing. I was apprehensive about going ahead with this latest insane plan but, once again, was in no position to argue.

I made my way on to the pitch to mild applause from the home support and took up my position.

"Ground control to Major Tam, eh'm floatin' in a maist peculiar way, aye. Wave at the bench if ye can hear iz, Lloyd."

I waved. He waved back.

"Hiya Lloyd! Hiya pal! Right, Jim Duffy's marking ye the day. Good defender but as slow as he is bald. Go and hae a word wi the cunt, noise him up."

Even with my limited knowledge of the Scottish game I knew Jim Duffy hadn't played for Partick Thistle for something like twenty-five years.

"Tell him eh shagged his wife in 1987, Lloyd. Tell him she was loving her slice o' Big Jocky. Get him telt, Lloyd."

I wandered up to Alan Archibald and delivered the good word. He looked at me as if I was absolutely mental, and with just cause. I could hear the gaffer laughing down the line.

"Tell him she went first class on the Jocky Express, Lloyd! Tell the baldy fucker eh pummelled her until her fuckin' teeth fell oot! GET JIM DUFFY TELT, LLOYD!"

Mercifully Davo Milne had intercepted a pass and knocked the ball out wide for me to chase. No sooner had I reached it and brought it under control than Archibald crashed into me and near enough put me in the Derry.

"Hud that by the way, wee man," came the harsh Glaswegian accent in my ear. I managed to utter an apology for bad-mouthing Mrs Archibald through gritted teeth as I lay pole-axed on turf.

"FUCKIN' BOOOOOOOOOOOO!"

The gaffer was none too pleased.

"Ya dirty bastard, Duffy! If ye were that dirty in bed the wife would never huv come lookin' meh way in the first place ya cunt!"

I dusted myself off and resolved to mime if instructed to deliver further insulting banter to Archibald.

The game was a classic rough-and-tumble midfield battle. Tackles both fair and otherwise flew in, keeping the referee and physios busy. I was kept on my toes by a still-irate "Jim Duffy", balls that broke my way from the midfield, and the stream of consciousness in my ear.

"Thing is Lloyd, eh wisnae tae ken Marvin Andrews wiz big on the whole God thing. Maist fowk at the perty thought it wiz funny as fuck haein' twa lesbo strippers kerryin' on wi' a crucifix dildo. Murdo MacLeod certainly did, and said as much in the letter o' thanks he wrote the following week."

As the game raged on, I heard all about Jocky's recent trip to the sexual health clinic ("Got the all clear nae bather. Well, Chlamydia, but naebody bathers aboot that, ken?"), his prowess at darts, golf and Hungry Hungry Hippos, and his cat (also called Jocky) allegedly having to go to the vets after fighting, and defeating, the top boy from the Ardler Pirates.

He became perplexed when, for the third home game in a row, there was some trouble among the away support. Once again the stewards were wading in among the visiting fans, and this time they were capturing them in big nets then using a crane to hoist them out like cod being plucked from the North Sea.

"Whaur the fuck are we hiring these cunts fae these days? Kirkton? There's nae need tae be treatin' fowk like that fur fuck sake."

Although the game's frantic pace didn't let up for a moment and I was seeing plenty of the ball, no clear-cut chances were being created. The clock was ticking, and with less than five minutes to go the frustration of another game going by without getting on the score sheet started to seep in.

"Patience Lloyd. There's still time. A chance will come your way." I looked over to the bench and saw the gaffer standing serenely cross-armed and looking back at me. I nodded back at him. Patience. I had to stay calm so that I was ready to take any chance that did eventually come my way.

As the fourth official's electronic board let us know there were three minutes of injury time to be played, Harry sent a long ball out wide-left for Chrissy Reilly to chase. He managed to keep the ball in play as it was mere inches away from rolling over the sideline.

"Mak' your run, Lloyd."

The calmly delivered instruction was unnecessary as I was already doing just that of my own accord. Chrissy darted toward the touchline and a roar of anticipation went up around the ground. I sprinted towards goal and, as if zigzagging trees in the Derry Jungle, cut left, snapped quickly back to run right, and broke free of Alan Archibald's attention. I was unmarked in the box.

"Stay cool, you've got this aine."

The cross was inch perfect, curling away from Thistle 'keeper Scott Fox's goal on a trajectory that ended on my right boot. For a fleeting moment I was playing fehve n' a boot at the swing park. I was cool, calm and coll-

"HIT IT YA CUNT!"

I made perfect contact and crashed a fierce volley at goal from the penalty spot. My heart leapt as it smashed the crossbar and came back out at me like a cannonball. Before I could react the ball hit me square in the face. It felt like being hit by a brick. I crumpled on impact. My vision spun, blurred then went black.

The sensation of a great deal of weight falling upon me brought me back round. The skies above were dank and grey, and a lone gull circled at an indeterminable height. The sound of cheering from all around started to fade in as if someone was gently turning up the volume.

I appeared to be at the bottom of a heap of bodies, one of which belonged to Davo. His face appeared directly above mine, his red eyes tiny slits in his smiling face.

"Fucking magic, Lloyd!"

In my ear there was hysterical laughter.

"By Christ that wiz funny as fuck! Eh've no' seen any cunt get smashed in the mooth like that since eh teabagged Joe Tortolano."

It all came flooding back as, one by one, my teammates extricated themselves from the pile and I was hauled back to my feet. Three sides of the ground were on their feet cheering and applauding. Scott Fox looked dejected as he punted the ball toward the centre circle.

It went in. The ball ricocheted off the bar, then my face, then crossed the line. I jogged back to the centre circle, still a little groggy and unsure what to do.

"Goalscorer for Dundee, claiming his first goal for the club: LLOOOOOOOYD GEOOOOOOOORGE!"

"Take a bow then ya daft cunt!" Jocky was still highly amused by the situation. I could see him wiping tears from his eyes as his own clapping hands added to the applause. I turned to the Derry, and raised a single clenched fist in their direction. The cheering went up a couple of notches.

By the time I felt fully in control of my senses again the full time whistle had sounded. We'd won 1-0, and I'd scored my first goal for Dundee. With any luck I'd be conscious to see the next one.

* * *

That night I sat in the tipi responding to Jimmy Anderson's message wishing me a happy birthday for the following day when a text from the gaffer came in.

"HIYA LLOYD! HIYA PAL! GET YOUR ARSE UP TAE THE FAIRMUIR FOR 8, CUNTO. LOL."

It was an unexpected order. The gaffer and the lads had showered and changed quickly after the game. Despite a good win and my first goal for the club, they were uncharacteristically quiet as they did so. It had left me feeling a little deflated, particularly as I was about to see in my 18th in the solitude of my humble Native American abode. Suddenly lifted by the invitation to join Jocky for what I could only assume would be post-match analysis over a Special or two, I hastily changed and headed out into the night.

I arrived to find I had been signed in in advance.

"In ye go, son. Jocky's a'ready sorted it oot fur ye."

I thanked the doorman, and gave him a smile over my shoulder when he called out, "Some goal today, by the way. How's yer pus?"

Assuming that the Sunday lunchtime pensioner rave to be something of a one-off, I expected a much more staid affair this time round. I was a fool to underestimate the Fairmuir clubbie.

"SURPRISE!"

The confetti cannons that exploded on either side of me as I entered the function suite nearly gave me a heart attack. The sight of a naked woman so fat a blunderbuss would have failed to halt her progress as she charged through a cloud of colourful paper towards me did nothing to slow my racing pulse either. As Stevie Wonder's *Happy Birthday* played through the sound system she effortlessly hoisted me up into a fireman's lift and carried me up the room through the crowd that had parted for her.

"Here comes the birthday boy! All the ladies in the hoose say 'Hiya Lloyd! Hiya pal!'"

The gaffer was behind the decks performing the dual role of DJ and MC. He cut the sound, and all the ladies present complied with his request. The one who had snared me dropped me on a chair in the centre of the dance floor.

"The lads chipped in tae get ye a lapdance fur yer birthday, Lloyd! Yassssss!"

I looked up to the decks to see he was giving me a double thumbs up like they'd bought me a season ticket in the dugout next to Sir Alex at Old Trafford.

"Get tore in there, Bertha!"

Bertha had tits like beach balls in bin liners. When she swung one in my face it was like being hit with a size 5 Mitre Delta all over again. I went sprawling to the floor to a massive cheer as the lads roared Bertha on from the sidelines.

"Alright Lloyd! Happy birthday for tomorrow, mate! If you hit her with an extra 50 quid she'll suck you off in the car park, eh."

Aye, cheers, Davo.

Bertha got on top of me in a 69 position and wiggled her arse in my face. The fart she blasted out turned out to be a blessing in disguise because, by the time I'd regained consciousness, she waddled out the room in a terry toweling robe to thunderous applause.

Thankfully that was the worst of it. The entire first team squad had assembled to celebrate my impending birthday in the company of the Fairmuir's regular clientele, for whom every day seemed to be a party. They bumped, grinded and bounced their way through the gaffer's hip hop set, and were looking suspiciously out their nuts when Tam McGinty took over behind the decks and started playing Chicago house.

After finishing his set and dedicating it to "a' meh homies" the gaffer joined the lads and me at our table.

"A-tae-the-muthafuckin'-K homeboys, wha's roond is it? Doug, you've no' bought aine since 1972. Get up there ya cunt."

Doug complained bitterly about his difficulties understanding the decimal system for a few minutes before accepting his fate and riding his mobility scooter to the bar.

"How's it goin', Lloyd? Good perty, eh?"

I raised my half-full glass and held it up in agreement and gratitude.

"Brilliant, gaffer. Thanks very much, this is really kind of you. I'm having a great time."

He nicked Eddie McGlone's pint and drained it.

"Nae bather, pal. This has been the venue fur a' kinds o' Dundee celebrations. Birthdays, big wins, Keith Wright's chin being made a National Heritage spot. Fairmuir fuckin' rules, aye."

I was coming round to the fact it did indeed rule. The punters were all wrecked, but very friendly at the same time. The music was good, the atmosphere incredibly lively, and the Special well poured and cheap. Most importantly, I was having a great time with my manager and teammates, who treated me as if I'd been one of the gang for years.

After my last experience with the Special, I was carefully pacing my intake but I consumed enough to make a schoolboy error when my stomach grumbled to signal that Eddie's pastry goods from earlier were ready to make their exit. As I sat in the cubicle reading the back of the door that the gaffer appeared to be using as a page on which to write his memoirs (the opening line read, "It was the maist teckle o' times, it was the pure shitiest o' times, ken?") I heard someone enter the next trap and unzip themselves.

"Well Davie, how are ye pal?"

A giant penis flopped through a hole I hadn't noticed due to its proximity to the toilet roll holder.

"Gaffer! No! Fucking hell, man!"

I shrieked and fled as far away from it as the cubicle's confines would allow, grateful to have already concluded the business that had led me there in the first place.

"Is that you, Lloyd? Yaassssssss!"

The cock slithered back out again.

"Sorry pal, eh thought auld Davie Morrison wiz in the night. Must o' misread the timetable behind the bar, eh! Sakes."

I waited until I heard the main toilet door creak shut before

103

wiping my arse, washing my hands and following him back to the function suite.

Once there, I fell under the gaze of the girl of my dreams.

Our eyes met across a crowded dance floor filled with ecto'd pensioners dancing like the NHS depended on it. She was buxom, blonde and looked like she could suck the colour out of a marble. As she eyeballed me with a look that was somewhere between a pout and a scowl she rested one hand on her hip as the other gripped a full bottle of Blue Wicked that she drained in one go without ever taking her eye off me.

As if in a trance I felt my feet move one ahead of the other. I was rubbish at picking up girls. The very thought of approaching a complete stranger of the opposite sex who I fancied terrified me. And yet I was walking through the throng of flailing limbs and walking sticks, pushing through the smoke that belched out from the DJ booth as my eyes remained unblinded by the lights and the sweep of the lasers. I walked right up to this tower block trophy wife and stood silently before her with my tongue hanging out. She looked me up and down me as if inspecting a newborn lamb up for sale in a farmer's market, licked her lips and growled, "Meh name's Charmaine, and you're comin' hame wi' me the night."

I nodded vacantly back at her. Having already scored earlier in the day it looked like I might make it a brace.

Things were most definitely looking up.

THIRD HALF

THIRD HALF

Charmaine McMaster, a 22-year-old bin lorry operative, was the last remaining resident of a multi-storey block in Lochee. As we made the ascent to her 14th floor flat in a lift that not only stunk of piss but also boasted a fairly substantial coil of human shite in its back corner, she explained, "The cooncil reckon they'll move iz oot tae Whitfield. That'll be fuckin' right – Whitfield's minky as fuck."

She had the voice of an angel, albeit one that smoked 80 Woodbine a day. It was so husky she made Mariella Frostrup sound like a prepubescent choirboy.

"Nae danger eh'm movin' oot the penthoose suite here. Any time the cunts come tae the door eh chase them doon the stairs wi' a giant dildo wrapped in barbed wire. The "Fanny Ripper", as eh call it. Christ knows there's plenty o' thum needin' ripped in that fuckin' cooncil, eh Lloyd."

I was about to agree despite knowing nothing of local politics when I was cut off with the umpteeth lustful kiss she'd laid on me since we met. I managed to deftly sidestep past the turd as Charmaine forced me back against the wall. I grabbed two handfuls of her ample, shapely arse and submitted to the tongue that was in about my mouth like there was treasure hidden in there.

We reached the top floor and, as she fumbled in her handbag to find her door key, Charmaine scattered a knife, a strip of condoms and what looked like a handful of human teeth across the landing. As she bent over to pick them up, I remembered the "be careful" look the gaffer had given me when we'd departed the Fairmuir.

The lads seemed to think Charmaine was brilliant, no doubt partly due to her ability to pop the cap off Doug's bottle of Sweetheart Stout with her cleavage. This move saw the old keeper's false teeth fly out his mouth and into Chrissy Reilly's pint of Special, eliciting a huge roar of approval from all present except Jocky.

"Wha signed ye in, doll? This is a members only clubbie and eh dinnae recall seein' your tits in here before."

She'd hesitated a second before answering, "An auld boy, think it was Bert somehin' or other. Eh dinnae ken, eh wiz just passin' and fancied a Blue Wicked. No' that it's any o' your business."

The gaffer had nearly choked on his pint.

"Nane o' meh business? Eh'm the tap boy in here! The Man in Cherge! Anyway, point oot this Bert o' yours; we've got aboot 40 Berts in here. If the place opened a dedicated Bert Lounge it would be packed oot."

She had a cursory glance over both shoulders before declaring that the Bert in question was nowhere to be seen. The gaffer said nothing more, but silently stared Charmaine down for most of the rest of the night.

"Mon in. Meh casa es su casa, aye."

She turned and gave me a cosmopolitan, woman-of-the-world look.

"That's Italian fur 'wipe yer fuckin' feet'."

I gave them a thorough rub on the filthy doormat that had the faded words 'HULLTOON HUNS' written on it and entered Chez Charmaine.

The "penthoose" was a rather ramshackle affair. I would guess it had last been decorated around the time monkeys were being sent up into space, while a deep-set odour suggested someone had died and lain undiscovered for some time prior to Charmaine getting the keys. Still, it was homely in a reminds-you-of-your-granny sort of way.

After fetching a couple of Blue Wickeds from a kitchen with dirty dishes piled almost to the ceiling on every available surface, Charmaine led me out to the flat's small balcony.

"Cracking view, Charmaine," I said, genuinely impressed as I leaned on the guardrail and sipped the toxic-tasting concoction that was a poor substitute for a good pint of Special.

"No' as good as this view, ya wee ride," said Charmaine as her black dress dropped to her ankles. My jaw hit the floor but the bottle fell some 14 floors further, causing me to shout "fuck!" after it.

"Dinnae worry aboot it," she said moving in behind me and sliding a hand round to give my crotch a squeeze, "Naebody bathers aboot chuckin' stuff oot the windie or aff the balcony here."

Her free hand directed me toward the multi opposite and what looked like a burning settee hurtling out from the 10th floor toward the car park below. She had my rapidly stiffening cock in her hand by the time the settee landed on what I hoped was an empty police patrol car and didn't let go until the opening bars of the dawn chorus. By the time I swaggered back into the lift some sleepless hours later, I'd been sucked, fucked, licked, bitten and, at one point, treated to the kind of experience that accidently happens when your bog roll isn't of the two-ply variety.

As far as birthday presents went, it wasn't too shabby.

* * *

I arrived at Dens for training to be told the gaffer wanted to see me in his office. I'd been drifting through the day in a post-sex daze, but the summons immediately set the butterflies fluttering. The sign on his office door that read "Abandon a' Hope a' ye wha' Enter" did little to ease my fears. I raised my fist to chap on the wood only to be halted by the sound of voices from beyond the door.

"It is absolutely imperative that Fong Du plays, Jocky. I cannot stress that highly enough. I have a lot riding on his continuing appearance on the pitch."

The club's CEO sounded none too pleased.

"Boaby, eh've got a tenner ridin' on the new Star Wars films bein' aboot Lando and Darth Vader startin' up a space chapter o' the Black Panthers, disnae mean it's gonnae happen though. The boy's fuckin' injured! Eh'm no a master o' the black arts wha can just voodoo him better, Boaby. Eh'm no' Jimmy Calderwood! The doc reckons he's gubbed fur six, mibbe seven weeks. Deal wi' it."

I bit my lip and backed away from the door a little, unsure whether to hang around or leave and come back later.

"Calm the fuckin' ham, Boaby. Young Lloyd's mair than capable o' daein' the damage up front. He just needs a wee bit more time tae find his feet aye."

Pride caused my chest to swell, only to be cut off at the pass the moment Bob McCracken spoke again.

"Don't give me that nonsense. The boy's no footballer. And that's to say nothing of his negligible marketing value."

My heart sank so far it almost hit the floor.

"He'll be twice the fucking player that heap of foreign import shite you signed will ever be, McCracken. Eh ken a futba player when eh see them; Lloyd's got what it taks. If we spent mair time bringin' boys like him on instead o' spendin' big bucks on mercenaries like Fong fuckin' Du the gemme wouldnae be in the state it is."

I could hear McCracken scoffing.

"You're the absolute last person to pass comment on the state of Scottish football, Jocky. Take a look in the mirror for goodness sake."

The sound of a chair sliding across the floor and footsteps making their way toward the door sent me scurrying up the corridor. I hid in the passageway that led to the dressing rooms and waited until I heard the gaffer's office door slam shut and McCracken stomp off in the direction of the boardroom.

I felt disappointed and betrayed but in no way surprised. The man had been full of shit from the start but they were still harsh words to hear. I took a breath and returned to the gaffer's office door. I knocked and popped my head into the room.

"Hello, gaffer. You wanted to..."

He was standing in the corner of the room with his jogging bottoms round his ankles pissing in a bucket. The letter 'J' was tattooed on his left buttock, and 'CKY' on his right.

"'Mon in, Lloyd. Grab a seat."

As I pulled up a chair he finished answering nature's call, bent over to pull his bottoms up, and revealed how human anatomy can cunningly be used to make savings in tattoo parlours.

"How ye gettin' on, son?"

I chose my words carefully so he wouldn't know I'd been eavesdropping. "I'm ok thanks gaffer. Did I, um, see Mr McCracken leaving as I came in there?"

"Auld Boaby? Aye, he wiz in fur a gemme o' Hungry Hungry Hippos."

He leaned forward, resting his elbows on the desk and explained, "The thing Boaby, and any other cunt wha wants tae get wide must remember, Lloyd, is that nae cunt's hippo is hungrier than mine. Nae cunt! Jocky's hippo nearly put Jimmy Chung oot o' business he wiz that hungry! It wiped out the whole fuckin' buffet nae bather! When the food wiz finished the mad bastard started eating chopsticks and drinking a' the soy sauce. Efter a' that he still wanted a chippy on the way back up the road. Meh hippo's fuckin' stervin'!"

Given the nature of his conversation with McCracken, I could understand the gaffer wanting to shield me from it. I let him thump away at an imaginary Hungry Hungry Hippos activation button until he was ready to speak about whatever it was I'd been summoned for.

A full five minutes later he finally stopped banging the desk and got to the point.

"Lloyd, Fong Du's oot for a while. Shame eh? No' really. Eh want you up front leadin' the attack, Lloyd. Yer playin' better beh the week as a subby; yer ready tae mak' a startin' appearance."

I felt my lip tremble just a little.

"Reckon ye can dae the damage, pal?"

He believed in me. With conviction, I replied, "Yeah, gaffer. I'm ready. I won't let you down."

Jocky raised his head, jutted his chin out and nodded once to confirm his approval at my self-belief.

"Good lad. Tell ye what, Lloyd, this is a good chance fur ye. If ye do well in the coming gemmes eh winnae drap a form player. Stake yer claim, laddie. Let's see what yer made o'."

My footballing ambitions had always revolved around personal glory but now I was determined to succeed so I could repay Jocky's faith in me. Getting it right up Bob McCracken would be an additional bonus we'd both enjoy.

With football business concluded, conversation turned to more informal matters.

"So, got yer hole on Saturday, eh?"

I could feel myself blushing a little. "I did, aye. Big time, gaffer."

His chuckle and raised eyebrow said "I bet you did."

"The Fairmuir's turning oot tae be a good huntin' ground for ye, eh? That's you pulled twice in twa visits. They'll be namin' a lounge efter ye if ye keep this up. Whaur did ye end up? Did ye gie her the totem pole in the tipi or wiz it back tae her hoose?"

"Her place. She lives in Lochee, in one of the multis."

He seemed vaguely impressed.

"Lochee burd, eh? Good stuff."

He gave his mouser a thoughtful stroke.

"Here, ask her if she kens Mad Alfie."

"Who?"

"Alfie's a pal o' mine fae Lochee. Mibbe Charmaine kens him tae, ken?"

There was something odd about the request, but I couldn't quite put my finger on it. I agreed to ask about this Mad Alfie character.

"Dundee's built on kennin' fowk, Lloyd. It gets good when the boy yer askin' fur's actually called Ken, tae. Dae ye ken Ken? Ken aye."

Dundonian was a bit like Swahili at times. I left him sitting repeatedly saying 'ken' to himself and headed down to the dressing room for training.

* * *

I feared the worst when Wally told us to board the team bus as soon as we'd changed into our training gear. Surely to fuck we weren't going back to Tesco. Seeing my ashen face and picking up on the heavy back-to-jail vibe I was giving off, he was quick to reassure me that nothing criminal was in the offing. "The gaffer's told us to meet down at his house; we'll be training there today. We're on the team bus, he's flying."

Thank Sir Alex for that.

A short while later we were driving through Broughty Ferry, which Eddie explained was Dundee's "posh bit". It was certainly a step or six up from the Hilltown. The homes here weren't stacked up on each other like the tenement and tower blocks at the "tap o' the hull" and the denizens of the area were neither clad in tracksuits nor obviously under the influence of drink or drugs. Although the bus windows weren't open I caught the unmistakeable whiff of money in the air. As such, I wasn't surprised that the impressive pile of bricks we pulled up alongside was situated in this affluent suburb. I was, however, astounded that my earthy gaffer called it home.

That fact did make the quirky touches and downright oddities easier to understand. As we disembarked, I noticed two flags flying high from the roof: one was a giant red, white and blue flag bearing the legend 'BIG JOCK'S HOOSE', and the other that staple of pirate ships around the seven seas, the skull 'n' crossbones. We passed through a gate on which a sign reading 'TRESSPASSERS WILL GET TELT' served as a warning to anyone who fancied a bit of backie trooping, ironic given the gaffer's own enthusiasm for the game. The team started up a meandering path which had been painted bright yellow, and silently nodded to a pair of midgets dressed as Munchkins as they tended to a flowerbed arranged to read 'THERE'S NAE PLACE LIKE HAME, AYE'.

Less quaint was the garden's water feature. Jocky had installed a life-size stone statue of himself in the trees to the right hand side of the path. Water spouted forth from the nose, ears, mouth and erect penis he'd fashioned from a huge piece of what I suspected was fireman's hose. As the hose swung round in a circular motion like a helicopter's rotor blade, it not only showcased the designer's talent but served as a useful means of watering the grass.

A half-dozen blow-up dolls dressed in Dundee United kits hung by their necks from the branches of a monkey puzzle tree. As I stood trying to comprehend the scene, Wally pressed the doorbell and unleashed an airhorn that would be heard on oil rigs in the North Sea and nearly caused the entire first team squad to miss the next game due to an outbreak of burst eardrums.

"I forget the doorbell every time. Sorry, lads," was what I think Wally said next but the ringing in my ears drowned him out. The excruciating siren faded as the door opened and I followed the rest of the lads inside the house.

"Hiya Lloyd! Hiya pal! Bonnie gairden, eh?"

He was wearing his usual trackie bottoms, but instead of football boots on his feet he was wearing a pair of giant novelty football boot slippers.

"They Munchkins dae a helluva good joab, like. Quite useful if ye come in pished and fancy a wrestle tae, ye kin knock fuck oot them and they cannae really fight back. 'Mon in, cunto."

As I accepted the offer and moved inside, a white cat strolled past my feet. It had a black moustache painted on its face. The gaffer scooped it up and kissed it square on the mouth for around 10 seconds longer than necessary.

"Hiya wee aine! Hiya pal! Check oot meh pussy cat, Lloyd. Called Jocky tae, likes. Trained in seven martial arts, a 33rd level Mason and a Grand Master at Connect 4. Good, eh?"

The alleged ninja cat gave me a withering look.

"Aye, brilliant, gaffer. Is he friendly?"

I lifted my hand to give the feline a stroke on the cheek. It made a low, guttural growling sound more likely to emanate from a guard dog whose knackers had been trod on by a clumsy burglar. My hand shot back.

"Friendly as fuck once ye get tae ken 'im, eh suppose, but until that time comes treat Wee Jocky wi' the same caution ye would a Great White shark if ye were oot sweemin' in tropical water wi' a pound o' raw mince doon yer shorts."

I jumped back as the cat leapt from his master's grasp and pushed through a door that I assumed led to the living room. I quite liked cats, but I'd be sure to avoid this one as best I could in future.

The day's exercise was training at its bizarre, shambolic best. While the gaffer wanted us to play head tennis, the game had to be played as we decorated his spare bedroom. One group went to work stripping wallpaper, another sanded down the wooden floors and a third went to work painting the ceiling.

"Keep that ba' movin', lads. And hurry the fuck up wi' the decorating; eh've got joiners comin' in the 'morra tae mak' this intae aine o' the rooms fae the Aztec Zone in 'The Crystal Maze'."

Several hours later the room was prepared for the joiners' arrival in the morning, and the lads began making their way back to the bus. Nature called, and I decided to quickly make use of the facilities before leaving. I nearly jumped of out my skin when I saw a familiar face standing in behind the toilet holding a towel.

"Dong Chu! Fuck sake, man, what a fright!"

He bowed serenely and replied, "Greetings, Mr Lloyd George. I am pleased to see you. When not interpreting for Fong Du I work for Mr Jocky. Toilet attendant and testicle washer jobs provide much needed additional income to send home to my family."

His sweet little smile betrayed the horror of his employment, and didn't make it particularly easy to take a slash either. I forced out a trickle, politely declined the offer of a nut scrub and headed out and down the stairs toward the front door.

When I reached it, I noticed the living room door was still ajar. Thinking I might say cheerio to the gaffer before depart-ing, and moving cautiously in case the cat was lurking in there, I slipped my head round the door.

"Gaffer? That's us away..."

The room was hands down the weirdest I'd ever encountered. Every inch of the floor was covered in sand, much of which had been used to build a hugely intricate sand-castle interpretation of Dens. Several deckchairs faced the biggest wall-mounted TV I'd ever seen. The opposite wall had been used in its entirety to recre-ate that famous painting of God reaching down from the heavens to touch the outreaching pointed finger of a man on Earth. A spark burst across the small gap between their fingers. The face of both God and his human creation had been replaced by that of the gaffer. Jocky creating Jocky. I shivered involuntarily.

I found myself wandering about the room marvelling at how fucking ridiculous it was. A stuffed bear standing on its hind legs was dressed in a Dundee strip with a novelty arrow positioned so that it appeared to have been short through the head. A lamp-post still bearing a 'Neighbourhood Watch' sign that had been stolen, cut in half and placed in the corner of the room illumi-nated the scene. There were framed photos all over the place. The ones of Jocky with various Scottish footballing luminaries looked authentic, but others with him cheerfully embracing celebrities including Dr Dre, Godzilla and the cast of *Saved by the Bell* had clearly been created by him cutting his own face from photo-graphs and sticking it on magazine pictures.

One of the few normal features was a bookcase. I browsed from shelf to shelf, impressed at the array of fancy authors and amused at his comprehensive collection of *The Broons* and *Oor Wullie* annuals.

"Meow."

I froze. After a few moments of inexplicable terror I slowly turned round, and saw the cat sitting in the centre circle of sand-castle Dens. He was staring right at me. He did not look amused.

"Eh, hello there, pussy cat."

He didn't respond. As I started inching cautiously toward the door, a beep from the bus's horn made me jump then freeze to the spot. The cat tilted its little moustachioed head to one side as if curious to see what my next move was. Mercifully Wee Jocky didn't budge an inch as I burst out the door and sprinted past the midgets, who lent on their spades, smoking and looking as if they were pining for the days when wicked witches were their main concern in life.

* * *

All of a sudden, I was scoring left, right and centre, and in more ways than one. I hit a blazing run of form that saw me find the back of the net five times in four matches as we extended our undefeated run and even won what the gaffer described as our "bogey fixture" – Queen of the South away. Apparently Dumfries was somewhere Dundee traditionally struggled to get a result, but the only problem on the day was our riotously drunken support. Having no doubt spent the three-hour journey south enjoying liquid refreshments and quite possibly a tenner ecto or two, they spilled out the stand onto the pitch in celebration of both goals. I couldn't help but notice that the stewards were much more forgiving than their counterparts at Dens, despite our travelling support behaving far worse than any I'd seen at our ground.

I was also doing more shagging than Ryan Giggs at a family reunion. Charmaine's sexual appetite was rampant and, despite the fact she was clearly as mental as Wesley Snipes is black, I was having the time of my life with her. Some of her moves could have been copied straight from schemiehoors, and I suspected the additional physical exertion was paying dividends on the pitch. An evening in Charmaine's bed left me more exhausted than any training session I'd undertaken with the team, including the time we had to race up the Law Hill on Space Hoppers then return to the bottom whilst doing "the worm". It was the very best of win-win situations.

I'd gained a great deal of insight into Charmaine's character through our post-coital conversations. When we weren't fucking in Balgay cemetery, in any number of dark closies, or, on one particularly memorable occasion, on the number 28 bus, we'd laze around in bed enjoying the free and easy nature of after-sex conversation.

"There's ayewiz three questions tae be answered when it comes tae losin' yer virginity, Lloyd. How auld were ye; wha wiz it wi'; dae ye wish ye'd waited fur someone ye loved. Tell iz whit your answers are, sugarcock."

I was too embarrassed to admit that the answers were 17 and eleven-twelfths, a woman old enough to be my gran, and yes, so I made something up about a mate's sister at a party a few years back. She coughed a "fair doos" between cheek-pinching draws of a roll-up cigarette.

"What about you, Char?"

She pulled me to her so I was squashed in against her ample bosom. The use of my ear as an ashtray probably wasn't intentional.

"Eh lost mine at meh Uncle Joe's hoose."

"What, did you sneak upstairs with a guy at a New Year party or something?"

"Nah, it was wi' Uncle Joe aine efternane efter he picked iz up fae the skail."

Horrified, I pulled myself free of her grasp to look at her and see if she was serious. The perfectly calm demeanour between relaxed puffs on her fag suggested she was.

"But that's..."

I knew the words I wanted to say but daren't utter them. Charmaine had no problem in doing so.

"Incest. Statutory rape. Morally reprehensible. Ken what else it wiz, Lloyd?"

I could only shake my head silently.

"Fuckin' class. Uncle Joe fair kent how tae push a green banana's love buttons, let me tell ye. Fuckin' great ride. We were shagging fur years. Probably still be at it nowadays if he hudnae keeled ower in the Planet Bar when that boy McFadden scored a screamer fur Scotland against France. God rest his soul, aye."

I slowly eased myself back down and clung to her like a newborn chimp embracing its mother. Anxious to change the subject I asked, "How did you get a job on the bin lorry, Char? No offence, but a scaffie's a fairly unusual gig for a lassie."

She flicked her cigarette butt toward the window. It wasn't open, so the remains of her roll-up merely bounced off the glass and landed on the carpet. I made a motion to go pick it up, but she eased me back down against her with a firm arm.

"Mibbe it is, sugarcock, but eh couldnae gie a fuck. It pays the bills, eh. Eh wiz wanderin' doon the High Street aine moarnin, jist headin' hame efter pumpin' some boy wha bides up Beachie, when eh passed the bin lorry and a' the boys wha were chuckin' bags o' rubbish in the back o' it. They a' started wolf whistlin' and giein' it, "get yer tits oot." The usual shite."

I had a fair idea where this was going so kept quiet to let her finish.

"Of course, eh duly oblehged. Aine boy goes, 'Crackin' bazookas, doll; fancy a ride in the lorry?' Now, eh'm no' sure if he meant sittin' in the cab up front or no', but twa meenits later eh wiz bent ower the back o' the thing takin' aine up the shitepipe as bin bags went flehin' ower iz intae the bit that chews it a' up, aye."

Remarkable stuff.

"And they gave you a job for that?"

She let go of me and perched herself on one elbow, lifted the duvet and let off a fart so resonant in tone it might have passed as an elongated note from a tuba.

"Nah, they didnae. What happened wiz the crew's gaffer went past in his motor and saw aine o' his lads on the joab whilst on the joab. The boy stopped and sacked the cunt wha' wiz ridin' iz on the spot. Apparently Dundee City Council frowns upon that kind o' behaviour."

She got up out of bed and draped a Playgirl nightgown over herself.

"Anyway, this a' happened jist eh'd been punted fae Lidl efter knockin' fuck oot these twa Polish boys in the car park efter they got wide at meh checkout, so eh says tae the gaffer boy, 'Go 'n gie iz that boy's joab, mate. The only cunt eh'll shag will be you, and we'll dae it somewhaur mair discreet than ootside The Bed Shed in broad daylight tae.' Boy wiz like that, 'Eh nae bather, aye.' That was 18 month ago."

As she made towards the door I pulled the duvet up to my chin and blurted out, "Are you still shagging him, Char? Your boss at work, I mean."

Seeing that I was somewhat wounded at the thought she cooed at me and came back to sit by my side. She ruffled my hair with one hand as the other slipped under the covers to gently stroke my member as if it were a cherished family pet.

"Awwww... is meh wee futba star jealous? Eh've only got eyes fur you now, sugarcock. Unless we're at an orgy or somethin' – which we might be if yer gemme fur it by the way – your toby is the only aine fur me."

She gave me a wee kiss on the forehead.

"Besides, the gaffer fucked aff tae bide in Arbroath when his missus, wha's fae a pure mental femly fae Fintry, came hame fae work early aine efternane and caught me goin' at his dowp wi' a cucumber. She wisnae happy, like. To be fair, neither would eh be if some cunt had stuff up their erse that wiz intended for meh piece the next day. Anyway, he fucked aff afore he got his legs broke."

She was quite the lady, and the more time we spent together the more I grew to like her. As long as she didn't get fresh with the contents of tomorrow's piece box I was ready for anything.

* * *

Although Jocky was unquestionably the "man in cherge" at the Fairmuir, on this particular Saturday night I felt like I owned the place.

"Here's tae the hat-trick hero. Well done, Lloyd."

I raised the pint of Special the gaffer insisted on buying me after the game and beamed from ear to ear as I clinked glasses with him and a few of the boys. It had been a fantastic afternoon. In the biggest game of the season so far we'd beaten our nearest rivals Falkirk 3-2 at Dens. Despite dominating possession, we somehow found ourselves two-down as we ate our half-time stovies. After a rousing team talk which involved the gaffer and Dong Chu acting out the final round of *Rocky II*, we'd gone out determined to get back in the game. We did just that when I nodded home a Kevin Rafferty cross a couple of minutes into the half. After I punished the Falkirk defence for some sloppy defending with 15 to go, there was only going to be one winner. When Harry sent a long ball over the top for me to run on to in the final minutes of the game I knew I was about to score my first senior hat-trick. Dens was in raptures well in advance of me rounding the 'keeper and slotting the ball into the empty net.

"Some atmosphere today, eh gaffer?"

Eddie might have been stating the obvious somewhat, but it was definitely a point worth making. The home support had remained behind us even when we went two-down and had played a big part in our comeback. When I wheeled away run towards the Bobby Cox Stand, the celebrations were no less enthusiastic than had the goal been scored at Hampden in a Cup Final.

"Oh eh, Eddie, it was braw. Me and auld Walzo were goin' fuckin' mental. Maistly 'cause we put 20 quid on us winnin' 3-2 in the dressing room efter you cunts went oot fur the second half. But it wiz a big win fur futba reasons tae, like. Thirteen points clear at the tap o' the league. Teckle!"

Once we'd shook hands with our opponents and the gaffer had sung a verse and chorus of *Oliver's Army* at Falkirk boss Steven Pressley ("Boy's called Elvis! Yaassssss!"), he ushered us toward each home section of the ground so we could give thanks to those who had cheered us on to victory. As I stood returning the applause, I appreciated Dens Park properly for the first time. Okay, it was a bit of a shithole by modern criteria, but there was absolutely no denying the buzz about the place on a day like today. I felt some kind of energy within the ground, like it had been charged up by an electrical current that ran through the stands and sparked out on to the pitch. I felt it earth right in my gut.

It was good to be out with the gaffer and the lads again. Although technically we were work colleagues and his subordinates, it felt like we were all pals together. Conversation was as free-flowing as the Special we happily necked away at, and the laughter plentiful. Once I reached the bottom of the glass of pint number four I felt brave enough to press the gaffer on something that had been on my mind since the day we'd trained at his house.

"Here gaffer, what's the score with that cat of yours? Is he really... well, mental?"

He wiped the froth from his moustache and gave me a serious look.

"Oh fuck aye. Much like the Wu Tang Clan, Wee Jocky ain't nothin' tae fuck wit'."

I sneaked a look at my teammates as I took my next sip. The raised eyebrows and faint smiles made me wonder what they knew about the gaffer's pet. Undaunted I pressed for more information.

"Mind if I ask where you got him, gaffer?"

He drained his pint with a satisfied gulp.

"Well, eh wiz in this weird wee shop in Chinatown, or the Keiller Centre as it's mair commonly known, lookin' fur a Christmas pressie fur Maurice Malpas. Eh wiz at the counter buyin' a giant black dildo wi' 'HIYA MO! HIYA PAL!' written doon the side o' it when eh spotted this cat sittin' up on the shelf behind the auld Chinese fella wha ran the show."

With my interest very much piqued I leaned in a little closer.

"Eh says tae the boy, 'Hola, cunto. Wha's in cherge here?' The boy said fuck all. Probably didnae understand English that well. Eh says, 'What's the score wi' thon pussy cat up there? He's fuckin' teckle lookin'!' The boy saw iz pointin' at it and understood what eh wiz meanin'. 'Not for sale, too much responsibility,' says auld Hong Kong Phooey behind the counter. 'Punch in the fuckin' pus time,' says Big Jocky."

He pummelled his fist into his other hand and pointed to his wrist to illustrate the point.

"The boy goes, 'Fuckin' chill oot big stuff, it's nae bather aye,' and sells iz the cat. Did a braw joab gift wrappin' Mo's dildo tae. Anyway, on the way oot the door the boy warns iz, 'Never expose it tae bright light, never get it wet and never feed it efter midnight.' Eh says, nae bather, pal. Cheery. Boy wiz talkin' a load ay shite, eh hud it in the bath eatin' stovies at three in the moarnin'; fuck all happened. There's a 100-watt bulb in meh bathroom, tae."

Chrissy coughed the word "Gremlins" and the gaffer was just spinning round to take him to task when my mobile vibrated into life on the table in front of me.

"*Just seen twa doags fuckin in the bushies, feelin pure horny as fuck. Get that toby of yours up here pronto, sugarcock. Luv Char X*"

Harry had picked up the drinks tray and was asking if it was the same again for everyone.

"Nah, I've got to make a move, Harry. Cheers though."

"Oh aye. That'll have been your burd then? Following orders already, you're well under the thumb there, mate."

The elbow nudge that accompanied the slagging let me know Davo was only being half-serious.

"It's been a good night and all that, lads, but y'know, I've only scored three times today and quite fancy a fourth."

Lewd banter didn't come naturally to me but Charmaine had taught me well over the past few weeks and, judging by the backslapping that followed my retort, I was getting better at it.

After a round of handshakes and good wishes, I slid out the booth and made to leave.

"Eh'll see ye oot, Lloyd."

The gaffer guided me through the crowd toward the door. I had to shake a few more hands on the way, and one guy called out, "Great gemme the day, son!" as I passed by his table. I could get used to this.

We pushed through the function suite doors into the corridor.

"Well done today, Lloyd. Outstandin' performance. Pleased fur ye, aye."

The words were spoken as seriously as any I'd heard him say since knowing him, and the blazing eyes that had once terrified me were now full of respect.

"Cheers, gaffer. I appreciate you giving me my chance. That was for you as much as anyone."

He winked and said it was nae bather.

As he walked me down to the door he seemed to be weighing something up, and cleared his throat before tentatively changing the subject.

"Lloyd pal, eh'm glad yer hain' a teckle time wi' this lassie ye met and a' that, but eh want ye tae mind how ye go wi' her. There's somethin' aboot her that's giein' me... eh dinnae ken... a wee bad feelin' or somethin', ken?"

"What makes you say that, gaffer?"

I stopped to face him. It clearly hadn't been easy for him to say what he had. I wasn't offended but the fact it wasn't like him to be mindful of his words meant I was definitely curious.

"Well, she seems pretty... what's the word... mental, ken? I'm sure she's lovely, pal, but that night eh met her she wiz pretty full on. No' really the kind o' dame eh wid picture you wi', ken?"

It was a fair point, although he thankfully wasn't privy to my Internet history and the gaffer calling someone mental was like Ruud van Nistelrooy drawing attention to a person's equinity.

"There's somethin' else tae. Mind she said she got signed in beh Bert?"

I nodded.

"Well... eh wiz a wee bit suspicious o' that, and when eh checked the book tae see a'body wha wiz signed in that night, she wisnae on it. Naebody called Bert, or anythin' else fur that matter, signed her in the clubbie that night ye met."

He gave his 'tache a thoughtful stroke and shrugged.

"I don't know what to tell you, gaffer," I said trying to make light of what was starting to feel like an awkward situation.

"Maybe the guy on the door let her through without putting her name down or something. Considering what she was wearing that night I can see why the guy got distracted."

We both looked down to the door and the old smoothie manning it turning on the charm with two elderly ladies as they entered.

"Mibbe, aye. Auld Johnnie there would o' been checkin' oot the twa Eammon Bannon nappers right enough."

I had no idea who Eammon Bannon was, but agreed with him. He lightened up.

"Fair doos, son. Nothin' tae worry aboot. Enjoy the rest o' yer night, eh?"

We shook hands again.

"Oh, and mind and ask if she kens Mad Alfie, Lloyd."

I'd forgotten all about that.

"Will do, gaffer. See you Monday."

As I was about to exit I turned to see if he was still there but saw only the double doors he'd departed into the main room through swinging back and forth until they creaked to a halt and closed behind him.

* * *

When I saw Bob McCracken approaching, my first instinct was to duck out the way. I'd seen him a few times in the weeks since I overheard the conversation in Jocky's office but never in a situation where we would have to talk directly. Unfortunately, the narrow corridor that led from the main entrance to the dressing rooms meant engagement with St Andrews' premier snake oil salesman was unavoidable.

"Lloyd my good man, how the devil are you?"

His smile came on full beam as if at the flick of a switch.

"Not bad thanks, Mr McCracken. Yourself?"

My interest in his wellbeing was minimal, but I sensed it wasn't in my interests to be anything other than civil with him.

"I see it all, Lloyd. You know how it goes."

He winked and wrapped an arm round my shoulder. I fought the urge to flinch out of his reach and McCracken started walking me back in the direction from which he came.

"You're on dazzling form at the moment, Lloyd. I'm glad you paid heed to my advice and watched Fong Du's game, it's paid off dividends for you. It's unfortunate for you that he'll be back as first choice striker now that he's on the verge of returning from injury."

Noting my wounded look, he continued, "You don't expect to be picked ahead of a first-class international striker, do you Lloyd? You may be scoring a goal here and there but you have to look at the situation rationally. Fong Du's presence means more than just goals; many of my future marketing and sponsorship plans depend on him being in the starting line up."

The gaffer had promised he wouldn't drop a form player, and I'd lived up to my end of the bargain. I wondered just how much sway McCracken had, and hoped it wasn't enough to see me back on the bench marking the gaffer's coupon.

We were outside the CEO's office now. He ushered me inside, lowered his voice a little and tapped his nose.

"Not to worry though Lloyd; I have a proposition that may see you move up in the world and maintain first team football. Come on in."

McCracken's office wasn't in the same league as Jocky's living room in terms of what-the-fuck factor, but it still stopped me in my tracks within a couple of steps of entering. The walls were adorned with three huge portraits in ostentatious frames. One was of Maggie Thatcher, another of some old businessman type whom I didn't recognise, and the third... Bob McCracken. I stood gaping at it. He'd had a painting done of himself attempting to look noble as he leaned against a grand wooden desk. When I turned back, the man was mimicking the pose against his own, much less impressive table. After a few seconds he broke the posture and looked more pleased with himself than was necessary.

Desperate to try and lessen the weirdness a little, I pointed to the painting of the guy I didn't recognise and asked who it was. McCracken re-engaged me in an over-the-shoulder hug and looked up at it wistfully.

"That gentleman – that hero – right there, Lloyd, is our lord and saviour Sir Fred Goodwin."

I'd heard the name from the news.

"The banker guy?"

Without taking his slightly misty-looking eyes off the painting he corrected me.

"To call Sir Fred a banker would be to call Lady Thatcher there a mere politician. Like the much-missed Iron Lady he was much more than that. When the economic crisis hit, someone had to carry the weight of responsibility, and poor Sir Freddie was quite viciously forced to suffer for all our sins. Is he capitalism's greatest martyr? Perhaps."

His voice broke and a tear spilled as he recalled, "They smashed the windows of his home, Lloyd. After all he'd done for us, they smashed the windows of his home. Forgive me; it's still hard to talk about."

He squeezed me tight and removed a monogrammed handkerchief from the top pocket of his moderately priced suit to wipe away his tears. After muttering, "Bless you, Sir Freddie Goodwin," he indicated I should take a seat at this desk. As he moved round the other side and eased himself into the kind of chair Bond villains stroke cats in, I had a quick glance over the things on his desk. Along with executive stress balls and one of those pin things you can leave imprints of your face in was a folder marked 'The St Andrews Project'. They do say a lot of business deals are cut on the golf course and the local putting green was probably more McCracken's style.

"So, Lloyd; let's talk business."

He'd reclined back into the black leather chair and was strumming his fingers on its armrests.

"Your recent run of form has not gone unnoticed, young man. There's been some interest in you from down south. From the Lancashire area, as it happens."

I sat bolt upright in my seat. Surely Man United weren't on to me already. McCracken laughed at my optimistic reaction.

"Settle down, Lloyd. You're not headed to the Theatre of Dreams quite yet. However, Accrington isn't too far away from it."

I gave myself a mental kick for giving McCracken a laugh at my expense.

"Accrington, Mr McCracken?"

"Accrington Stanley, Lloyd. A fine League Two outfit who have been scouring the lower leagues of Scotland for up-and-coming young players. You caught their attention, and I'm reliably informed they had someone up watching you in the defeat of Falkirk at the weekend."

I was flattered, and nodded thoughtfully. McCracken leaned forward on his elbows and made his proposition.

"What would you say to a move, Lloyd? I can strike a deal on your behalf. The £10,000 I could sell you for would be put to very good use in building this club's future. We need a new corporate logo you know. At the same time, you would be a step closer to fulfilling your ambition both career-wise and geographically. This might be a great opportunity for you, Lloyd."

It was a most unexpected development. I exhaled loudly.

"Wow. I'm not sure what to say, Mr McCracken. It hadn't crossed my mind for a second that I might move on so quickly. I've only just found my feet, y'know?"

McCracken leaned even further over the desk. I thought he was going to reach out and take me by the hand.

"Lloyd, in business you should always strike while the iron is hot, and when opportunities come along you grab them with both hands. Do some blue sky thinking with me on this one; think of the possibilities!"

I became restless in my seat and started fidgeting about.

"I dunno, Mr McCracken. It's a bit too soon, or something. I kinda like it at Dundee. It's good here."

He looked at me like I'd just suggested burying Thatcher in a coal mine.

"You like it here? Lloyd, frequenting that class-forsaken club with Jocky and hanging around with Lochee scrubbers appears to be pickling your brain somewhat. Accrington is a proud club in a country where football isn't run and played by drunks and amateurs; a move to England is a huge step up from Scottish football. At least until after my revolution anyway."

Despite McCracken's protestations, it wasn't for me. I was genuinely was enjoying my time at Dundee both on and off the park.

"What's Jocky saying to all this, Mr McCracken? I wouldn't have thought he'd want to let me go quite so soon."

Realising I wasn't going for the carrot he was dangling, McCracken sat back in his chair again.

"His opinion is of little concern to me, Lloyd. This one was between you and I. Do me a favour; give it some thought. Perhaps come the end of the season you'll have seen sense on the matter and a move to the Vegas of the North West will happen."

"Is it not Blackpool they call the Vegas of the North West?"

"No, it's definitely Accrington."

I left his office feeling like I needed to take a shower, and wondering how he knew I'd fallen in love with a Lochee scrubber.

* * *

Even on a Thursday night, Dundee city centre was not for the faint-hearted. Groups of loud and lairy young guys strutted their way through the streets like pack animals while screeching groups of girls wearing much less than the temperature required teetered on the brink of broken ankles in comfort-denying high heels. They yelled and laughed and vomited their way from pub to pub creating the kind of scene worthy of being filmed by camera crews following emergency service units on a night shift.

The moment I met Charmaine that night, I detected a slight tension in the air. I caught sight of her as I approached our designated meeting point outside a fashionable bar at the bottom of the Perth Road and was almost stopped dead in my tracks. Her long blonde hair extensions spilled down the flesh exposed by her backless red dress, one that barely covered her modesty and offered a full view of long, toned legs and knee-high black leather boots. She looked absolutely stunning, but her smile betrayed a vulnerability I hadn't thought she possessed.

When I'd suggested a night on the town she'd been a little reluctant, wanting instead to have a drink at her place or one of the deathly quiet old man pubs in the Lochee area. Fancying a change of scenery I'd insisted on treating her to a night out in some of the city's more salubrious nightspots. It took a little persuasion, but she eventually agreed.

With the trendy bar we'd met outside deemed "full o' pretentious cunts" she led me across the road to a traditional-looking pub called the Phoenix. I ordered a Blue Wicked for Char and a standard lager for me (no Special available), as she secured a pair of seats behind a stained glass screen right by the toilets, an odd choice given the other options available.

Though she was happy enough to engage in the bouts of snogging that interspersed our drinking, Charmaine smacked my hand when I tried to finger her under the table, which really wasn't like her.

"Save it for when we get up the road, sugarcock," she reprimanded me with a smile.

"You ok, Char? You seem a bit on edge or something."

Her eyes darted round the room as if she were a fugitive from the law.

"Eh'm fine, aye. It's just that this isnae really meh scene, ken?"

Charmaine's discomfort was compounded when my newfound minor fame saw our company temporarily grow.

"Here Simmy man, check wha' it is! Alright Lloyd!"

A couple of well-dressed guys a couple of years older than me thrust their hands out to be shaken.

"Fuckin' good tae meet ye, man! We're Derry boys, aye. This is Simmy and eh'm Robbo."

Intrusive and fairly well on with drink though they were, they couldn't have been friendlier. Simmy and Robbo were polite in greeting Charmaine, chatted away about football for a minute (Simmy had been lifted at the Queen of the South game, and couldn't be prouder of it) and wished me all the best. Just as they were about to head towards the exit for a fag, Robbo turned back with a look of curiosity and approached Charmaine.

"Sorry tae bather ye again, but do eh ken you, pal? Ye look affy familiar somehow."

Charmaine was uncharacteristically flustered and, when she replied, "Eh, nut. Dinnae 'hink so, like," her voice seemed to lift an octave or two before she regained her composure and gave a more convincing, "Probably jist seen iz aboot the toon or somethin', aye."

The guy took a couple more seconds to consider her face then said that probably was the case right enough. The second he got out of the door Charmaine's hand found my crotch and the girl I knew returned.

"Right, fuck this city centre shite; mon we'll go up tae mine and ye kin lick marmalade aff meh tits."

I was quite partial to marmalade. With command of my decision making faculties now handed over to my penis all thoughts of a night in the town were jettisoned. We drank up and departed.

As we were walking by the nearby theatre looking for a taxi I spotted a familiar face lurking in the shadows of a doorway.

"Alright Davo! How's it going, mate?"

Davo took his hood down and gave me a fist-bump and hug.

"Alright Lloyd, no' bad, dude. This your lass then is it?"

I introduced the pair of them. Davo, being a gentlemanly stoner, offered a courteous little bow as he took her hand and said it was a pleasure to meet her.

"What you up to Davo? Out for a drink?"

"Nah mate, just waiting for a pal. He's after a wee bit of smoke, like."

That got Charmaine's attention.

"You a dealer, aye."

Davo seemed mortified at the notion.

"Nah, fuck that. I just sort out my mates if they need a bit."

"Fair doos."

A car pulled up beside us and Davo gave the driver a thumbs up.

"That's my pal now. Lloyd, see ya tomorrow, mate. Last day of training before the Scottish Cup on Saturday; be great to get a wee cup run on the go, eh? Charmaine, lovely to meet you, pal. If you ever need a smoke give me a shout. Lloyd'll give you my number."

The dulcet tones of Snoop Dogg poured out the car as Davo got inside, and as soon as he the door closed they pulled off.

"A futba player wha deals weed? What kind o' team are you playin' fur exactly?"

She was smiling as she said it. I grinned back and replied, "One that's top of the league, sweetheart."

I flagged a taxi and we sped off toward Lochee.

* * *

Much is said about the romance of the cup. It's a competition where anything can happen, where the minnows get the chance to swim with the big fish, and where footballing dreams can come true. At the end of the day, football is just 11 men against 11 men and, over the course of a one-off 90 minute game, sometimes the magic actually happens.

Unfortunately it wasn't to be for second division newcomers The Rangers. The plucky underdogs came to Dens full of giant-killing dreams that were quickly shattered as the gulf in class between a relatively big club and one still wet behind the ears like the Govan outfit became all too apparent. The gaffer told us to lay off them in the second half as he had us down on his coupon to win by no more than a six-goal margin.

With the formalities out the way, we showered quickly and gathered in front of the dressing room TV to watch the quarter-final draw being broadcast live from Hampden. The smaller clubs left in the draw were few and far between and, as we speculated about who we might face with mounting excitement, the gaffer left us in no doubt as to who he wanted.

"United."

He was stood right in front of the screen, clad as always in tracksuit bottoms and football boots. His hands were balled into fists, every muscle in his sinewy body was tense and the veins in his neck popped out.

"United."

He repeated this at intervals of around 10 seconds in a low, matter-of-fact tone. He even ignored one of the lads' attempts at humour when he asked the gaffer who he really fancied playing. On any other occasion, a weak joke like this would have elicited a caustic 'telt', but every ounce of energy the topless Trapattoni could muster was focused on trying to influence the draw's outcome by some form of telekinesis. As the minor footballing celebrities charged with plucking balls from a velvet bag took their place in the studio, he shifted his weight from foot to foot, unclenching his fists momentarily to slowly wiggle his fingers like a gunslinger ready to draw his pistol at dawn before clenching them tighter still and this time whispering, "United".

Willie Dawes was one of the faded stars who would be making the draw, and once more I was impressed by his ease in front of camera as he smiled and wished all clubs the best of luck before dipping his hand in the bag and rummaging deeply. He pulled out a white ball with the number '3' printed on it and passed it to an SFA official who announced, "Number three: Dundee United."

A cheer went up and was quickly extinguished by a knot that spontaneously arose in our collective stomach. The only noise that could be heard was nervous laughter bouncing around the tiled walls. Down front, the gaffer tucked his thumbs under the waistband of his tracksuit bottoms, bent double as he thrust them down around his ankles and shot bolt upright into the wide-stretched-arms "come ahead" pose he usually reserved for opposing managers, linesman and teenagers glaring out bus windows on their way to housing schemes he wasn't particularly fond of.

As the next ball came out the bag he shouted, "OW! UNIT-ED! WHA'S IN FUCKIN CHERGE HERE?" The official who was passed the ball turned its number to face the camera and, with a broad grin, declared, "Will play number two... Dundee."

The dressing room erupted.

As the lads cheered, hugged and slapped each other on the back the gaffer let his head tip back and unleashed a "FUUUK-KKKINNGGGGG YAAAAAAAAAAAAASSSSSSSSSSSS!!" that nearly put a hole in the ceiling. His enormo-cock reared up like an elephant's trunk, swaying to-and-fro like an unmanned firehose for a few seconds before stiffening into an erection that could have been used to hit home runs. He swivelled on his heel, bat-dick swinging so that those standing in close proximity had to leap out the way mid-section first in order to avoid contact with the meaty colossus. The man's eyes had rolled back in his head to leave them completely white and even more terrifying than the wild deep black pools usually on display. He raised his fists to the sky, shaking them so violently that the reverberation ran down the length of his arms and engulfed his entire body. He looked like he might take off and he wasn't even wearing his jetpack. A stream of gibberish began pouring out his mouth as if he had been possessed by a drunken demon. He rattled and shook until finally, like an old washing machine coming to the end of its spin cycle, he gradually slowed down and came shuddering to a halt. His tongue fell from his mouth, eyes rolled back around into position and he came to rest with a weary exhalation. He looked at his players who, to a man, had long since stopped celebrating the draw, fallen silent and stared back at their leader with terror in their eyes.

"United at Tannadice, eh?" His grin took about 30 years off him. "THAT'S WHAT EH'M TALKIN' ABOOT! THUN-DERCATS – HOOOOOOOOO!"

And with that he kicked his trackies off and bolted out the dressing room door, naked but for his football boots. We stood in shocked silence, mouths agape, for a second before bursting into life and charging after him.

Both sets of double doors leading to Sandeman Street had been taken off their hinges as if they'd been hit by a cannonball. When we reached the street we heard unintelligible shouting and followed the noise to discover a trail of bodies lying in his wake. At sporadic intervals lay a boy of about 13 who'd been taken clean of his BMX, a middle-aged woman whose shopping from Lidl was rolling back down the street, and an unfortunate pensioner who hadn't had the chance to use his walking stick to defend himself. The gaffer was delivering clothesline after clothesline to anyone who stood in his way whether they were attempting to hinder his progress or not. As we attempted to keep up with him he veered off the pavement and headed straight for the nearest part of Tannadice, a brick wall that formed the ground's westernmost boundary. A dozen variations on "Gaffer! Stop!" cried out into the early evening air. Instead of slowing down he accelerated and launched himself at the wall like a drone missile hitting an Afghani orphanage. The team trailing behind him faltered and winced collectively before hurrying to attend to our fallen leader.

He lay in a heap by the wall he'd smashed into, semi-conscious and mumbling, "Drinks on a tray, ya cunt... Wha's in cherge here?... Big Jock's in cherge here, a'body kens that..." We crowded round as Harry knelt by his side and to slap some sense into him.

"Gaffer! Fucking hell, man, are ye all right? Gaffer!" He came around slowly, looking dazed and confused. With some assistance he started to get his bearings again, looking up at those around him and laughing, "Fuck sake, eh've no' seen as many concerned faces as this since the Civil Service Clubbie announced they were puttin' on a dubstep night. The fuck's happenin' here like?"

He was pulled back into an upright position and, noticing that we were stood in the shadow of our local rivals' stadium, remembered the circumstances that had led him here.

"Oh eh! United at Tannadice! Fucking yas!"

The good feeling that had been present before he went loco returned, and we began celebrating the big news again. It had been a number of years since the Dundee clubs had faced each other. The Scottish Cup quarter-final Dundee derby would be a momentous occasion for both sides and for the city itself.

As we made our way back up the road to Dens Jocky led the singing.

"When the Dees! Go up! Tae lift the Scottish Cup, we'll be there, we'll be there!"

The whole team joined in and the gaffer he dropped back through the ranks to fall in line by my side.

"Hiya Lloyd! Hiya pal. Eh've a wee favour tae ask ye, cunto."

"What's that then, gaffer?"

"Eh've got aine o' they gairden hooses fae the B&Q, but ye hae tae build the cunts yersel and it's no' really a one-man joab. Any chance ye could fire doon the hoose and gie Big Jock a hand putting it up?"

Even though I didn't know what a "gairden hoose" was, I had no qualms about helping out and was chuffed to be asked. This wasn't football business. This was the kind of favour a friend asks of another friend and I instantly said I'd be happy to help. He gave me a pat on the back and a "Cheers pal" before joining in the singing again. Exhilarated at the prospect of my the biggest game of my career to date, I joined the impromptu Sandeman Street choir with gusto. The blare of the emergency service sirens approaching in the distance did little to drown out our voices.

FOURTH HALF

FOURTH HALF

I hit the eardrum-shattering airhorn at Jocky's front door in a state of unprecedented, pant-shitting terror.

"Alright, Lloyd? What's the dae wi' ye? Ye look like a lion's just jumped oot the bushies at ye."

Which was exactly what had happened. I'd come up the garden path and said hello to the Munchkins, who were erecting a scarecrow by the flowerbed as a Tin Man with a body of silver foil and head of bucket (face drawn on it in marker) watched over the scene. I walked up the path only to discover a lion whose defining characteristic was most certainly not cowardice lurking in the bushes. Its swiping paw came to within about six inches of my face before the dog leash used to secure the animal to a tree strained to its full length.

"Gaffer, what the fuck, man? Where in the name of fuck did you get a lion from?" I panted as I held my hand to my chest in an attempt to prevent my heart making its escape.

He hurled a mince pie at the lion, who caught it in its mouth and devoured it in an instant.

"Eddie got iz it. Phoned him at the back o' six last night and he wandered in wi' it on a doag lead at eight o'clock. Says he'll hae a wicked witch fae the west here by Tuesday."

With my heart still pounding I followed him through the house. After my shoes had filled with sand as we passed through the living room we reached the enormous kitchen. This room was

143

dominated by a cauldron so big he had to climb a step ladder to stir its contents with an oar-sized spoon. The meaty aroma of stovies filled the room, which was murderously hot due to the fire pit underneath the cauldron. The gaffer seemed not to notice the flames that licked menacingly close to his football boots.

"Cheers fur comin' doon, Lloyd. They gairden hooses are a cunt ti dae yersel'."

Leaving the giant oar-spoon to stand of its own accord in the corned beef and potato delight he hopped off the steps, opened a walk-in refrigerator stacked ceiling to floor with Tartan Special, and grabbed a four pack. He opened each can in turn before casually lobbing them into the pot, aluminium and all.

He led the way outside to the back garden, which was surprisingly conventional in comparison to the rest of the estate. A small children's paddling pool filled with icy-looking water sat on the left side of a paved patio that led to a rectangular patch of grass bordered by thin strips of brown earth and encased by a wooden fence around six feet tall. An unopened box marked 'Garden Shed' lay to the right of the paddling pool, although the latter word had been scored out and replaced by "hoose" and an "i" had been inserted in the former. Beyond that, the only real weirdness to speak of were the Dundee flags planted at intervals around the soil border where ordinary people would have placed bushes and flowers, and the dozen or so pairs of tracksuit bottoms hanging on the washing line.

The gaffer pulled his current pair down, his cock tumbling down his legs like a python being released from a sack as he did so, and stepped into the paddling pool. He lowered himself into the water without flinching at its temperature, sipped from a can of Special he'd left by the poolside, pointed towards the assembly kit and instructed me to get tore in.

Realising this wasn't going to be a case of me helping Jocky build the shed so much as me doing it myself, I opened the flat pack and looked blankly at a collection of panels, hinges, nuts and bolts. As I did so, my manager started bellowing a Dundee song about keeping the blue flag flying high as he waved a large red, white and blue flag bearing the words 'FUCK THE SHED' that he hadn't got around to planting yet.

"Why have you got that written on your Dundee flag, gaffer?" I asked ten minutes later when he finally stopped singing that same song over and over.

"Eh'm glad ye asked, cunto."

He sat up in the paddling pool and looked deadly serious.

"Ken how Dundee's got the Derry, Lloyd, and we're a' Dundee Derry Boys?"

I remembered Davo explaining it to me, and had picked up on it further through hearing the fans' songs during games.

"The Shed's the United version. It's whaur their fans yased tae sit at Tannadice, and they call themselves Shed Boys. We're Derry, they're Shed, even if the daft cunts give up their spiritual home to away fans. Eh dinnae hate the Shed as much as eh love the Derry, but it's no' far aff it. Ken whit eh mean?"

I nodded, understanding now why he had chosen to rename a fairly innocuous domestic storage building. I went back to work and the singing and flag waving started up again.

Putting a gairden hoose together on your own is an arduous task, and it quickly became apparent that I lacked the dexterity and technical nous required to become a competent shed-builder. Nevertheless, I persevered and, with sweat lashing off me and a final determined grunt, I shifted the roof into position atop the somewhat shaky-looking structure. I crumpled into a seated position for several minutes. Once I had caught my breath I asked if I could use the toilet.

"Providing ye can answer a question, aye."

I hoped the test would be easy because my back teeth were floating.

"Wha dae the Derry hate, Lloyd?"

Though puzzled by the question's relevance, I knew the answer, and responded swiftly.

"The Shed."

"Spot on, cunto. Ye ken whaur the bog is. Nae solids, there's a compost heap roond the side o' the hoose if ye're in need of a shite."

I wandered inside and climbed the stairs to the toilet, where the presence of Dong Chu once again caused me to jump out my skin.

"Mr Lloyd George, a pleasure to see you once again."

"Hi, Dong Chu. How's tricks?"

He went about sorting the array of aftershave bottles, all of which were something called 'Brut,' that sat in front of a sign saying, 'FRESH FOR THE PUSSY'.

"Tricks are good, Mr Lloyd. That is what eh am talking aboot."

After accepting a quick squirt of Brut and unloading all the change from my pocket into his donation basket I headed back downstairs. As soon as I entered the living room I saw Wee Jocky sitting on top of the bookcase. He was perched above a book that sat out of place in the row as if it had been pulled out recently and hadn't been replaced properly. Seeming to follow my gaze the cat looked down at the book, back up at me and meowed.

"Hello, Wee Jocky. Who's a good pussy cat?"

He eyed me suspiciously and offered no response. I'm not sure why I even expected one. Taking carefully measured steps I slowly moved through the room into the kitchen and out the back to find a sight that left me gobsmacked.

The shed I'd spent the afternoon building was ablaze and collapsing as flames engulfed it. The gaffer was nowhere to be seen. I called out for him but received no response. What the fuck had happened?

Quite stunned I hurried back into the house calling his name. Again receiving no response, I ventured round the side of the house and almost fell face-first into a compost heap so big it probably qualified as a Munro. Unsure what to do, I marched round the monstrous pile and down the garden path, where I was pleased to see the lion sleeping off its pie.

When I reached the front gate I heard a cat meow from

behind me in. With the day's light fading fast, I couldn't see clearly and was about to carry on again when I spotted what very much looked like Wee Jocky standing on his hind legs performing a Tai-Chi routine at the front door. The light must surely have been playing tricks on me. I turned and started a walk that very quickly became a full-pelt run down the street.

* * *

It was clear things weren't going to go our way almost from kick-off. Most of our ever-inebriated away support hadn't even made it into the ground yet when my left-foot drive hit the inside of one post, then the other before landing safely in the arms of the befuddled Alloa goalkeeper. A minute later, Kev Rafferty was harshly deemed to have led with his elbow in an aerial challenge and headed for a bath so early he'd have to put the hot water on himself. No one within earshot was surprised when the gaffer was told to follow him after unleashing a tirade of megaphone-enhanced abuse at the ref that would surely have earned him a world record for 'Most Repeated Use of the Word "Cunt" in a Single Sentence' had Guinness been represented at Recreation Park that afternoon.

For the first time since my arrival at the club, the carry-out on the bus home was consumed to drown sorrows rather than celebrate another point or three in the bag. Unused to losing as we were, the mood was one of sombre reflection as our Special combated the bitter taste of defeat. Seemingly preoccupied with texting someone on his phone, even the gaffer was unusually quiet.

Not for long though.

"Right lads, fuckin' battle stations. The Aiberdeen casuals are stoppin' at Stirling services on the way back fae Parkheid; eh telt them we'd meet them there fur a square-go."

I expected groans of disapproval and calls for reason from my fellow travellers. What I heard was an audible surge of excitement and a distinct lift in mood.

"Fuckin' class, man," chimed in the ever-pink-eyed Davo as he leaned over the seat behind me. "We've no' had a proper swedge since that time we met Hibs off the train at the station in Dundee. The gaffer was picking them up, flying them halfway across the Tay and dropping them. First time in recorded history the Coast Guard had to be called out to a football hooliganism incident."

As we pulled off the motorway and into the service station forecourt I spotted a group of about 50 guys ranging from teenagers to those those in early-middle age. They were immaculately dressed in designer labels, and looked like they might smell of Aggro by Calvin Klein. I felt like a lamb being led to the slaughter, appropriate given the livestock-menacing reputation of the combatants.

"Right lads, usual tactics; eh'll dae the pleasantries and lead the cherge. A'body pile in efter iz and be back on the bus in twa minutes. Eh've got a helluva good perty tae be at the night and need tae spruce the auld ba'bag before headin' oot. Let's get the ASC telt, aye."

With Wally right behind him he hopped down the stairs and off. We filed out in turn after them. With my stomach more knotted than a pack of Scouts off their nuts on speed could have managed, I was the only one hesitant to follow.

"It's cool, Lloyd. The gaffer does most of the work. They'll probably run like fuck the minute he takes off and flies at them. Stay by me, I'll keep an eye on you."

Neither Davo's words nor calming pat in the back did anything to put me at ease. I hadn't been in a fight since a Primary Three kid knocked fuck out me after school one day. I was in Primary Seven at the time. I did my best to hide at the back of the group that gathered across the forecourt from the Aberdeen mob.

"Furry boots are youse fae, min? Fit? Fit?"

The top boy from Aberdeen looked somewhat perplexed at the distinctly non-casual group now facing him.

"There's nae furry boots here, cunto. Only futba baits, and

auld Walzo here occasionally rocks cowboy aines when he's doon at the line dancin'. Ye ready tae git yer cunt kicked in, big aine?"

The casual guffawed.

"You muppets canna be the Scumdee Utility, surely? Fit? Fit like min? Fit?"

The gaffer took a few steps toward him at a nonchalant pace.

"Eh'm Utility, Lochee Fleet, tap boy at the Fairmuir and an honorary member o' the Nation o' Islam. Wha the fuck are you, ya workin'-on-the-rigs, granite-hoosed cunt?"

The Aberdeen guy burst out laughing and said "fit?" five or six more times. The gaffer turned to us amused at the situation.

"This boy's braw, eh?" In an instant his demeanour changed and he growled, "He's fuckin' mine."

With that, he sprinted at the Aberdeen man out front, igniting his jetpack as he went, leaped forward into a horizontal position and hit him with a flying clothesline that damn near took the guy's head off.

Despite the casuals outnumbering us by more than two-to-one, the team, Wally and Harry's squad of barbers showed no fear, let out a roar and charged headlong at the bewildered Aberdeen mob. Carnage ensued. Fists, feet and football managers were flying everywhere. I had no idea what to do, so I just stood there with my fists clenched making as much noise as possible. My lack of participation made little difference as the lads were clearing house. Wally was knocking boys spark out with one punch. Old Doug had attached a cattle catcher, the kind of thing you might see on the front an old mid-west locomotive, to the front of his mobility scooter and was running anyone in his path down. The gaffer had the top boy's jeans round his ankles and a nozzle jammed up his arse as he carefully watched the dial on the pump spin round so he could get exactly £10 worth of diesel in him.

"Lloyd, go inside and gie the wummin a tenner. Eh'll pay ye back efter."

I went inside to settle the bill with the counter assistant, who was quite understandably freaking out. I didn't want to add to her trauma, so politely said, "Pump number five please," and left my money for her to pop in the till at her own convenience.

With the Aberdeen casuals vanquished, and indeed topped up with enough fuel to get most of the way home, we piled back on the bus and made our getaway. The mood was jubilant until we realised there was a man down.

Chrissy Reilly was grimacing and groaning in his seat. A concerned Jocky bounded up the aisle to tend to him.

"Chrissy pal, are ye a'right? Did ye get a doing?"

He tried to straighten up a little but couldn't. His arms were hugging his chest tightly.

"I pure tripped up in the melee, gaffer. One of them got me with a hefty boot in the ribs. It's sore as fuck."

He looked like he was in a lot of pain. He definitely needed medical attention.

"Right, we'll get ye up tae Ninewells pronto when we get back. Hud tight, pal."

He ruffled Chrissy's hair then told the driver to step on it. We'd be home in less than an hour. I'd still have time to get changed and join Charmaine, who was taking me to a "special" party she'd been invited to. She'd neglected to provide further details, but had promised "the night o' yer fuckin' life, sugarcock."

It was with a blend of both concern for my injured comrade and anticipation of my own night ahead that I eagerly awaited the sight of Bonnie Dundee emerging over the horizon.

* * *

The alleged "night of my fucking life" was set to take place in a multi-story block at the bottom of the Hilltown. The event?

"An orgy, Lloyd. Beats a night in the Phoenix any day o' the week, let me tell ye."

She announced this at the foot of the multi, leaving me little room to back out should I have reservations. Which I did. By the bucketful.

"An orgy, Char? What, like loads of people shagging everywhere and all that?"

She pouted and took a handful of my crotch.

"Exactly, Lloyd. It'll be like thon film Caligula, only wi' Dundee fowk instead o' a' they Romanians. It's a pity Helen Mirren's no' gonnae be here though; eh'd be in aboot her fanny like a spastic eatin' a choc ice."

Seeing that I was having massive doubts, she grinded up against me and promised I could shag whoever I wanted or watch her shag whoever I wanted. "And it'll only be lassies eh'll shag tae," she added.

Sweet Bobby Charlton's comb-over. I looked up at the monolithic block towering into the dark sky above and slowly exhaled as she took my hand and led me inside.

Whilst this lift was much less toilet-like the one that lead to Charmaine's penthouse, it did have its own unique character in the form of a junkie lying in a crumpled heap with a syringe sticking out his arm. Char seemed not to notice, and calmly led me inside to turn and face the door as it closed behind us.

"12th floor please, bellhop."

She looked down at the junkie, then at me, and burst out laughing.

"Eh'm only kiddin', Lloyd. The Hulltoon multis dinnae hae bellhops. Plus, that boy's broon breid, ken?"

She hit the button for '12' before I could hit the one that would open the door again, and the lift creaked into life.

Trying gamely to ignore the dead body less than two feet away from us I thought of the practicalities of what was about to happen.

"I take it you've got condoms, Char?"

She looked at me like I'd just asked if she had a mummified skull freshly excavated from an Egyptian tomb in her handbag.

"Johnnies? At an orgy? Lloyd, that wid be like goin' tae the Stand 'n' Tan wi' yer trackies on."

She positively exuded wisdom sometimes.

We left our deceased companion behind and hit the doorbell of the flat in which the "party" was taking place. Charmaine quickly explained that she'd found out about it on a website dedicated to this sort of thing, and that the hostess had been really friendly as they made arrangements for the night via email.

Sure enough the hostess was indeed very pleasant, and offered us as a warm welcome. Not that it put me at ease any. Betty was somewhere around my granny's age. Unlike my Granny she was clad in thigh-high black leather boots, a skirt that laughed heartily in the face of modesty and a bra that required more wire than an early telephone network.

"Charmaine is it? Mon in, sweetheart. Dinnae mind the dug, he winnae bite."

The naked middle-aged man she had attached to a lead barked at us, and received a swift boot in reprimand.

"Shut it, cunt! Awa' back tae yer kennel!"

The man scurried off on all fours into a cupboard, and closed the door behind him.

"That's meh lad, Derek. If he comes up tae ye wi' a ba' in his mooth, dinnae throw it; he'll be pesterin' ye tae keep daein' it a' night."

Betty explained how things worked. The living room was the primary sex room where anything and everything went; the double bedroom was for voyeurs who wished to watch the night's feature couple ("Sandra fae doonstairs and this black boy wha came tae the door sellin' Betterware catalogues") go at it, and the spare bedroom was a chill-out room for drinking and mingling with other guests. There were only two rules: "Hae a good time, and wash yer hands before touchin' the buffet in the kitchen. There'll be sassij rolls oot the oven aboot the back o' 11."

I badly needed a drink or five before this was going to seem like a good idea. The fridge was well stocked, so I grabbed a couple of cans of Special (an unexpected bonus amongst the lager and wine) and was quite firm in declaring our first port of call would be the spare bedroom and not the living room that Char was anxious to get to.

Sober as a judge or not, the moment I opened the chill-out room door I wished I'd followed her wishes.

"Hiya Lloyd! Hiya pal!"

For fuck sake. Though I was unsure what to expect from my first orgy, finding the gaffer with a bin bag tied round his cock and playing darts with a semi-naked group of women I recognised from Frews, was well down the list.

"Twa seconds, pal, eh'm a double ten awa' fae beatin' this boy here."

The dart found its mark, and a "That's what eh'm talkin' aboot!" later he was over shaking my hand and Charmaine's.

"Didnae ken you were intae this sort o' kerry on, Lloyd."

He stood with his hands on his hips without a care in the world. Before I could respond, Char interrupted.

"Nivir mind Lloyd – what the fuck are you daein' here? And how huv ye got a bag on yer dong?"

His smile faded ever so slightly before he addressed her questions.

"Eh'm an auld hand at these gigs, doll. Used tae host them misel' till the boy next door caught auld Walzo pumpin' twa Scandinavian burds in his greenhoose. Ye get awa' wi' that sort o' thing at this end o' the toon, but no' doon the Ferry. As fur this," he shook his hips so his cock swung from side to side like a pendulum, "well they dinnae dae johnnies in meh sehze, and if there's one thing eh truly believe in, apert fae Jim McLean bein' Bible John, it's safe sex. Eh've got a crash helmet ben the hoose tae!"

The three of us blethered away over a few drinks. I was pleased to see the gaffer making an effort to get on with Charmaine in spite of his doubts about her. I was also pleased that Char was asking lots of questions in an attempt to get to know him better, too. He also managed to get an answer to a question of his own, one that I'd completely forgotten to ask her.

"Mad Alfie? Wha's that, exactly?"

His jaw tightened just a fraction.

"Dae ye no' ken Alfie?"

She shook her head. He said it didn't matter and pressed on telling the story he'd managed to drop the question into.

Despite the gaffer being even less dressed than normal I was glad he was here and, had it not been for the occasional naked and visibly aroused person strolling in asking if the sausage rolls were on the go yet, I might have quite forgotten where I was. Charmaine was seemingly now of a similar mind, and made no inclination toward heading through to another room.

"Check this oot, Lloyd. Sair aine on the coupon the day."

He reached round himself and grimaced slightly as he pulled a rolled up bookie slip out his arse. He went to hand it to me, immediately understood why I baulked at the notion and unravelled it himself.

"Fuckin' Farfar let iz doon fur three grand. Bridie-munchin' bastards."

I looked at his accumulator and was horrified to see he'd backed Alloa to win. "Gaffer! You had us down to lose today?"

He became only slightly defensive.

"Fuckin' chill there, Cochise. Only 'cause eh spoke tae meh Granny last night and she telt iz what would happen at the gemme. She's rarely wrang on the futba predications."

He was a good age himself so I had to ask how old his grandmother was.

"She's been deid 20 years. Eh wiz speakin' tae her on the Ouija board, likes. It's like a chatroom whaur dead cunts hing aboot, only withoot any cunt pretending they're 15 year old lassies. Or black guys. Lloyd, never request tae private message Black_as_Fuck_Ken? on these things; it's jist me, aye."

I knew that name from…

I managed to hold the mouthful of drink that tried to hurtle its way through any available orifice and swallow it with a chest-thumping cough. He crumpled his coupon and chucked it on the floor.

"Ow! Respect the wummin's hoose you, eh? There's a fuckin' bin."

Just as Charmaine scowled at him and went after the litter so she could do the right thing on his behalf there was a scream from one of the other rooms. Seconds later a woman wearing a substantial strap-on dildo came through in a state of panic.

"Susan and Tracy have hud an accident!"

The ladies from Frews gasped, dropped their drinks and darts and quickly followed their friend. The rest of us did likewise.

I've watched a lot of porn in my time, and in the past month or so at least, had a lot of sex. I'd never seen a woman with her foot lodged up another woman's vagina though.

"In the name o' the wee man, what the fuck were you twa trehin' tae dae?"

The woman who was almost calf-deep in her lover tried to explain, "Eh slipped! We've done fingers, dildos and half the fruit and veg aisle in Lidl; a foot seemed like the next logical step. Are ye a'right, Tracy honey?"

Tracy could only wail and cry for someone to get it the fuck out of her. Perhaps used to tending to orgy-related injuries the gaffer got down to help. He tried taking careful tugs at Susan's leg, but couldn't budge it. She was stuck fast. Betty reluctantly called an ambulance.

As the group of 20-odd party goers in various states of dress and arousal hung around awkwardly the gaffer took command.

"Right a'body, the dame's in pain here so let's treh 'n chill things the fuck oot. How aboot a singsong?"

He stroked Tracy's hair tenderly, asking, "Ye wantin' a wee singsong, pal? It's nae bather aye, ye'll be fine."

He looked up toward the ceiling deep in thought for a second, then started whistling something. I didn't recognise it. The girls in the darts team seemed to and, when Jocky started belting out something about a 'constant craving', they all joined in.

"Lloyd, we should go, eh?" whispered Charmaine.

I wasn't slow in agreeing with her. I motioned toward the door at the gaffer, but he shook his head.

"Nah, pal, eh'm stayin'. Once this foot's oot that fanny'll be loose enough tae tak' meh cock in a oner. Fuckin' yassss! See ye at trainin' on Monday."

After all that I barely noticed the dead junkie in the lift. We headed back to Charmaine's and, for the first time since meeting, went straight to bed without having sex.

* * *

We arrived at Dens on Monday morning wondering where Doug Roberts was. The ageing stopper was always first at the ground and would be moaning about how a dose of National Service would help the youth of today get out of their beds when we arrived. His absence was notable, but instantly put to the back of our minds when Wally walked in with bad news.

"Chrissy's got a cracked rib, boys. He's going to be out for weeks."

The mood plummeted like Gillette's stock the week Harry decided to try waxing. Chrissy was one of the first names on the team sheet every week and would be a real loss at Tannadice. Coming on the back of our first defeat in months, the news brought the dressing room to a standstill.

"Lads, let's pick ourselves back up here, eh?"

Harry's barbers stopped hacking away at their best and constant customer, standing to one side so he could say his piece.

"Chrissy would be pissed right off if he saw us like this. He took a kicking fighting for the Derry, so let's fight like Derry and win it for him on Saturday."

The sound of hearty agreement filled the room.

"And forget the result on Saturday, it was a fluke. Those jammy Alloa cunts should never have beaten us. Total coupon burster, like."

Unless your dead gran had told you about it in advance, at least.

The captain had done his job well. By the time we made our way out the dressing room the buzz I'd grown used to revelling in had returned. We were still top of the league; we were still in a strong position despite losing one of our top boys.

We came out the tunnel to find the pitch already a hive of activity. A giant catapult was stationed on the Bobby Cox side of the pitch and a couple of dozen midgets dressed in Dundee strips laboured away round it. Most were busy shovelling what looked, and most certainly smelled like, a giant compost heap into the weapon's ammunition chamber. Jocky's own compost collection looked like a cow pat in comparison.

"The big pile o' dung," explained the gaffer before anyone had the chance to ask what the merry hell was going on "comes courtesy o' meh auld pal Geoff Broon. Boy's a fermer! He assures me this is grade-A Perthshire coo shit, the very best o' the teckle. Because we're pals he threw in a couple of barrels o' St Johnstone player turd tae."

By now each and every player had pulled their training top up over their nose. The stench was biohazard-level awful.

"The wee guys come fae Peter Marr's latest business venture. Boy runs pubs, nurseries and a taxi firm. The next logical step wiz obviously formin' 'Dial-a-Dwarf'. Got a joab tae dae? Canna be bathered daein' it? Fuck it, get the midgets in."

They were certainly an industrious bunch. One who appeared to be the foreman of the crew blew his whistle, a signal that saw his workers move behind the catapult and give the gaffer a group thumbs-up. "Gentleman, the Dundee derby is this comin' Saturday. As such we'll be gettin' the week under way wi' a bit o' psychological warfare using a technique straight fae Sun Tzu's Art o' War known as 'flingin' giant piles of keech at United!'"

He raised his hand and returned the thumbs up to the dwarf foreman, who reacted by sounding another blast of his whistle. The firing mechanism was initiated, and the catapult burst into life. With a creek and a mighty whoosh the arm jacked up and unleashed its payload. An enormous brown lump was sent hurtling out of the ground. As it passed overhead, little droplets fell to the ground, scattering the players as we ran screaming in every direction to avoid being hit. The gaffer didn't budge an inch and remained perfectly calm when a snowball-sized chunk hit him on the left shoulder. To everyone's horror he leaned into it, took a lick and looked thoughtful in the way a wine taster might when judging a New World chardonnay.

Silence fell as we wondered what would happen next. The gaffer and his team of shite-hurling midgets stood motionless and expectant. Our attention was drawn to a dwarf with the role of lookout positioned in the nearest floodlight and, as he started cheering and punching the air with both fists, his Dial-a-Dwarf colleagues erupted into celebration.

"A direct hit! That's what eh'm talkin' aboot!"

Jocky was ecstatic, and applauded the team of happy workers at the catapult. He got his megaphone out and announced, "WELL DONE, LADS. KEEP UP THE GOOD WORK. PINTS ON ME AT THE END O' THE DAY. THERE'S A FEW BOYS AT THE FAIRMUIR WANTING TAE REEN-ACT THE BATTLE O' ENDOR IF ANY CUNT FANCIES A BIT O' EWOK OVERTIME."

As they started beavering away to reload the catapult the gaffer took his phone out, dialled and awaited a response.

"Hiya Dave Mackay! Hiya pal! It's Jocky... eh no' bad, pal. Dave, guess what eh've just licked aff meh shudder'?... No, guess... keep guessing... close! Your shite! Ken aye, no' done it for pure ages. How ye keepin'?"

With St Johnstone players's faeces periodically flying overhead we trained hard under the gaffer's watchful eye. As we were put through our paces executing fitness drills and ball work exercises he talked of how we were still the big team in Dundee, the older, more successful "city club" as opposed to "they East Angus mongrels", who would be shown who really ruled Sandeman Street. He was commanding and articulate, his words laced with passion and a belief in his team and the club as a whole.

As we finished the session off with a bounce game against the wee guys who had decorated Tannadice with such aplomb, we were interrupted by the gaffer shouting, "aw fur fuck sake, man" into his phone. Players from both teams jogged over to him and awaited an explanation. He was listening intently, saying nothing, and slicing a hand across his throat to signal bad news.

The phone came down from his ear, and with a look of utter misery he quietly announced, "Doug's been put intae an auld folks' home. Some cunt phoned Social Services 'cause he wiz goin' doon the Kingsway on that mobility scooter o' his at fehve mile-per-hour. Six-mile tailback, apparently."

It was terrible news. Despite being older than the Sidlaws, Doug was worth 20 points a season, and was one of the main reasons we were standing clear at the top of the league. Losing an experienced goalkeeper was a savage blow.

"Eh'll play fur ye."

The midget who'd been in goal for the little people during our bounce game boldly stepped up to offer his services. Jocky walked up to him, scooped him up onto his shoulder and gave him a Tombstone Piledriver.

"Any cunt ken a goalie? Tell him tae gie iz a text."

The air was thick with the stench of dung and pre-derby tension as we tried to make sense of the triple-blow we had received in the past couple of days.

* * *

There was a discernible change in the mood of the city in the build up to the derby. I found myself receiving the good wishes of Dundee-supporting passers-by on the streets and around the golf course, while United fans weren't shy in telling me the Shed ruled as they shouted from passing cars. My hand was shaken, back slapped and ears filled with words of encouragement and abuse from people in the grip of big match fever. The derby was no ordinary game of football; it was a clash of the city's two tribes, a game in which victory would bring either elation and bragging rights for days, weeks and months to comes, or abject misery in the face of the gloating opposition. To those who wore their dark blue or tangerine hearts on their sleeve it meant absolutely everything. The sense of anticipation was palpable.

No one was more hyped up about it than Jocky. As the days went by his body language aped that of a prize fighter preparing for a shot at the title. His physical presence seemed to grow with every passing moment, and the fire in his eyes brurned ever brighter until the blaze within was ferocious.

On the Wednesday before the match, two pieces of big news landed. The first was that Charmaine was going to be in attendance, which pleased me no end. She'd never been to a game before but, realising the magnitude of the occasion, said she would come along to offer her support.

"Mind n' whip yer tap aff if ye score, ya wee ride," was her only stipulation on attending. I'd be happy to oblige in the event of hitting the back of the net.

The second revelation was another brutal blow.

'DUNDEE STAR IN DRUGS BUST SHOCK' blared the headline from the sandwich boards outside every newsagent on the Hilltown. Davo had been busted. Acting on an anonymous tip-off his flat had been raided and they'd found a couple of marijuana plants he was cultivating in the broom cupboard. Three key players were now set to miss the big game and, in Davo and Doug's cases, out indefinitely.

After a final training session on Friday morning that saw us lined up outside Tannadice pissing against the Main Stand while Jocky spraypainted 'DFC #1' on every car parked nearby, we were as ready as we were ever going to be.

Or so I thought. The gaffer had an 'additional training exercise' planned for me in the afternoon, and told me to be at his house for 3pm.

After hurling the lion a couple of pies I'd brought to distract him and taking a mouthful of abuse off the old Glaswegian woman in a witch's costume who'd been painted green, I reached the front door to find a note sticking out the letterbox.

'HIYA LLOYD, HIYA PAL! DINNAE GET WIDE WITH THE WICKED WITCH, SHE'S ALREADY SET HER ARMY OF WINGED MONKEYS ON THE POSTIE. DOOR'S OPEN, 'MON IN AND FIRE ROOND THE BACK.'

As advertised the door swung open when I tried the handle.

I wandered inside and tip-toed through the sandy living room in case the cat was there again. There was no sign of him anywhere.

I looked over and saw the book that had sat out of place last time I'd been here was still poking out of line. Curious as to what the gaffer might have been reading of late I approached it and saw that it was Mary Shelley's *Frankenstein*. I fingered the book's spine.

"Meow."

I gasped and spun round. The cat was poking its head through the living room door looking at me. I bolted through to the kitchen and burst out the back door.

"Hiya Lloyd! Hiya pal! Wi' a' the shaggin' you're doing of late ye might want tae get the auld ball bag spruced up a bit, eh? Dive in, the water's freezin'!"

The gaffer was lying naked in the paddling pool as Dong Chu, clad only in a thong, manfully worked the oversized scrubbing brush over his employer's groin. He paused to bow gracefully in my direction before resuming his task.

I declined a scrotal scrub and tried to look anywhere but at the scene in front of me. I couldn't help but notice there was a garden shed in a box on the grass.

"Welcome tae training, cunto. There seemed tae be technical issues wi' that last gairden hoose ye built, so get busy."

I looked at it then turned to the gaffer. He was smiling right back at me as he soaped up his moustache with a toothbrush. I looked back at the garden shed and, with shoulders heavily slumped and profane frustration that I kept under my breath, I set about it.

He left me to work in silence. Sitting in a paddling pool drinking beer as a young South Korean boy scrubbed his scrotum, he couldn't have been more relaxed. I, on the other hand, was trying my hardest not to be overcome by a brewing foul mood as I once again struggled to put a fucking garden shed together.

"Lloyd, eh think yer burd's at it."

I stopped what I was doing and looked over at him.

"What are you on about?"

He told Dong Chu to go inside before continuing. The wee man bowed and scurried off.

"She claims tae be fae Lochee but disnae ken Alfie. Every cunt in Lochee and beyond kens Alfie. There's somethin' no' right aboot that lassie. Fuck knows what, exactly, but she's definitely at it."

Did he honestly think the world revolves around his and his daftie pals? Honest to fuck. I couldn't be bothered listening to him bad mouth my girlfriend so I ignored him and got back to work on the shed.

"Biggest gemme o' the season the 'morra, Lloyd. Ye ready fur it?"

Through gritted teeth I replied, "As ready as I'll ever be."

With the benefit of experience it didn't take as long to build the thing as it had the first time, and I was soon attempting to hoist the roof up into place. Panting and unable to prevent a few choice words from filling the calm Broughty Ferry air, I felt my grip on the roof slip and was about to see it tumble when the weight was suddenly shared.

"United fans are gonna gie you doags abuse the morra, Lloyd. You're oor danger man, and the danger men ayewiz git targeted."

With two men – one of whom was stark bullock naked – handling the task the roof went up and into place much more easily. I slumped to the grass and lay back on my elbows as I sucked some air down.

"They'll be callin' ye a wee prick, a blue nose bastard and a Derry wanker. If they're half as quick as Mikey fae the Hulltoon Huns they'll be callin' ye "Mongo-Lloyd", which will admittedly be pretty funny."

I considered it for a moment, sat back up with my head turned to one side so I didn't have to face his penis and told him I could handle it. The words "can ye now" were faint, and when I turned my head back I saw that he'd walked away into the kitchen. Seconds later he reappeared with a jerry can.

"The key thing when ye get abuse aff opposition fans, Lloyd, is tae use it tae yer advantage."

He unscrewed the cap, dropped it and started throwing the clear liquid inside over the newly constructed shed.

"Gaffer? What are you doing?"

He blanked me and maintained his own thread. "Thrive on the shite they're giein' ye! Dinnae fold under it; feed aff it."

With the last remaining contents of the can now dribbling out he threw it over the fence into the neighbour's garden. He took his penis in one hand, pulled his foreskin back and plucked a Zippo lighter off the bulbous exposed head. He'd rolled the skin back in place before I could distinguish whether he was, as I suspected, storing Jaffa Cakes in there, or perhaps had some hideous venereal disease.

"Get it right fucking up them, Lloyd. The mair they scream abuse the harder you should be tryin' tae shut them the fuck up beh playin' better and scorin' goals."

He flipped the lighter's lid, the flame automatically flickering into life.

"Lloyd?"

There was fire in his eyes and soon to be one in his garden as well.

"Get United telt."

And with that he casually flipped the lighter at the shed.

I'd managed to scramble several feet backward before it hit the nearest wooden panel and burst into flames with a tremendous whoosh and blast of heat. I shielded my face from the inferno with my forearm as I got back to my feet and backed away further still. He sauntered over to stand by my side and watch the flames engulf the fruit of my physical efforts.

"Here, Lloyd; favour tae ask ye, cunto."

I looked at him long and hard before replying, "What?"

"Fancy giein' iz a hand building meh new gairden hoose?" He turned and pointed out yet another box from the B&Q that sat at the back of the garden. I couldn't believe it.

"What?"

"A gairden hoose. Eh'm needin' somewhaur tae keep Dong Chu when the decorator comes in tae turn the bog intae a replica o' the place in LA whaur Dode Michael got caught wankin' aff polis."

He looked at me like butter wouldn't melt in his mouth. I was stunned, and not to mention pissed right off. I sputtered, "Gaffer, I've built you a shed twice already! You just set that one on fire right in front of me!"

I turned and walked away as he continued to plead with me, seemingly unaware of what the problem was and continued, "But what aboot the gairden hoose Lloyd? What aboot the shed?"

Trying not to explode was a struggle that was getting the better of me. I spun round again to face him.

"Sorry but fuck the shed, gaffer!"

Something inside him changed. He straightened up and the confused look that had been on his face fell away.

"What was that, Lloyd?"

I'd sworn at him, and although I felt it was a mistake to talk in such a manner to my manager I was unable to prevent myself repeating it.

"I said, fuck the shed."

He screwed a finger into his ear and again asked, "Sorry Lloyd, eh didnae catch ye; what was that?"

Exasperated, I spat it out, one word at a time, "Fuck. The. Shed!"

He clenched his fists and cheered, "Yaasssss! And again, Lloyd!"

"What on earth...FUCK THE SHED!"

"One mair time!"

"Have you gone deaf? I said..."

The penny dropped. The crazy old bastard. He stepped forward, put both hands on my shoulders and waited my saying it just once more. Despite the lunatic method by which he'd got me there I said it with pure conviction.

"Fuck the Shed."

He smiled and gave me a playful little slap in the cheeks.

"Exactly, Lloyd. Ex-fuckin'-actly."

With that he walked off past the blazing remains of the garden storage unit, still as naked as the day he was born. I looked up to watch the huge plume of black smoke as it rose into the sky above, heard the now-familiar cry of emergency sirens approaching and nodded to myself.

I was ready for the Dundee derby.

* * *

I'd arrived at Dens expecting an atmosphere electricrified with anticipation and excitement. What I found was a mood of dejection.

"Harry's been captured."

The gaffer looked as if he'd been kicked in the nuts which, for all intents and purposes, he had been.

"Captured? What d'ya mean he's been captured?"

"Some Yeti hunter caught him. The barbers ended up on the lash last night and didnae turn up at his hoose this moarnin tae shave him. When he went oot to get a hunner-pack o' Bics the boy shot him wi' a dart gun and took him awa' in a big net. He'll be in a documentary on the National Geographic channel next week."

Of all the men we could do without losing, our inspirational skipper was the one we'd miss most. Eddie McGlone was handed the captain's armband and we were told to get ready to leave for Tannadice.

The Dundee Derby is unique in that it is almost certainly the only game in the world where the visiting team walks to the opposition ground. The gaffer had led us out of Dens and lined us up in a flying V-formation and we walked down the middle of the road towards Tannadice in this manner. Amid the songs, taunts and chants from both sets of fans, the gaffer could be heard loudly enquiring as to whether Operation Yewtree had claimed Jim McLean yet.

As soon as we got in the away dressing room, he and Wally went to work decorating it with giant Dundee flags on every wall. As we stripped for our warm up the gaffer rigged up a TV set and DVD player on the massage table.

"Hi! Eh'm Big Jocky. You may remember me from pre-match instructional videos such as 'To Hell and Back: A Guide to Surviving a Trip to Love Street' and 'Hiya Roy Aitken! Hiya pal!'"

The video was a montage of key moments from the *Rocky* series, Luke Skywalker blowing up the Death Star, a full episode of *Saved by the Bell: The College Years* and footage of Hulk Hogan leg-dropping and pinning Sergeant Slaughter at Wrestlemania VII. By the time we'd gone out to warm up we were almost back in the zone, and when we came back inside with the roar of the huge Dundee support ringing in our ears, thinking about the key players who wouldn't join us on the pitch only bolstered our determination to look adversity in the eye and offer it a square-go.

Ten minutes later we sat round the dressing room listening as the gaffer delivered his final instructions.

"We shall fight on the pitch, we shall fight in the dugoots, we shall fight on the Hulltoon and, if any cunt can be bathered gettin' the bus doon the Ferry, we shall fight them on the beaches; we shall never surrender."

Standing there bare-chested and ripped to the tits on adrenaline he appeared to be 10 foot tall.

"Dae it fur Harry. Dae it fur Doug, Chrissy, and fur auld Walzo here wha's been diagnosed wi' cancer and only has twa weeks tae live."

We gasped as our eyes shot to Wally Gordon, who looked to Jocky in bewilderment. After a second, he twigged and looked round the room nodding in sombre agreement.

"This, lads, is the Dundee fuckin' derby, and by Christ are United awa' tae get telt."

He was psyched, and it was infectious. I could sense the spirit and will to win building with every word that came out his mouth.

"Wha's in cherge here, United?"

A cheer went up.

"The Dees are running the fucking show here, aye!"

Another cheer from the players, a little louder this time.

"WHA'S IN FUCKING CHERGE HERE, UNITED?"

To a man we jumped to our feet and let out a roar. The gaffer dropped his tracksuit bottoms, shook his hips so that his giant penis almost wrapped round his waist like a bullwhip and let out a primal scream that threatened to shake the tiles free from the walls.

"COME ON DUUUUUUNDEEEEEEEEEHHHH! THUNDERCATS! HOOOOOOOOOOOOO!"

We cried 'HOOOOOOOOOOOOOOO!' in unison and made our way into the tunnel, where we found the United team lined up looking at us as if they were about to play a team from the local mental hospital. They must have heard everything.

Good.

The noise out in the ground was incredible. Both sets of fans were belting out their respective songs in full voice and creating a fantastic atmosphere. A huge surge of excitement flowed through me and goosebumps popped up on my goosebumps.

"Let's fucking go, Dundee! C'mon!"

Eddie's battle cry dominoed down the line and, as we began moving forward, we all verbalised our urge to get the task at hand under way. I was breathing heavily, sweating and all of a sudden feeling rather faint.

Just as I feared for my ability to continue I came out into the sunshine and my nervous tension was swept away by a wave of awe and wonder. The full-to-bursting ground was a sight to behold. To my right, a sea of solid tangerine and black lifted like high tide behind the ocean spray of confetti thrown skyward from behind the goal. Streamers and toilet rolls arced high before plummeting down to cover the track and goalmouth. To my left and directly ahead, a twirling mass of blue and white scarves were partially obstructed from view by the fog pouring out of the smoke bombs that had been launched to greet our arrival. The decibel level was such that the singing, shouting and screaming from all corners of the ground merged into one indistinguishable, passionately delivered noise.

This was what it was all about. This justified every sacrifice I ever made to fulfil my dream of becoming a footballer.

We made our way to our end of the pitch and offered applause to the massed ranks of the Dundee support. They were ready, and so were we. Our numbers had been bolstered by the gaffer cleverly exploiting bureaucratic loopholes and calling in favours from underworld acquaintances to secure the emergency signings of Lochee United captain Craig Robertson and former Dee 'keeper Dennis "Soapy" Soutar, reputed to be the best testicle scrubber in the country. Members of the youth team had been drafted in to fill the bench.

As Eddie and United's captain oversaw the coin toss I watched the gaffer and Wally make their way down the track. As they passed the home dugout, United boss Jackie McNamara greeted his opposite number with the extension of his hand. The gaffer accepted it, shook it and quickly used it to gain leverage by pulling the young manager into a chest-to-chest confrontation. Wally was in quickly to pull them apart and guide his over-stimulated colleague away. McNamara looked thoroughly shaken by the incident and slunk back into the dugout and the soothing embrace of his assistant, Simon Donnelly.

The referee's whistle rang out and he signalled the teams to remain where they were. We'd be shooting into the opposition support in the first half. As the noise emanating from the stands reached a deafening crescendo the game began.

* * *

The first serious piece of action came not on the park but on the sidelines. There was a commotion in the home dugout and, as I followed play across the halfway line, I saw that the gaffer had hurled himself in among the United management team and substitutes. He was clawing at Jackie McNamara's face as if trying to pull it clean off. As Wally, the fourth official and a couple of stewards tried to drag him out of there I could hear him shouting, "IT'S A FUCKN' MASK! EH KEN IT'S YOU McLEAN YA BALDY CUNT! UNVEIL YERSELF!"

With roughly 60 seconds on the clock the gaffer had been sent from the dugout to watch the match from the stand. The home support were delighted and goaded him as he trudged along the track toward the tunnel he'd emerged from only a few minutes ago. When he reached the corner of the East Stand he stopped in front of the United support and faced them down with the now-familiar arms-outstretched pose until four stewards were forced to pick him up and physically carry his crucifix-rigid torso down the tunnel and out of sight.

Before he would even have made it to whichever new vantage point he was headed, the situation had deteriorated on the park. Eddie had followed pre-match instruction to a tee and booted Gary Mackay-Steven on to the running track the first time he'd tried to dribble his way down the wing. While taking United's star player out had been at least a temporary success, the resulting free kick had been floated into the box and met by the towering head of Jon Daly. The net rippled, half the ground exploded with noise and the odds on a home victory were slashed.

"Keep the heid, lads. It's nae bather, we'll come back fae that."

The gaffer was putting his megaphone to good use and was managing to direct things from the front of the stand he'd been banished to.

"Hiya Jackie McNagoodaine, hiya pal! Big Jocky's got a peace offering for ye: fancy a Jaffa Cake?"

United rode the high of their early goal to seize the momentum. They dominated the opening exchanges, pushing us hard from midfield and breaking forward quickly in numbers. Only some valiant last-gasp defending and acrobatic stops from Soapy kept the deficit down at the half-hour mark.

A desperate clearance up the park led to our first chance of the game. As he attempted to control Eddie's aimless hoof upfield, I stole the ball off the toe of Sean Dillon and made headway toward goal. With the sticks in clear sight I cracked a left-foot shot high toward the top corner and was only denied by a brilliant diving fingertip save from United's keeper.

It was important to keep momentum up, so I darted after the ball and gestured for the ballboy to get it to me quickly. As I caught it and rolled it over to the corner flag and I found myself only a few feet from United's most vociferous fans.

"YOU'RE FUCKING SHITE, YA WEE PRICK!"

"GET TAE FUCK YA BLUE NOSED BASTARD!"

"FUCK YOU YA DERRY WANKER!"

"GRANNY SHAGGER!"

It was the tirade of abuse the gaffer had told me to expect. Only the last shout surprised me.

"Dinnae fall under it; feed aff it."

The gaffer's words of advice came to mind as if he were whispering in my ear. I clenched my fists, steeling myself against the fearsome wave of derogatory remarks as I positioned myself in the penalty box, started jostling for space and willed Kev Rafferty to drop the ball right on my head.

He must have heard me thinking. His in-swinger was inch perfect and I met the ball with a deft flick of the head which neither the defender, goalkeeper or front post could do anything about it. There was a split second of silence, then an almighty roar from the far side of the ground. Dundee United 1 – 1 Dundee.

As I broke away from the crowded box to celebrate I brought my index finger up to my mouth and pressed it against my lips. The explosion of rage it elicited was almost comical in its ferocity, especially given the obscenities coming my way seconds earlier. I didn't get much time to enjoy the moment of revenge as I was quickly engulfed by my teammates as they joined me in celebration.

As we made our way back to our half of the field I looked towards the away support and grinned at the incredible sight around me. Thousands were wildly celebrating a goal I had just scored in a game that meant so much to so many people. It was almost overwhelming. I turned to the dugout and shook my fist happily at Wally, who returned the gesture. When I looked up into the stand the gaffer was too busy initiating a one-man Derry Rhumba and taunting the suited-and-booted United fans in the hospitality section to share a similar moment with me. Fair enough.

The barrage of abuse I was getting had increased ten-fold in the wake of the "hush" gesture I'd offered after my goal. Most disconcerting of all was a song that went up from the United fans.

"GEORGE SHAGGED A GRANNY! OH, LLOYD GEORGE SHAGGED A GRANNY!"

What the fuck? It rang out loud and clear until a song from the jubilant away support drowned it out. I'd shagged a granny? I hadn't sha-

Jeannie McKay. Fuck. I actually had shagged a granny, perhaps even a great-granny. But how did the United supporters know about it?

It was on my mind right up until half time, where we found the gaffer was waiting for us in the dressing room.

"Here, nae cunt telt me Jackie McNagoodaine and Dougie Donnelly's laddie were merried. Fuckin' trehed tae rip the poor boy's face aff in front o' his wife there, he was like that, 'you ya big ride, get aff meh hubby!' Eh says, 'It's Jim Mc-fuckin'-Lean ya daft bint! Open yer mince pehs!'"

The halftime team talk was an open discussion on whether the Mystery Machine would beat the A Team van in a race from the Swallow circle to Asda at the far end of the Kingsway. There wasn't enough time for us all to offer our thoughts on which member of the crack commando unit you'd have sex with if the plan coming together depended on it (the gaffer asserted that he'd go with Mr T because "ye'd be as well goin' the whole hog and trehin the black aine.") before the buzzer signalled the end of the interval.

As we filed back out the gaffer grabbed hold of me and kissed me on the cheek.

"Fucking perfect timing wi' that goal, son. That got us back in the gemme at just the right time. The wee shut-yer-pus-ya-Arab-cunts celebration was maist teckle tae."

"Cheers, gaffer. Hey, did you catch that song they were singing about me? About shagging a granny?"

He looked sympathetic and concerned.

"Eh did, aye. Ye hae tae ignore that kind o' shite though. Mind what eh said: thrive on the abuse. Get it right back up them."

As I made to leave he called my name so I turned round again. He pointed at my chest before cocking his thumb back at his heart. I looked down, saw the Dundee badge and knew what he meant. I gave it a little pat with a clenched fist and walked back out smiling as the United support treated my return as if they'd just been told it was their granny I'd shagged.

Despite starting brightly and quickly gaining the upper hand we were soon 2-1 down. United broke out from a corner with lightning speed, catching us cold to score their second goal of the afternoon. It was a cruel blow, and one that deflated us. The momentum switched again, and if United scored the third goal they were threatening it would be all over.

It took chasing a lost cause of a long ball to spark a revival. As I slowly wound my stride down to a stuttering, frustrated halt right against the advertisement boards behind the goal, I realised I was looking at a familiar face in the crowd.

"Come on, Lloyd, keep it goin', man!"

Mikey the Hulltoon Hun was in the front row, his pals from the game of "fehve n' a boot" flanking him. I acknowledged them with a nod. Belief and determination was etched in each of their faces, and it stoked my own fire. As I stepped back I roused the Shed with a get-up-and-get-behind-us gesture that had an instant effect. Within seconds the whole enclosure was on its feet, and the stand that ran down the touchline were spurred into doing the same. The spark leapt on to the pitch and flashed from player to player like a lightning bolt.

The tide turned once again. All of a sudden we were stronger, faster and looking more dangerous.

But we couldn't break them down. Our final ball was gobbled up by United's big, sturdy backline time and time again. We pressed and pressed but couldn't find a way through.

As United's entire support began singing again in anticipation of an imminent victory I realised it was now or never. I looked up into the stand and saw the gaffer looking right back at me with three fingers raised. There were times I was sure he was somehow reading my mind. I passed the word round the players in order to galvanise them for one final throw of the dice.

We poured forward, won three corners in a row and still we couldn't break through. United hoofed the ball back down the field and I felt sure that was it. The ref checked his watch but, despite thousands of United fans mimicking the sound they wanted to hear from him, his whistle remained in his hand.

Soapy collected the ball midway in our half and an almighty roar went up from the Dundee support, the soundtrack of those who refuse to give up until the bitter end. With every outfield player we had now in an attacking position the ball was launched forward. It was met by Dee and Arab heads simultaneously, and spun high in the air over my shoulder. I didn't take my eye off it for a second. Some 25 yards out I was there to meet it on the turning volley when it dropped to waist height. I knew it was in the second it left my boot.

2-2.

Cue pandemonium. With no apparent control over my actions I ran headlong in a straight line in the direction I was facing, screaming like a banshee until I was swallowed up by the front row of the Shed. The players piled in behind me in equally delirious fashion. The fans were going several shades of crazy, piling over seats, each other and on to the pitch. It was an explosion of pure, unadulterated joy shared with players they'd cheered on relentlessly all afternoon.

All their lives, in fact. As I was hauled back onto the playing field and looked among their number I felt privileged to be part of the kind of epic moment that would be cemented in their memory as long as they lived.

"FUUUUUUUUUUUUUUUUUUUUCKKKKKKKK-KKKKKKKKKKKKKKKKKKKKING YAAAAAAAAAAAAAAAA AAAAAAAAAAAAAAAAAAAAAAAAAAAAASSSSSSSSSSSSSSSSSS SSSSSSSSSSSSSSSSSSSSSSSS!!!

The gaffer seemed happy too. So much so he'd jumped out of the stand and made a belated entry to the piley-on that was now dispersing as the dozens who'd invaded the pitch headed in the opposite direction. His tears of joy wet my own cheeks, leaving a residue of what it means to be a Dundee fan on my face before he was hauled off to the sin bin once again.

We'd earned ourselves a replay.

* * *

Jocky stood tall in the middle of the away dressing room. He took the time to look round at all of his players, ensuring he was making eye contact with each and every one of us as he went. Having swept the room he smiled at some thought that went unshared. Once it had passed he spoke.

"Lads, eh'm as proud o' you tonight as eh huv been o' any team eh've ever played fur or managed. Eh mean that. Eh ken eh speak a load o' shite on occasion, but eh do want ye tae ken eh mean that. Thank you. Ye didnae deserve tae lose that gemme today."

Heads hung heavily on bodies slumped into their seats. We all heard the gaffer and knew he was genuine in what he said. All we could meet it with was silence. Dejected, soul-crushing silence.

As we lined up for the restart, shaking with adrenaline, the fourth official indicated there would be two minutes of injury time. United lumped the ball forward toward our goal and we instantly returned it to them. This pattern was repeated two or three times to no effect before the ball finally landed at the feet of Willo Flood some 30 yards from goal. The referee was bringing his whistle to his lips when the United midfielder unleashed a desperate long-range effort that was heading high and wide until a wicked deflection saw it change course. Soapy did everything in his power to scramble across his goal to keep it out, and even managed to get a hand to it, but it wasn't enough. United celebrated as wildly as we had just a minute or two earlier as every player in dark blue crumpled in a stunned, disbelieving heap on the turf.

"Ken the song 'Up Wi' the Bonnets'? The Dundee sang. Meh favourite line's ayewiz been, 'for the brave boys who wear the dark blue of Dundee'. You cunts lived up tae that line tonight. Brave as fuck, aye."

His voice cracked and he seemed to ponder as to whether he'd fight the tear in his eye. He wasn't one for disguising his emotions and decided let it go free. He looked round the room, grinning at us before wiping his face with his forearms.

"Fucking Willo Flood. It took an extraterrestrial gettin' a wild deflection tae beat us here, lads. Nae shame in it. Boy'll be anally probing rednecks the night thinking, 'Dundee deserved a draw, aye. I'll add that tae the list o' kinds ay close encounter'."

The streets were quiet by the time we shuffled out of Tannadice. United had taken their celebrations to the pub, while those of a dark blue persuasion headed home to hide from the world for a while.

I had three missed calls from Charmaine, so called her back. She didn't greet me sympathetically, as I has expected, and instead jumped straight to a question.

"What's a' this aboot you shagging a granny? When wiz this?"

Shit. There was no point in denying it, so I told her the story.

"Eh thought eh wiz the second lassie ye shagged, Lloyd? Ye lost yer virginity tae yer mate's sister, then there wiz me."

Fuck. I stuttered and struggled to form an explanation, telling her I'd been too embarrassed to admit to Jeanie to her. It cut me no slack.

"You fuckin' LIED tae me ya wee prick. Eh'll tolerate a' sorts o' shite, Lloyd, but eh willnae tolerate bein' bullshitted. You're fucking dumped!"

She hung up on me. Fighting tears, I tried calling back but her phone appeared to be switched off.

"A'right there, Lloyd?"

The gaffer was coming out of Tannadice behind me.

"I've... I've been binned. Charmaine just dumped me."

He didn't look entirely surprised.

"Efter that gemme as well? Shite, sorry to hear that, pal. What happened?"

I explained the situation. He listened intently and sympathetically.

"She'll mibbe come around, pal. Gie her a wee bit o' time tae calm doon, eh."

I declined the offer of a lift home via Air Jocky. I had never been dumped before so didn't know what to do. Sadness began to overwhelm me and, in a daze, I bade the gaffer farewell. With shoulders heavily slumped I started walking slowly up the road that would eventually lead me back to my lonely tipi.

"Lloyd."

He stood in the same spot and had watched me walk 10 or so paces before shouting to me.

"Question fur ye, cunto – how hungry's yer hippo?

He remained straight-faced as he awaited an answer, but his right hand began tapping away as if making that hippo of his eat something.

"Gaffer, it's not really the time..."

"I repeat, cunto – how hungry's yer hippo?"

It took a few seconds for me to figure out why he asked, and when I did I was humbled for his efforts. In spite of the crushing pain I felt, I couldn't help but smile as he continued to tap ever faster.

"To be honest, gaffer, it's considered to be among the very hungriest of the hippos. Ravenous so he is."

He spread his arms out and looked disgusted.

"Hungrier than meh hippo?"

I walked a few steps back toward him.

"Apparently, word on the street has it that your hippo's just a wee bit peckish as opposed to actually being properly hungry."

His arms dropped to his sides, genuinely concerned by what he was hearing.

"Are you bein' serious? Has some cunt actually been sayin' that or is it just part o' the mon-back-tae-mine routine we're daein' here?"

I couldn't help but laugh.

"I'm just kidding, your hippo's reputation remains intact. For the moment, anyway."

He phewed and backtracked.

"Eh fuckin' kent that, it's nae bather aye. Get strapped in then ya cunt, it's time tae separate the Hungry Hungry Hippos fae the merely Hungry Hippos."

Minutes later I'd received my welcome from the flight deck and safety instructions. We took to the air, and after veering over Tannadice so he could deposit the contents of his lungs on the pitch, made our way towards Broughty Ferry.

* * *

I was still hungover as fuck on Sunday evening. The gaffer and I had powered into the Special and stovies the minute we arrived at his place and hadn't stopped until the early hours. Not that I had any recollection of going to sleep; the first thing I knew about it was waking up face down in the sand somewhere around lunchtime.

Getting out of it had been the only way to finish the day. After the defeat to United and being dumped by Charmaine, whose phone remained switched off all night, we'd needed something to take our minds off of things.

For all his bluster the gaffer wasn't even that good a Hungry

Hungry Hippos player. The way he talked I'd expected him to be some kind of quick-fingered hippo master, yet I found myself winning the first few games quite easily. After that I had to subtly control my hippo's food intake so as not to send my opponent into a rage that probably would have seen him raze the surrounding neighbourhood to the ground.

I'd left just after lunchtime. Jocky had invited me to join him down at the Broughty Ferry Green crazy golf course, where he was meeting Wally for a game.

"Loves a gemme o' crazy golf does auld Walzo. Fucks his heid up a wee bit though. He usually gets to aboot the 8th hole before he starts giggling at the hole design, sayin' there's too many colours to smell and not enough sound to feed the souls that tread the path into the light and shite like that. He chills oot once he gets a choc ice fae Visocchi's doon his pus."

Tempting though it had been, I just wasn't in the mood. I needed to speak to Charmaine. With her phone still switched off I decided to take direct action and pay her a visit at home.

* * *

The only problem was she no longer lived there. I knew this because an enormous pile of rubble had replaced the multi-storey block that once stood tall over Lochee. The taxi driver told me that it'd been demolished that morning. I had to pinch myself to check I wasn't living some kind of bad dream. With the hangover, heavy heart and the vacant space where my girlfriend and I had re-enacted graphic content from schemiehoors just days earlier, I found myself wondering whether I had somehow become detached from reality.

I spent most of the day suffering in bed at the tipi. Every time my phone buzzed my wrecked body and mind jumped back into life and desperately hoped the message was from Charmaine, but inevitably it was another update from the gaffer.

"WALZO'S CLAIMING THAT WHEN YOU REALLY THINK ABOUT IT, HIS PUTTER'S NO LESS HUMAN THAN

*YOU OR I. WE'RE ONLY ON THE SECOND HOLE. FUCK
SAKE AYE. LOL X"*

Then, later:

*"HAEIN' A BRAW TIME, YOU SHOULD FIRE DOON. I'D
SAY WALZO'S ASKIN FOR YE BUT HE'S PEERING DOWN
THE HOLE ON THE NINTH SPEAKING TO SOME CUNT
HE KENS DOON THERE. FUCKIN' LOL X"*

When sleep finally claimed me it was interrupted by a ring
tone that instantly slapped me awake more effectively than any
alarm clock ever could as my mind jumped to the gravest possible
explanation for the nocturnal phone call.

It was 3:43 on Monday morning, an unusual time even for
Jocky to call. I braced myself as I pushed "answer".

"Gaffer. What's up? You OK there?"

There was no response, but I could hear the sound of liquid
pouring out of its receptacle and knew it was only a drinking pause.
There was a gasp as it hit the spot, then, "Lloyd? Hiya pal. Hiya."

He sounded incredibly down. It wasn't like him at all.

"Hiya gaffer. Is everything ok? You've got me worried here..."

His speech wasn't slurred but measured. It was freaking me
out.

"Aye, eh just wanted tae hae a blether, likes."

I waited for him to get going.

"Ok... go on..."

"Walzo and eh finished up the crazy golf aboot seven just as
the bothy was closing up for the night. Fehve fuckin' hours tae
play a roond o' crazy golf. Walzo said foursome always tak' longer.
When eh asked what the fuck he was on aboot he said oor spirit
guides were playin' tae. Eh wiz like that, 'Walzo we need tae stop
comin' here fur fuck sake, it's gettin' ridiculous'."

I would've laughed had the tone of his delivery not indicated
it would be inappropriate.

"So eh telt him we'll fire up here and hing aboot a bit. Eh
agreed the spirit guides could come tae, assuming they'd behave.
His is a big native Amercian fella and probably aware o' guest eti-

quette. At your hoose he would, fuckin' right. Apparently mine's a fox though, and they're no' really known fur respecting yer wishes no' tae eat things and piss a'place."

"True enough. Rare to see a fox indoors, it's not really their cup of tea."

"Exactly, Lloyd. So we're sittin' strugglin' tae play Twister 'cause the Indian cunt was haein' problems spinning the dial or something, fuck knows, but it wisnae movin'. Eh says, 'fuck this. We'll dae somethin' these lads will be able tae grasp; eh'll get the Ouija board oot'. So we get it fired up and ask the usual warm up questions. The gless is sliding back and forth and Walzo's fuckin' right intae it, goin' 'fuck me Jock, this is wild'. Now, Lloyd, eh ayewiz ask it, 'wha's in cherge here?' And it spells oot J-O-C-K-Y. Every time, 'cause when eh say 'a'body kens that' eh do mean on every plain o' existence and no' just this aine whaur we bide."

I let him go on without offering any response.

"But this time, Lloyd? Nothing. Didnae move. Did not budge an inch."

I was struggling to offer any meaningful feedback.

"Eh, maybe it was just a bad connection or something? I don't know what to tell you, gaffer, I've never used one of those things."

"Well, that's what eh thought at first. The big chief asks it how Hiawatha's getting on and the glass bursts back into life saying he's fine, and awa' up tae the shops fur baccy and fag papers. The board wisnae broken. Fuckin' freaked right oot, aye."

Exasperated, I told him not to worry and that he remained very much in cherge.

"Dinnae ken, pal. Eh've got a feeling in meh water something's awa' tae go doon. Fuck knows what, but somethin'."

"Gaffer... You're going to be fine, there's nothing that'll stop you being in cherge of anything. You're probably just done in from having to look after Wally and his pals all day. After a big night last night too, it's probably just catching up on you."

The words seemed to soothe him, and there was a noticeable lightening in his tone.

"True enough, pal. Ye were right no' tae get wired in aboot they tenner ectos. Gettin' auld tae; eh'll be 118 next year. Dinnae look it, eh?"

I had no chance to probe him further on the incredulous claim as he announced, "Fuckin' hell, that fox left a puddle o' piss on the kitchen flair. Fuckin' telt Walzo they were bad news! Right, better mop it up and hit the scratcher. See ye at trainin, cunto. Cheery."

The line went dead.

It was an odd call all right. Though the tale was no more outlandish than most of the gaffer's utterings, his state of mind had clearly not been healthy. To hear a man normally so rip-roaringly full of vitality so obviously on a downer concerned me. I resolved to speak to him privately after training.

I tried to get back to sleep but each time I shut my eyes a sense of dread washed over me. Though I was no devotee of the Ouija board, I couldn't help but feel the gaffer might just have been on to something.

* * *

'DENS ROCKED BY DOUBLE SCANDAL IN WAKE OF DERBY DEFEAT.'

As far as headlines went it was as jarring as any I'd seen outside a newsagent to date. When I went in to buy a paper I was horrified to see Jeanie McKay's face on the front page of a tabloid under the headline, 'BY GEORGE! GRANDMOTHER SPEAKS OF NIGHT OF PASSION WITH HER TEENAGE FOOTBALLER LOVER.' I swayed back on my heels thinking I was going to faint. Jeanie had sold her story to the papers.

It got worse. The Courier's front page read, 'DENS BOSS EMBROILED IN BETTING SCANDAL.' A quick skim read of the cover story informed me that Jocky had been accused of backing his side to lose.

I walked down Provost Road in a daze. This couldn't be happening. As soon as I turned the corner and saw the ruck of press hanging about outside the player's entrance I knew it really was.

It only took one reporter to spot me and break away from the pack before the rest followed his lead. A barrage of questions came my way as I put my head down and pushed through them to get inside.

"Does Jeanie spit or swallow, Lloyd?"

"What can you tell us about Jocky's gambling habits?"

"Will this derail Dundee's promotion bid?"

I barged past without saying a word. By the time I reached the safety of the other side of the door I felt like bursting into tears.

The dressing room was like a morgue. My arrival at least inspired a few warnings to stay away from their grandmothers. I was mortified at the situation, but a little gentle humour eased the pain somewhat.

My inclusion in the morning news was nothing compared to what was happening with the gaffer. A sex scandal, embarrassing though it was, was little more than tabloid fodder. The allegations made against Jocky were no laughing matter.

"Lads, the gaffer's on the telly."

Wally pointed to the screen and we all looked up expecting to see him sitting on the toilet at his house. Instead the TV was tuned to BBC News 24. Footage from the derby played as they discussed allegations of match fixing.

Dumbfounded, we watched and listened as the reporter explained that Jocky stood accused of not only gambling on games involving Dundee, but also plotting to see us lose so that he could gain from bets placed on opposition victory.

That simply wasn't true. Anyone who knew him would verify it was a claim so wide off the mark it was offensive. Yeah, he'd bet on Dundee losing against Alloa but only on his dead grandmother's say so. Surely common sense would prevail.

It was only then that I realised just how ridiculous that would sound to anyone who wasn't part of our inner circle of benevolent insanity.

How did word get out though? He'd shown me his burst coupon at the orgy the previous week, but he'd thrown it in the bin immediately after.

The world stopped spinning on its axis as I remembered he hadn't put it in the bin.

Charmaine had.

The gaffer's words boomed out in my mind as he were delivering directly into my ear through his megaphone.

"Lloyd, eh think yer burd's at it."

Surely to fuck...

"There's somethin' no' right aboot that lassie."

She couldn't possibly have...

"Fuck knows what, exactly, but she's definitely at it."

Every fibre of my being fought valiantly to deny it but there was a white hot lump of reality burning in the pit of my stomach. Charmaine was involved in this somehow. She'd sold Jocky out.

But why?

The dressing room door swung open and Jocky entered the room. He looked like he'd seen a ghost, and not his dead granny's.

"Gaffer! What the hell is going on?"

The whole room jumped into life, rising to greet him with desperation etched on each and every face. He raised his hands to prevent anyone coming closer, and to hush us. He took a moment as if to steady himself before talking in an uncharacteristically low, soft voice.

"Eh've just handed in meh resignation."

The air was sucked out the room.

"Ye a' ken eh hae a gamble on the futba, and on the Dees tae, ken? McCracken kens an' a' now and is bein' a total cunt aboot it. The cunt's angling it like eh've been fucking match fixing."

He looked off into the middle distance, an incredulous look of innocence on his face.

"Me, fixin' it so we lost! He's aff his fucking nut!"

A few voices spoke brief words of agreement before he continued, "But he's got iz beh the balls, aye. Big time."

As he looked up and his eyes found mine the sad smile on his face nearly broke my heart.

"He's got proof that eh put a bet on Alloa tae win last Saturday."

Charmaine. Fuck no.

"Your gran gave you a tip, didn't she, Jock," said Wally, who immediately understood what had happened.

Jocky smiled weakly at the old friend who knew him all too well.

"As ayewiz, Walzo, you ken the score."

He straightened up and cast an eye round the room.

"Lads, youse ken me; eh wid never, ever, dae anythin' tae dae this team herm. Eh'm Dundee to the fuckin' core. McCracken kens that, but he doesnae gie a fuck. The slimy bastard's been dying tae get me oot since the day he slithered through the door so he's grabbing this opportunity wi' baith hands. What's important tae me is that you boys ken the truth."

Every single man in the room confirmed they knew it full well. There wasn't one iota of doubt. He appreciated it.

"If eh hudnae resigned McCracken would o' sacked iz anyway. The gemme's up the poley fur auld Jocky here, lads."

His voice cracked a little as the dam that held his emotions in place became in serious risk of being breeched, but Wally's strong arm was round his shoulder in time to hold him together. The gaffer gave the hand that hung over his chest a pat of gratitude, and held firm.

Eddie McGlone, his voice as thin as a wisp of smoke, spoke up. "But there's only, what? Seven or eight games left to play? I can't believe this is happening now, right at the end of the season when we're top of the league. It's just... crazy."

The gaffer stiffened up and spoke with far more conviction than he had since entering the room.

"And ye'll stay tap o' the league, Edwardo."

He wiped his face and slipped into team talk-mode for the last time.

"Do not fuck up on the pitch because o' this. Ye hear iz? Ye hae tae stay strong and fight on otherwise it's punch in the pus time for every aine o' you cunts. The league is ours, yours, for the taking."

Pulling Wally in close to him again he pointed at his friend's face.

"Fuck knows what'll happen in the next wee while, but Walzo's still gonnae be here. It's just me that's goin', at least so far. Walzo can run the show here. He kens the score better than any cunt. Pay attention tae him, he'll see ye through."

They exchanged the kind of look only old friends can as Wally, fighting back the tears himself, nodded in agreement. Jocky added, "Tell ye what, he's got a no' bad toby on him tae, eh pal?" and a few of those tears slipped out along with the laughter the joke merited.

He made his way round the room thanking each player for their efforts during his reign. Hands were shaken, hugs were exchanged and grown men cried like babies. When he reached me I was unable to make a start on all the things I wanted to say before he cut me off with a single raised finger. As we embraced he whispered, "It wisnae your fault," held my face in one hand, and winked. I felt like curling up in a ball and dying.

"It's been a pleasure, boys. Yer a good bunch o' laddies, and eh'll miss ye."

He sucked it up one more time and backed out the room. With a final flicker of that fire in his eyes he parted on, "Away the Dees."

And with that he was gone.

There was no training that day at Dens. We sat stupefied for the best part of a half hour with barely a word spoken in the funereal atmosphere. Eventually Wally told us to take the day off and to gather as normal the following day.

I went home via the pub, and fitted right in among the day-time drinkers sat staring silently into pints nursed to ensure they wouldn't have to face the outside world again too soon. I ignored the funny looks and witty comments about Jeanie that came my way. I was in no mood for them.

Some time later I returned to the tipi and found someone had paid me a visit and left a gift.

Mary Shelley's *Frankenstein* sat on my fold-out bed.

I sat down and picked it up. Tucked inbetween the inside cover and front page, a handwritten note.

"Hiya Lloyd! Hiya pal! Wee Jocky reckons you'll like this aine. Eh'm gonna lie low for a wee while, but eh'lll be in touch. Speak soon, cunto. LOL. Jocky x"

What the hell was going on with this book? There was a lot more to it than met the eye. Whatever it was, Big Jocky knew. Wee Jocky knew, too.

I settled down to get some reading done.

FIFTH HALF

FIFTH HALF

The week that followed was possibly the worst of my life. My early days of struggle at the club were nothing in comparison to the depression that took root in the aftermath of Jocky's departure. Wally was holding things together as best he could and we worked harder than ever, but our efforts were compromised by the events of the past few days. Whilst the team was there in body, our spirit had walked out the door with allegations of impropriety hanging over him on Monday morning.

Though the gaffer had said he'd be in touch I couldn't wait for him to make the first move. I phoned, but he didn't answer. I sent long, rambling text messages trying to articulate my feelings of guilt and shame. I told him that I owed him everything and would give anything to turn back the clock and change things. He didn't reply.

The veil of silence stretched to cover Charmaine. Her phone remained resolutely switched off, and after a few days her number was no longer recognised when I dialled it. As soon as I had realised that it was her who'd shafted Jocky my heart had sunk to a place from which it had not yet risen. There were so many unanswered questions, the most troubling of which was simply why?

Friday morning saw us arrive for training to find the press had gathered outside Dens once again. They'd been around a lot at the start of the week then lost interest as time went by, perhaps because the players offered nothing beyond "no comment" as we waited for Allan in Bangladesh to arrange for our entry. While Jocky seemed to have gone into hiding, Bob McCracken had never been out of the papers or off the screen. He was receiving plaudits for his supposedly dignified response, saying he was assisting with inquiries, pledging to drag Scottish football into the 21st century and announcing plans to bring in an interim manager to see the season out. It was the latter that brought the press corps out again.

"Salutations, gentlemen. I trust you're all well and enjoying this fine spring weather we're having."

Bob McCracken breezed into the dressing room for the first time since I'd arrived at Dens. This wasn't his territory, but with the gaffer gone he was feeling brave all of a sudden. He cast his eye around the place with a vaguely disgusted look. Bar the odd crushed empty and the lingering smell of stale smoke it wasn't actually in that bad a state.

"This, gentleman," he said whilst plucking an old Special can from the massage table between his thumb and forefinger and holding it as if it were hazardous waste, "stops right here. I know the kind of savagery Jocky not only let you away with but actively encouraged."

The can fell from his fingers and was deftly drop-kicked between Kevin Rafferty's open legs.

"It stops right here. Breaking the club's professional code of conduct – and yes, there is such a thing! – will result in immediate termination of contract. Do I make myself clear?"

The whole room bristled, but not one word of response was offered. McCracken's smile eased seamlessly into a sneer and a forced chuckle.

There was a sudden bang against the door, and a muffled call of, "MR BOBBY! LET ME IN, MR BOBBY!" could be heard behind it.

McCracken's smile returned at full beam.

"Ah! Gentlemen, it is my pleasure to introduce the man who

will be your manager until the end of this season. I'm sure most of you will be familiar with him."

Every head in the room turned to follow McCracken as he went to the door and swung it open with a dramatic flourish. Every mouth in the room fell open when we saw who it was.

"WILLIE LIKES FUTBA!"

Our new manager entered on a kiddie's tricycle. He wore a nappy, bib and a multi-coloured hat with a little propeller on top. He veered sharply to the right and disappeared inside the shower room, hollering, "WILLIE SLEEPS WITH THE LIGHT ON 'CAUSE HE'S SCARED OF PAPA SHANGO!" He did a quick lap, came back out and only stopped after crashing into the bath Doug once used to soak his aches and pains away.

"WILLIE! LIKES! FUTBA!"

Former player and TV pundit Willie Dawes had arrived, and apparently he liked futba. He jumped off the tricycle and launched himself at McCracken, hugging him hard round the waist and shyly burying his face against his stomach.

"Gentleman, this is Willie Dawes. Willie's going to be my man in the dugout for the remainder of the season. Isn't that right, Willie?"

Dawes looked up at him and smiled like a kid would at a beloved grandparent.

"Hi Mr Bobby."

McCracken gave his propeller a spin and told him he was a good boy.

Wally Gordon stepped up to the plate and asked the question on everyone's lips.

"Bob, what the hell is happening here? What's... what's wrong with him?"

Dawes let go of McCracken and sat cross-legged whilst using his index finger to investigate the goings-on in his nose. The results were fascinating enough to eat.

"Though it's largely unknown in the public domain Willie has a rare mental syndrome that sees him act in an adult, professional, and analytical manner when a camera or microphone is pointed at him. The rest of the time he's a man-child with the intellect of a pot of those stovies Jocky was forever stuffing his face with."

Dawes had gotten up off the floor and walked over to show Eddie a particularly interesting specimen from his nasal passage. He gave it a brief inspection and offered a thumbs up, which sent him running off giggling to search for more nose bounty.

A somewhat perplexed Wally pressed for answers.

"So why have you brought him in as manager then? I'm assuming he's wearing velcro shoes for good reason there; what chance does he have of managing a football team?"

McCracken slipped his thumbs beneath the braces under his open suit jacket and swayed back on his heels.

"Because, Walter, it's vital that we have a good media man at the helm. Someone who knows how to handle the press, to say the right things for the papers. It's a vital function that has been sadly lacking at this club all these years."

There would be no prizes for guessing who'd be keeping a tight check on what the manager would be saying to the press.

"As for the football side of things, all the great business minds of our time – Steve Jobs, Richard Branson, Craig Whyte, Sir Fred and myself among them – understand that the product is secondary to the brand. Get your marketing and PR right and the markets will take care of the rest. Anyway, enough chit-chat; time is money, gentlemen."

With a regal bow and self-satisfied smile he bid us good day. How could he be so unconcerned with events on the pitch? Did he really think a positive media profile helps you grind out wins at Cappielow when the rain is pissing down and the Young Branny Toi are threatening to stab yer maw? Whatever his misgivings about the club, surely he wanted us to win the league for no other reason than promotion meaning more money to rake in.

Though the stench that filled the room transpired to be coming from our new manager's nappy, it could have been our promotion hopes starting to decompose.

* * *

The post-Jocky era got off to a late start. 2am on Sunday morning, to be precise.

In order to appease the South Korean market who'd be watching the game live, McCracken had arranged for our game against Cowdenbeath to kick off at a time when most footballers were falling out of nightclubs. The palms of those running the game, who I didn't doubt were as money-hungry as McCracken himself, had surely been greased heavily. The result was a sporting contest deemed worthy of transmitting live to Fong Du's homeland being attended by only a few hundred insomniacs and nocturnally inclined diehards. It was just as well none of our young fans were allowed up this late as Deewok the bear was unable to entertain them due to him hibernating.

For the first time in months I took my place not on the pitch but on the bench. The news I'd been dropped came via a team sheet written in brightly coloured crayon on paper headed '*From the office of Bob McCracken CEO.*'

"This is a new low, Lloyd. In all my years in football I've never known anything like it."

Wally looked ready for his bed. He was in good company alongside Willie Dawes, who was sound asleep with his thumb in his mouth in a small Moses basket at his feet.

"Kicking off at two in the morning? The chairman picking the team? It's ridiculous."

Coming from someone who'd spent years working with a man who travelled by jetpack, chose to cover his living room floor with sand, and re-enacted much-loved children's films in his garden, it was as damning an indictment of the McCracken regime as you're likely to hear.

"Have you heard from Jocky, Wally? He left me a message saying he'd be in touch but I haven't heard from him since."

Wally was now staring into the distance ahead of him. When his wrinkled face began rearranging itself into a grin I followed the gaze and saw for myself the catalyst for his first smile of the week.

'McCRACKEN OOT. BOABY'S A TOBY,' read the crudely spray painted bedsheet that had been stretched across the corrugated iron wall at the back of the Derry.

"I haven't heard from him, no, but I wouldn't be surprised if he's not too far away."

Within seconds there was movement from the stewards. Half-a-dozen of them descended on the back of the Derry and a skirmish broke out. The handful of fans in the vicinity turned to watch and loud boos of protest emerged as the stewards fought – actually fought – people in the back row. Whoever started the altercation was unceremoniously ejected before Wally or I were able to confirm whether it had in fact been the gaffer.

"In the name o' the wee man, this stewarding is getting beyond the joke. They're fighting people up there! Home fans, too. I've seen it bad in the away end but never our own mob. This is getting beyond the joke."

As the game struggled to get out of first gear one thing quickly became apparent – Fong Du wasn't fully fit. Laziness had been the main limiting factor previously, but his lack of mobility tonight was clearly as a result of his persistent injury. When he pulled up chasing a through ball, Wally checked the sleeping Willie Dawes, popped his dummy in his mouth and told me to get warmed up.

As I ran down the touchline the handful of fans sat in the Main and Bobby Cox stands rose to give me a standing ovation. With hands above my head I returned their applause. When a song went up declaring me to be blue, white and fucking dynamite, I momentarily forgot all my troubles and felt like a World Cup winner.

After a few minutes of bending and stretching I noticed two stewards had approached the dugout to engage with Wally. Curious, I jogged back and caught the tail-end of the conversation.

"Mr McCracken's running things round here, and he'll decide if Fong Du plays or not. Got it?"

The one with 'Head of Security' on his jacket was as big as a bear and possessed a threatening growl to match. His body language suggested he was not averse to physical confrontations similar to the one in the Derry earlier. When they departed Wally called me over.

"You heard it clear enough; Fong Du's to stay on. Orders from that prick in the director's box."

He shook his head half in despair, half in disgust.

The PA ding-donged into life and a recorded voice announced, "Rong Un Industries: For all your future business solution needs."

The entire ground asked itself, "What the fucking hell was that?"

"Mid-game advertising announcements," sighed Wally. "It gets worse by the minute. Auld Jock would never have allowed any of this shite to happen."

Half time came and went. Despite Wally's best efforts to breathe some life into the team, they fared no better in the second half than they had in the dull-as-dishwater first. Although we had the majority of possession there was no cutting edge to carve through the resolute Cowden defence. When the bold Fife outfit broke up field and scored with their first and only chance of the game, no one was particularly surprised. The small band of supporters who'd paid good money to watch us at this unholy hour weren't shy in letting us know exactly how they felt about a third defeat in a row.

Of all the weird and surreal things I'd seen during my time at Dens none were as confounding as that which I laid my tired eyes on later that day. Having got to the tipi somewhere around 6am, I slept through until afternoon. Upon rising I'd immediately submitted to the pangs of hunger and headed toward the Hulltoon. Frews did hot pies as well as Special; it was exactly the type of breakfast of champions I was after.

Keen to keep the slaggings about Jeanie and football banter with the public to a minimum I took my food and drink through to the lounge. The big screen TV wasn't showing the football that everyone's eyes were glued to through in the bar, but I was prepared to suffer a soap opera for some escape.

My first forkful of pie didn't make it as far as my mouth. It was poised an inch or so from my face when I recognised a face on TV.

Charmaine.

In *River City*.

The piece of pie dropped off my fork back on to the plate.

She looked a lot different to the girl I knew, but it was undoubtedly her. While her long blonde hair was shorn into a shorter brunette style, her skin was bereft of the fake tan she usually doused herself in and she wore far less make up, there was no question it was her. Those bright blue eyes, the high cheek bones and the gorgeous face – Charmaine all over.

I sat staring at the screen with my mouth hanging open, stunned and shocked to the core. When the credits finally rolled I learned that 'Charmaine' was an actress called Anastacia Farmer. Had I managed to get that first bite of pie in my mouth I'd have asked the bar staff whether it had been laced with some form of hallucinogenic drug.

I watched a double episode of *EastEnders* and *Songs of Praise* before feeling steady enough on my feet to go home.

* * *

I doubt many footballers opt not to get back on the team bus so they can stay in town after a game at Dumbarton. I'd waved the lads off after a 1-1 draw with the Sons of the Rock claiming I wanted to visit an aunt who lived in the area. The real reason I chose to hang around on the Clyde Riviera was the town's television studio.

It had been a month since I'd seen Charmaine on River City. I'd spent a fair portion of that time finding out whatever I could about Anastacia Farmer. She had attended Dundee High School, the private school in the centre of town whose current pupils I'd seen in various expensive eateries on my excursions south of the Hulltoon. Her acting credits prior to landing a plum role as Shellsuit Bob's heroin-addicted half-sister amounted to minor parts in little-known Scottish dramas. My newfound knowledge of the girl still didn't satisfy the aching curiosity and hurt that was embedded in my gut.

A passing comment in the dressing room triggered what I thought might be a solution. After a run of games that had seen us pick up two points from a possible nine and our lead reduced to a mere five points, we were looking forward to visiting Dumbarton as it was seen as one of the easier fixtures in the league. Someone suggested going to The Tall Ship for a pint as the Scottish soap that featured both the fictional pub and the girl I knew as Charmaine was filmed in the town. Kicking myself for not thinking of it sooner, I decided to use the trip west as an excuse to visit to the set.

By 7:30pm I was having my doubts as to whether it was a good idea after all. A security guard at the site had confirmed filming was taking place but there were no signs of anyone leaving.

Just as I was starting to make plans to catch a bus to Glasgow so I could transfer to Dundee, people started to trickle out of the set. I recognised a couple of faces from that afternoon in Frews. Five minutes later, Anastacia Farmer made her way on to the street.

She was dressed much more modestly than I'd seen previously, in jeans, trainers and a light jacket. Preoccupied with her phone she didn't spot me until she was on the verge of bumping into me.

"Hello Charmaine."

She nearly jumped out her skin. When the initial shock passed she hung her head low, looking to the ground as if willing it to open up and swallow her. When she raised it her eyes were filled with tears.

"Lloyd. Darling. I am so, so sorry."

Agreeing that we needed to talk we went to a nearby pub, a lively little place with old men lining the bar like sentinels and middle-aged couples preparing for whatever a night on the town entailed round these parts. We found a table in the corner and, with a pint and a gin and tonic in front of us, the truth came out.

"Bob McCracken got in touch and said he had an acting job for me. I had no idea who he was and assumed he was an agent or something."

Her voice was soft, her accent still bearing a tinge of Dundonian through the practised elocution of her RADA training.

"I met him at the Old Course Hotel one afternoon. When he explained what he wanted me to do I nearly threw my glass of Chateau Neuf du Pape over that cheap suit of his. When he showed me the cheque he was going to give me I..."

Her beautiful blue eyes began swimming in tears again.

"I couldn't say no. Acting is a vocation, though not a well-paid one for the most part. Everybody has a price, darling."

She wiped her eyes, took a stiff swig of gin, checked out her own reflection in the nearest mirror and flicked her hair into shape again. I didn't feel sorry for her. Nor did I feel angry at her. My mind was filled with Bob McCracken.

"So he paid you to go out with me?"

"To go out with you and to find out what was going on with your team. Especially with your manager. He had a real bee in his bonnet about the guy and wanted rid of him as quickly as possible. Something to do with reputation management ahead of a necessary strategic branding correction."

Unbelievable. I was stunned at the lengths McCracken had gone to.

"McCracken explained the character he wanted me to play. He was very specific about it. What to wear, how to act, what to... you know... do. He said Charmaine was your type."

She bit her lip, the shame forcing her to break eye contact. It gave me a second to ponder how exactly McCracken knew what my type was.

"I told myself it was just like being an undercover spy, like a Bond girl or something. At first it was exciting, pretending to be an awful chav, saying things I would never say, doing things I would never do. Oh, darling I felt so alive! It was the role of a lifetime and perfect practice for my part in this show. But it got harder as time went by because... because I really grew to like you, Lloyd. You're such a sweetheart. I'm so sorry I did this to you. And to your manager and friend with the weed."

Poor Davo. The humble stoner didn't deserve to get caught up in all of this.

"What about Harry and Doug? Did you shaft them as well?

Her face contorted at the prospect of yet more confessions. "I might have got some pals from college to distract the barbers. McCracken set up the rest. As for your goalie, well he's just senile as fuck these days." She paused and looked at me for the first time in minutes. "I know it's too late to change anything, Lloyd, but I regret what I did. I'm sorry, darling."

By this time I was just staring vacantly into space. As far as head-fucks went, this was off the scale. Sensing I'd heard enough she drank up, wished me well for the future and took liberties by giving me an unwanted kiss on the cheek before departing.

The trip back to Dundee was a long and lonely one. Glasgow city centre was in full swing as I made my way from the bus station to Queen Street via a carry-out shop. Several drinks were absolutely necessary.

My mind was like a bee hive of incoherent thoughts that all led to Bob McCracken's vicious smiling face filling my inner vision. I fucking despised the man.

I needed to speak to Jocky. He was the one man whom I could talk to about this. I missed my gaffer. I missed my friend.

When I got back to the tipi I found a four-pack of Special waiting for me on the bed along with a note asking whether I fancied a game of golf the following morning. I was absolutely elated.

* * *

The sun was shining brightly on the home of golf. St Andrews was only 15 miles from Dundee on the other side of the Tay but it might as well have been on another planet to the Hulltoon I had grown to love. Yeah, it might boast one of the world's best universities and its most famous golf course but I bet you couldn't get a decent pint of Special anywhere and the wit appeared to be native to America and the Home Counties. As I awaited the gaffer's arrival, tourists, well-to-do students and golfers from all over the globe mingled and created what was a fairly cosmopolitan vibe considering it was Fife.

The roar of jet engines from nearby RAF Leuchars meant I didn't hear the gaffer approaching, but I got visual ID as he passed directly over the base's airspace. As he descended over St Andrews' west sands, a EuroFighter jet scrambled from the runway and veered sharply in his direction.

"Oh fuck," I muttered, suddenly afraid the gaffer might find himself engaged in a dogfight with a fighter jet. Knowing his fearless nature, I doubted he'd shy away from a fight that would be a bigger mismatch than his arm wrestling contests with the Frews' ladies' darts team. Thankfully he was already close enough to his destination to avoid such a confrontation and, as he landed in the car park, the jet passed by overhead and steered away from the town again.

"Ow! You fuckin' tailgating me ya Top Gun cunt? 'Mon then!"

He started to take off again and was a few feet off the ground when he saw me running toward him shouting, "Gaffer! No!" He offered the "Top Gun cunt" a middle finger and came back down to earth.

"Hiya Lloyd! Hiya pal! Did ye see fuckin' Ice Man there? Awa' back tae yer homoerotic shenanigans wi' Tam Cruise and Goose ya cunt! He'll be gettin' telt on the way hame, like."

He slipped out the jetpack, stood it up in a disabled parking space and strode toward me with a massive smile on his face and his arms open. Considering what had happened I'd been a little nervous about meeting him, but there were no traces of animosity. We embraced in a tight hug.

"Good tae see ye, pal."

"Good to see you too, gaffer. How you getting on? Have you managed to win at arm wrestling yet?"

He blew air through pursed lips and exclaimed, "Whit!

Lloyd, if it wisnae fur fowk turnin' up at inopportune moments eh'd be undefeated against they boys."

The snort of laughter snuck out before I could stop it.

"What you fuckin' laughing at ya cunt? They lads huv hud tae start playin' dominos 'cause eh've fucked up their darts arms! They're thinkin' aboot gettin' some toby on the go 'cause they cannae finger each other any mair! They're..." He surrendered to the laughter himself before continuing, "they're harder than Justin Fashanu that time eh went in the wrang showers at Airdrie."

He took me back for another quick back-slapping hug.

"I like your golf outfit, gaffer."

He was wearing appropriate attire for the occasion. Well, sort of. The gaffer had foregone his trackie bottoms in favour of a pair of tartan plus-fours which were matched with an oversized bonnet complete with giant pompom. Unfortunately, he'd accessorised with a pair of white Donnay socks and muddy old Umbro football boots. As always the man was topless, and he'd written "Pringle" just above his left nipple in black Biro.

"Cheers eh. Like the t-shirt? Jimmy Monaghan's daein' three fur 20 quid up the Fairmuir, hae a word next time yer up. He's got red and blue aines tae."

"Ehrrm, I will do. Cheers for the heads up."

The gaffer told a passing American tourist that a saxophone-wielding President Clinton was busking outside a public toilet round the corner and offered to "look after" his bag while he checked it out. As a result we made our way to the first tee with a full set of clubs, which the gaffer told me I wouldn't be needing as my function was to be that of caddy.

"Pass the drehvur, Lloyd. Big Jocky'll show ye how tae get a golf ba' telt."

I passed the driver and he lined up his first swing.

"So, how are things pal? Eh tak' it Char-fuckin'-maine husnae been back in touch."

He smashed the ball off the tee, screamed, "IN THE FUCK-IN' HOLE!" and passed the club back to me. I brought him up to speed on Chamaine actually being an actress hired by Bob McCracken. He was as incredulous at the story as I had been, and it took a few minutes for him to compute it.

"It wisane your fault, pal. Well, beyond the fact ye should o' learned yer lesson aboot pulling in the Fairmuir efter ye tromboned Jeanie McKay."

The very thought of it still made me shudder.

"I still can't believe Jeanie sold her story to the papers."

He asked for a 7-iron as we reached the ball that lay dead centre on the fairway.

"Eh got Jeanie telt aboot that aine. It transpires that oor pal Boaby paid her tae dae it."

"What?!"

"Aye. He gave her a hefty wedge. Enough tae see her retire tae the Red Lion Caravan Park in Arbroath wi' a season ticket tae Pleasureland. The hing eh dinnae get is how the devious cunt found oot aboot you and her in the first place."

He swung his club screaming 'IN THE FUCKIN' HOLE!' and dropped his ball to within about five feet of the pin. He was a better golfer than he was a Hungry Hungry Hippos player.

"Auld Boaby McCracken. The cunt wiz fuckin' jiggin' when he pulled me intae his office that Monday mornin'. Eh wiz just aboot as pissed aff that he got one-up on iz as eh wiz aboot haein' tae leave. Devious bastard, eh cannae fuckin' stand the cunt. Worried aboot what's gonnae happen at Dens now that eh'm no' there tae. Fuckin' gemmes at twa in the moarnin'? He's turnin' futba intae a farce."

I remembered the banner that had been unfurled that night.

"Were you at the Cowdenbeath game, gaffer? There was a bit of a set-to in the Derry. We thought you might have been in there."

He turned to me with a smile.

"Did ye like the flag? 'Boaby's a toby!' It's funny 'cause it rhymes, ken? Eh'm a wee bit like thon Wullie Shakespeare, or Rabbie 'Third Degree' Burns."

"The flag was brilliant, gaffer. I can't say the same about the stewards' reaction though."

He grimaced and requested his putter as we approached the green.

"The stewards are McCracken's doing tae, Lloyd. They're nothin' but thugs brought in tae sanitise and suck the life oot the gemme. They've been at it wi' away fans fur a good while now, being dicks tae fowk wha are just haein' a good day oot travellin' the country and gettin' on the tenner ectos tae support their team. It's a fuckin' bad sign that the hame fans are gettin' it tight tae now. There's gonna be a riot at that bottom corner o' the Derry if it ever kicks aff wi' a' they young lads wha look like they're in The View. That lot are as bold as brass, they'll no' back doon fae a fight."

He sunk his putt. I marked his card with a birdie three. As we left the green I turned to look back and saw a party making their way up the fairway. They were still some distance off, but somehow they seemed familiar. I put a hand over my brow and strained my eyes.

"Gaffer, that group playing behind us…do they seem familiar to you? I can't quite make them out."

There was no response.

"Gaffer?"

When I turned round again he was nowhere to be seen. A little louder I called out again.

"Eh'm just in the bunker, pal. Gies a minute."

Curious as to what he was doing in there I walked over to the steep sand hazard that lay at the back-left of the first green and peered in. I should have stayed by the bag and waited.

"Hiya pal! Eh cannae think o' a mair appropriate place tae say eh'm daein' a "Tom Kite", can you? Boy's a golfer!"

He squatted with his trousers round his ankles, as a shit emerged from his arse. It sent me reeling back reviled.

"Gaffer, for fuck sake!"

I had to fight back the vomit.

"You got the dreh boak there, pal? Yassssss! Here, go and check if thon septic tank's got any bog roll in his bag. If he disnae, any chance eh can borrow aine o' yer socks?"

I dashed off toward the bag as quickly as possible and found a packet of tissues in the side pocket that saved my sock from unimaginable horror. With no desire to return to the crime scene, I hurled the pack into the bunker, got a "Cheers pal!" and left him to it.

As I waited for him to emerge my attentions returned to the party playing behind us. They were closer now. I didn't have to strain my eyes too hard before a gasp of recognition shot down into my lungs. I scurried over to the bunker and found Jocky burying his shite in the sand.

"Gaffer! Bob McCracken's playing behind us!"

His eyes widened and he stood staring at me for a second before jumping into action. He clambered up the inside wall of the bunker until his head poked over the edge. He looked like a soldier about to charge over the top of a trench.

"Boaby, Boaby, Boaby, fuckin' toby, it's a rich man's world," he sang in a familiar melody. "Are ye an Abba fan, Lloyd?"

"What? Not really, no."

He looked philosophical for a moment.

"Me neither. Ayewiz find m'self up dancin' when that Fifer tribute band Dancing Neebs play the clubbie though."

He stroked his moustache and looked thoughtfully to the sky before snapping back into action and sliding back down the bunker.

"Lloyd! Hide the clubs and get in the bunker!"

"What, next to the load you've just dropped out your arse? That'll be right!"

He started digging round the spot where he'd done his business.

"The shite's coming back oot! Get in ya cunt!"

Making sure there was plenty sand between his hand and the log he'd squeezed out moments earlier he scooped it out, clambered out the bunker and ran onto the green where he dropped the shite in the hole.

"What the fuck are you doing?"

He signalled for me to join him as he ran back toward the bunker.

"A wee surprise fur Boaby when he picks his ba' oot!"

The pair of us jumped in the bunker and lay flat on our backs. The gaffer started squirming around and burying himself in the sand. Very cautiously I climbed up to peek over the edge and watch the approaching party. McCracken and a small party of what looked like Korean associates were hitting shots toward the green. The first ball was McCracken's, and it landed a couple of feet from the hole. As I watched the other players take less accurate shots toward the pin I asked, "What if McCracken doesn't hole his ball first?"

"Fur a' his cuntishness, Boaby's a teckle golfer. Meh money's on him sinking it first. If no', well, aine o' his pals is still gettin' a handful o' meh shite and a degree o' teckle is achieved."

With all players now making their way to the green I slid back down into position. The gaffer had buried all but his head and arms and built himself a not inconsiderable pair of sand-tits.

"Here Lloyd, go and touch meh tits."

I slapped a hand over my mouth to stop the laughter giving our position away.

"Get to fuck, touch your own tits!"

He did so, and started writhing around caressing himself and quietly moaning, "Mind that goal ye scored against United, pal? Tell ye what, eh ken how auld Jeanie McKay felt when ye gave her a slice o' Big Lloyd, like. Ooft!"

The pair of us giggled like school kids, but the sound of approaching voices quickly shut us up. McCracken was holding court. The man loved the sound of his own voice.

"It's an ideal location in so many ways; the crown jewel of the north east. The majority of the population here are cut above the riff-raff on the other side of the Tay. We'll see a better class of spectator in attendance, both from the local area and abroad... Good putt, sir, hard luck... The student and tourist population is transient, but the Scottish diaspora are essential to my long-term plan to capture the international market and, of course, we already have a toehold in your fine country. By deploying the marketing strategy I have been working on we'll have them coming into the Rong Un Industries Stadium in their droves."

The Rong Un Industries Stadium? That was the company who were advertised mid-game at Dens recently. I whispered as much to the gaffer, who said he already knew as he'd jetpacked his way to the roof of the Main Stand to watch the remainder of the Cowdenbeath game after being kicked out the Derry.

"Excuse me, gentlemen, I'll just sink this putt and we'll carry on talking business."

Jocky grabbed my arm and looked ready to explode. Heavily accented voices offered congratulations on a good putt. McCracken thanked them.

"What the... WHAT IN THE NAME OF SIR FREDDIE GOODWIN! OH FOR THE LOVE OF GOD. WHAT KIND OF MONSTER WOULD DO THIS?"

A series of retching sounds followed as a silently hysterical Jocky mouthed, "That's meh shite! Yasssssssss!" and groped his sand tits. I had to bite down hard on my forearm so as not to let the laughter erupt.

"Gentlemen, let me assure you this is level of depravity is highly unusual in St Andrews, and the greenkeeper will find himself in hot water the moment I find him. This is beyond vile!"

There was much chattering in a foreign tongue.

"This is the kind of behaviour one might expect on a Dundonian municipal course! Gentlemen, please be assured that when we move Dundee Football Club to this beautiful town and rename them St Andrews-Seoul Rong Un Dragons I will see to it that reprehensible behaviour such as this is eradicated. You have my word on that. Of course, we will face a certain degree of opposition from the knuckle-draggers but overcoming it will be much easier for a first division club whose only alternative is liquidation rather than a newly promoted one with money in the bank."

The gaffer and I sat staring at each other in shock and abject horror long after the voices from the green moved out of earshot.

"Did ye hear that, Lloyd?"

I nodded, but could offer no words as we waited for our opportunity to escape our bunker. It was only when a golfer from the party behind McCracken's picked his ball out the hole and went mental that we silently made our way off the course.

* * *

The thread title on the unofficial web forum Dundee Mad screamed out: "McCRACKEN WANTS TO DO A WIMBLE-DON TO THE DEE!!1!11!" The opening post, by new user "Black_as_Fuck_Ken?" read: "It's got fuck all to dae wi' tennis ya daft internet cunt, eh mean a Wimbledon FC moving tae Milton Keynes joab! As Boabby Cox is meh witness eh wiz on St Andrews golf course earlier and heard Boab McCracken speakin' tae a bunch of Korean business cunts aboot MOVING DUNDEE TAE ST ANDREWS! CALLING US ST ANDREWS-SEOUL RONG UN DRAGONS! PLAYING IN THE RONG UN INDUSTRIES STADIUM!1!! MCCRACKEN WANTS TAE KILL THE DEES – SPREAD THE WORD!! CUNT STEALS TIPPEX TAE! HE MUST BE STOPPED. OOR FUTBA LIVES DEPEND ON IT!!!1!"

We were sat in gaffer's living room. After a brief skirmish with a EuroFighter over Tentsmuir Forest we'd spent the jetpack journey home discussing McCracken's plan and how it could be foiled.

"We need tae spread the word, Lloyd, and fast," he'd shouted over his engine as he gunned it over the Tay. "If only there wiz some kind o' communication network that near enough a'body huz access tae and any cunt can say whatever they like and it'll spread like wildfire. Mibbe it could hae hunners o' porn on it tae."

I wasn't sure if he was kidding or not, but ventured, "the internet?" just in case.

"The internet! Brilliant, Lloyd! Up here fur thinkin', doon there fur dancin'. Eh'll fire up the Etch-a-Sketch when we get hame."

I thought he'd been kidding about the Etch-a-Sketch too, but as soon as we got in the door he'd grabbed one out the cupboard and given it a good shake. By some miracle of technology, the Google homepage appeared. He used the dials to draw in the search term "Dundee fans needin' telt aboot something aye", given it another shake and lo and behold he was on Dundee Mad.

"Eh've tried puttin' it on the official site tae, but nae danger the moderators will let it go up. McCracken's doing, he's got a tight grip on the reins there. Eh put it on that Peh and Bovril site tae though. Some wee cunt fae Greenock's sayin' eh'm on the "verge of tears." Gies a minute and eh'll tell him he's on the verge o' being hunted down, killed and used tae mak' packets o' Cunt Munch at that sweetie factory the Morton chairman owns."

As we sat sipping Special and he read out strange excerpts from a blog former Dundee and Hibs striker Leigh Griffiths had supposedly written, the word began to spread. In among the requests for evidence, general abuse and accusations of nazi-ism were other posts confirming sightings of McCracken in the company of foreign business associates and people pointing out the links between Fong Du, the mid-game announcements and these latest rumours.

The gaffer didn't stop at the Internet either; as the flames were fanned online he contacted the football writers at DC Thomson.

"Tam ya miserable fuck, it's Jocky... eh no' bad pal... eh couldnae gie a fuck aboot the rash on yer groin ya dippit cunt, shut yer pus and listen..."

Discredited by the allegations still hanging over him, the gaffer was unable to put his name to the story and insisted on being refered to only as an undisclosed source. He made similar calls to the daily nationals before ringing up the guy at the Sunday Post who writes *The Broons*, insisting it would be a "maist teckle" storyline for the next edition.

After a few cans my bladder reached capacity and I made a trip up the stairs to the toilet.

"Eh've got somethin' tae show ye when ye get back, Lloyd."

His grin was mischievous, and made me a tad apprehensive.

I was considering the endless possibilities of what lay in store for me when I entered the bathroom. I was ready for Dong Chu this time, but not the sight of Wee Jocky standing up on his hind legs on the toilet seat taking a piss.

"Mr Lloyd George, so teckle to see you again," said the ever-courteous Dong Chu.

"Meow," said the cat. He used his little head to indicate the flow of urine had stopped since I entered. Who'd have thought cats got stage fright too? I looked away and the tinkle of a stream of urine hitting the target below resumed.

Wee Jocky finished his business, closed the lid as he got down from its perch and made his way out the door. As he passed by me, he rubbed himself against my leg and purred. The simple things can make you so happy sometimes.

The cat was waiting for me when I left the bathroom.

"Hiya Wee Jocky, hiya pal."

He turned and started slinking his was down the stairs, pausing a few steps down to turn and meow again as if instructing me to follow. Cautiously, I did so. He paused again at the living room door, waited for me to reach the bottom of the stairs then moved inside.

When I reached the open door he was sitting by the bookcase, which had opened like a bascule bridge. Wee Jocky wandered through the gap into whatever lay beyond.

What on earth was going on? I called out for the gaffer and heard a faint meow in response. Several different voices could be heard from the darkness. Under the watchful eyes of the figures in the Jocky-creating-Jocky painting opposite I slowly approached the bookcase. Feeling my heart thump and my limbs tremble, I took a long, slow breath before taking tentative steps inside.

* * *

"Like a' the maist teckle endeavours in scientific experimentation and discovery, Lloyd, the initial idea came durin' a post-dominos swally up the Fairmuir."

Jocky had a secret laboratory in his house. It was an incredible sight. After walking down half-a-dozen stone steps I found myself in a huge room not dissimilar to Bruce Wayne's basement. The place was crammed with computer equipment, giant screens displaying mathematical data, bizarre-looking medical equipment and bubbling beakers of brightly coloured liquid.

A massage table that I suspected was once property of Dundee Football Club lay in the dead centre of the room with a white sheet draped over something. Jocky stood by the table alongside a small group of men and women in white lab coats. He shook hands with each of them before they departed the lab leaving only me, Big Jocky and Wee Jocky behind. The bookcase/door slammed shut behind them. I apprehensively made my way to the centre of the room and the gaffer. My only question had been, "What in the name of fuck is going on here?"

"It wiz years back, and a few o' the lads and m'self were debating which characteristics the greatest futba player o' a' time would hae. Stuff like Cruyff's shuffle, Maradona's balance and Pele's ability tae score goals. And Viagra. No' that eh need any o' that shite tae get a root on. Ye ken the score."

We stood over the table while Wee Jocky prowled round looking moody.

"Efter eh left the clubbie that night eh started thinkin' tae m'self, what would the greatest Scottish player hae in terms o' combined attributes? If eh could sign the ultimate Scottish player, what would he be like?"

I looked down at the bulk under the sheet and started feeling rather scared of what was underneath it.

"Gaffer, where are you going with this? This is getting really fucking weird, even by your high standards."

Exasperated, he replied, "The ultimate player wouldnae hae your fuckin' patience, cunto, that's fur sure. Or yer taste in wummin for that matter. Let iz finish the story, eh?"

I apologised and let him continue speaking.

"The thought stayed in meh heid fur a while until one night eh wiz at Hamish McAlpine's book club, and the book wi' hud tae read fur the following meeting wiz Mary Shelley's Frankenstein.

Dame bided in Stoabie! Eh wiz like that readin' it, 'creating yer aine monster fae scratch! That's a fuckin' teckle idea. Eh should dae that and get the ultimate Scottish futba player on the go.'"

I looked down at the table again, and took a step back from it. Jocky started pacing round the table.

"Now, eh initially tried makin' it oot o' toilet roll tubes and paper mache like some whacky Blue Peter project, but it didnae really cut the mustard. Eh needed money tae buy science and a' that shite. As coincidence might have it, eh'd recently hud a big win at the bookies. Eh'd gone in pished and thought, ken what? Let's get aine o' they crazy bets on. So eh stuck a quid on a World Trade Centre collapsing/Partick Thistle winning the first division double at a odds o' a hunner million tae one. Couldnae believe it when it actually came up."

He paused for a moment and looked up to the ceiling with his head shaking in disbelief.

"The Harry Wraggs winning promotion to the SPL; fuckin' crazy stuff. Anyway, 12 years later here we are."

He wheeled a strange contraption across the room. Two large silver orbs hung loose from the stanchion and base that held them. Once in place behind the top end of the table, Jocky lowered the orbs so that they were positioned level with, and about a foot away from, either side of the top of the bulge beneath the sheet.

"Gaffer... what the actual fuck is happening here? You can't possibly have..."

"The winnings aff that line paid fur a fuckload o' science, Lloyd. A fair bit o' corned beef tae. Eh've hud the tap scientists on the planet workin' doon here and munching a' the auld Jon Bons they could eat fur mair than a decade now. Cunt's probably could've cured cancer beh now."

He walked back to the wall facing the foot of the table and threw me a pair of safety goggles. He placed a tiny pair over Wee Jocky's eyes and put on a pair himself. I looked down at the table and quickly ran over to stand by them as he took hold of a huge lever on the wall.

"Something teckle this way comes, pals. Wee Jocky, Lloyd: Behold! The ultimate Scottish futba player."

He pulled the lever. Immediately a thrumming sound began to build and grow louder, a deep vibration that I could feel run all the way up my body from my feet. Just as it felt like something was destined to explode, a whooshing sound burst forth and thin strands of lightning fired out each of the orbs and connected with what I could now only assume was a head beneath the sheets. Sparks flew everywhere, equipment burst into flames and glass smashed right across the lab. As I cowered against the wall the gaffer started shouting, "YASSSSS!" and Wee Jocky meowed in unison. The white sheet flew off the table and the body below shuddered. Its arms stretched out and its fingers began to wiggle.

"HE'S ALEHVE! HE'S ALEHVE!"

The gaffer looked demented to the point I expected lightning to bolt out from his eyes.

With one final eruption that blew every piece of equipment in the room to smithereens, the electricity stopped flowing and the thrum faded until the room fell quiet. The only sound to be heard was our starving lungs desperately sucking down oxygen. Nobody moved. All eyes were on the table.

When Jocky's monster sat bolt upright and bellowed, "HIYA JOCKY! HIYA PAL!" my scream must have curdled blood as far away as St Andrews.

"Oh ya cunt, it worked! Fucking yassss!"

The gaffer was beyond ecstatic. He started riding an imaginary horse round the debris-strewn room, hopping gracelessly from foot to foot and slapping his invisible steed's hindquarters.

"This must be how God feels!" he exclaimed before running out of breath and slowing down. "It's no' any different tae bein' on three tenner ectos, really."

Jocky's monster remained sitting up on the table. When I gained the nerve to look at it properly I couldn't help but notice it was already dressed in a full Dundee kit and struck a startling resemblance to someone I had gotten to know over the past few months.

"Gaffer, why does it look like Fong Du?"

He stroked his creation's cheek lovingly before giving it a little kiss.

"That's an easy aine, cunto – it's Fong Du's face."

"What do you mean it's Fong Du's face? How can it possibly be Fong Du's face?"

"Ever seen that Nicholas Cage and John Travolta film? Uncle Buck or whatever it's called. Eh took his pus aff and put it on this fella."

I looked on aghast with my hands on my head. It was mind-bogglingly horrifying.

"Dinnae look a' freaked oot, pal, eh gave Fong the Mong a new face, it's nae bather. Made an improvement on the cunt, even."

"Whose face did you give to Fong Du?"

"This deid junkie eh found in a lift up the Hulltoon. He wisnae needin' it any mair, ken?"

Fucking hell.

"But why Fong Du?"

He put a finger in the monster's nose, pulled it back out thought about putting it in his mouth for a taste then decided just to wipe it on the table.

"Eh've hud this thing registered as a Dundee player a' season. Kent he'd probably be ready in time tae get a gemme. The face wiz aine o' the last bits tae go on. Efter a'hin that happened eh though the gemme wiz up the poley. Then eh realised it wiz just a case o' makin' it look like some cunt auld Boaby a'ready kent."

At least there was some form of method in this particular strand of his complete and utter madness.

I looked the monster up and down. He was vaguely athletic looking, and certainly big and strong.

"But how did you... how did you build him? What did you use? He looks human. Kinda."

The more I looked at it the more I became impressed at the scale of the gaffer's achievement, morally questionable as it was.

"Graverobbin' played a big part in the proceedings."

I felt my legs start to give way and took a grip of the table's edge.

"Eh needed a basic body tae work with so eh went and took aine fae Balgay cemetery. Went up wi' a few lads fae the Fairmuir. Kerry oot, a few spades. Turned oot tae be a no' bad night, actually."

I felt my mouth fill with saliva and my thighs tremble. I couldn't believe what I was hearing. I felt ready to puke.

"Eh made a few alterations o' meh aine though. See that left foot? Davie Cooper's. The right aine? Tommy Burns'. Eh wisnae really wantin' Tommy's but if there's one thing eh've learned aboot dealin' wi' the Auld Firm it's that if ye rob aine o' their legend's grave then ye hae dae the same fur the other side tae so's tae keep the peace."

Three graverobbings. I put a hand over my mouth and fought hard to keep the contents of my stomach down there.

"Other attributes were developed via DNA samples taken aff hair eh pinched aff cunts' heids when eh took them up the Fairmuir and got them pished. They include Duncan Ferguson's ability tae heider ba's and uppity defenders, Ally McCoist's poaching, Stevie Nicol's engine, Alex McLeish's complexion, Chic Charnley's bevvyin' ability, Stevie Fulton's belly, Pat Nevin's taste in music, Henry Smith's hairdo and last, but certainly not least, meh fuckin' mouser."

I'd been so busy trying to process the "pus aff" situation I hadn't even noticed the big, bristling, black moustache on "Fong Du's" upper lip.

"That's the ultimate Scottish footballer?"

This was insanity taken to a new level.

"Fuckin' right. This boy right here's gonna lead the Dees back tae the SPL and beyond. Good eh?"

I dropped to sit on the floor with my head in my hands. This was a fully-formed nightmare of unprecedented proportions.

"Here Lloyd, ken what his name is? Hae a guess."

I gave it some consideration and concluded there was only

one answer. I stood up to find him grinning like a kid on Christmas morning, an arm draped round his creation's shoulder as if they were old buddies.

"Jocky?"

He burst into a "Yasssss!" and reached over to congratulate me with a pat on the bicep.

"Ye ken the score, pal. Jocky's a fuckin' teckle name!"

Monster Jocky suddenly shouted, "KEN AYE!" and sent his creator into raptures. The cat jumped up on the table and meowed wildly at me. Light-headedness kicked in with a vengeance, spun my world around and sent me slumping into darkness.

* * *

The city was awash with rumours regarding Bob McCracken's plans to move Dundee to St Andrews. Both the local and national press ran with the story the gaffer had leaked, and the corner of the cyberspace where such matters were of concern took what I knew to be fact and added not only arms and legs to the story, but a tail, a false nose and a substantial afro wig. No matter – the original intention of spreading the word, getting people asking questions and most importantly having the Dundee support mobilised into opposing the move, had been achieved.

McCracken refused to make any meaningful comment on the matter beyond making it clear that all avenues would be explored in the quest for fresh investment. Like a skilled politician, he was a master of obfuscation and his lengthy responses failed to answer simple yes-or-no questions. While the coverage was unlikely to prevent him attempting to carry out his devious plan he must certainly have been given some food for thought by its public revelation and subsequent derision.

Having shared his own quite literally monstrous agenda, Jocky informed me he had a plan to return to the fold at Dens, with Monster Jocky (or "Fong Du" as he would be called in an attempt to somehow fool McCracken) in tow. I reminded him there were only two games left to play and pressed him for further details on his plan but he fished a pair of headphones from his trackie pockets, placed them in my ears and played the X Files theme to me from his phone.

In the build up to the vital penultimate game of the season, the real Fong Du was nowhere to be seen. Word eventually reached us that he had returned to his homeland to deal with an urgent family matter. It was an explanation far easier to digest than "he no longer has a face."

Though I sympathised with the fact he'd be wandering around South Korea with a Hulltoon junkie's face, Fong Du wouldn't be missed on the park. Spurred on by Jocky and a desire to get it so far up Bob McCracken it would come out his mouth, I initiated rescue operations for our erstwhile team mates.

Getting Big Doug out the old folks' home had been easier than expected. I went in saying I was his great-grandson and, in spite of him protesting that he'd never seen me in his life, I wheeled him out for a walk and never took him back. Soapy had done a great job filling in for oldest goalie but it was good to have our number one choice back between the sticks. Though clearly now in an advanced stage of dementia, Doug's reflexes continued to defy conventional medical wisdom whenever an air-filled leather sphere was punted at him.

Davo Milne had been banned for the rest of the season for drug misuse, but his presence in the dressing room would be key to lifting our team spirit. He was sitting at home in a cloud of pungent smoke wearing a marijuana leaf t-shirt modified to read '*Free the ~~Weed~~ DAVO*' when we found him. He was happy to come back and join the title push any which way he could, so long as he got to finish his second packet of Jammie Dodgers first.

Liberating Harry had been an altogether more difficult task. He was in a caged pen in Camperdown Zoo, and it required me and a crack unit of youth team players to launch a midnight raid in order to free him. The man was hairier than a woolly mammoth when we found him. After breaking into the pen using plastic explosives provided by Eddie McGlone, it took five of us working a lawnmower each to get him down to a moderate growth that wouldn't hinder his progress as he bolted from captivity. Our captain was back.

Back at training, our new manager was proving to be every bit as hopeless as our initial impressions suggested. In spite of repeated insistence that he loved futba, Willie was as ill-equipped to prepare a team for a vital title-dependant clash as was to be expected of a man with the IQ of a three-year-old. When an inflatable bouncy castle appeared on the pitch at training on Wednesday we thought he'd devised a fun, team-bonding session of the type Jocky specialised in. This faint glimmer of hope was extinguished when we attempted to join Willie and he flew into a red-faced, scream-the-place-down tantrum, curled up in the foetal position and burst into tears until we agreed to leave his toys alone.

With Fong Du off the radar, no doubt to Bob McCracken's chagrin, I was back on the colourfully drawn team sheet for the game against promotion rivals Dunfermline at Dens. Wally had drilled it into us all week long: we had to get at least a point in order to go into the last game of the season with matters still in our own hands. His team talk was as heartfelt and passionate as any Jocky had delivered, and he did so in spite of Willie Dawes' repeated interjections.

"Forget the past few games, they mean fuck all."

"I NEED CHANGED."

"Play with yer hearts on yer sleeves and fight for every single ball."

"WILLIE'S DONE A JOBBY."

"Play like I, and every one of you, know you can."

"WILLIE'S EATING BUM CHOCOLATE."

"Get stuck right intae them!"

As Willie smeared the contents of his nappy over his face we got up to head out on to the pitch. Wally stopped us with one final pre-match word of encouragement.

"Oh and by the way, I was speaking to Jocky earlier."

These were words that stopped us dead in our tracks.

"He was saying he'd be up today and wanted you to know he'd be cheering you on."

The lift in mood was tangible. Several voices spoke one after another asking if the gaffer was well and whether he'd said anything else. Wily old fox that he is, Wally milked the moment to maximum effect.

"He's well, aye. Still full of fire for this club. Still a Dundee man to the core."

He looked around the room making sure he had our undivided attention, which he absolutely did.

"Go out there and do it for your gaffer. In his very own words, get out there and get Dunfermline fucking telt cuntos."

A determined roar laced with laughter went up and we practically sprinted out the door. Right there and then we all knew there was absolutely no way we were losing this one.

* * *

Which turned out to be true. It was a hard-fought battle against a team still vying for promotion, but we wanted it more. Even when the Pars opened the scoring on the hour-mark it did nothing but galvanise us. With five minutes left the midfield general we'd missed so much hit a stunning 30-yard free kick into the top corner that sent Dens mental.

A curious thing happened as we celebrated the goal. Harry had gone sliding head first across the turf in front of the Derry and been engulfed by every outfield player as we joined him in a piley-on. When an 11th body jumped on top of the heap we assumed it was Doug but he remained in his goalmouth, looking confused and muttering about prices these days. Deewok the bear had run across the pitch and dived in among us. He normally spent games whipping up excitement at the family section, but he's never got this involved before. His participation in the celebrations was well received by the players, fans and photographers behind the goal who now had the perfect lead shot for the newspapers and websites as a result.

Things became more curious still when we made a jubilant return to the dressing room and found Deewok sitting waiting for us.

He didn't respond to our jokey hellos and reminders that Camperdown Zoo was miles away, so it was left to Wally Gordon to deal with him.

"What the hell are you doing in here you big daftie? Away you go – this room's for players and management only."

Deewok just sat there looking at him, the fixed grin of his bear head suddenly a little unnerving.

"Look, son, your place is on the pitch entertaining bairns; you've no right to be in here. Move it, please."

Deewok picked up a can of Special from the bench next to him. Using both paws, he tipped it back and let its contents shower his face. Wally stared him down, then broke into a grin.

"Well, Jock. Enjoy the game?"

Deewok ditched the empty, lifted his head off, and said, "Wisane bad, Walzo. Hud it doon as 2-1 us on the coupon, like, but cannae complain."

With a tremendous cheer the players swamped our rather sweaty leader in a mass of hugs and kisses. When our overjoyed new mascot finally managed to get to his feet he started body-popping in the centre of the room. We egged him on, forming a circle round him and yelling, "GO! GO! GO! GO!" After pulling a few moves he went into rapper mode and laid down a verse.

"Straight oot o' Dundee! Crazy muthafucka named Jocky! See yer arm? No as big as meh cock, eh? A pair o' braces, a leather belt – pull yer breeks up or yer gettin' fuckin' telt! Straight oot o' Dundee."

The room dissolved into laughter as he started doing the robot and shouting, "Bit o' NWeh? fur ye there lads! Wha's in cherge here?"

"You are, gaffer!" we chorused.

"Fucking great to see ya, gaffer."

Harry's sentiment was shared by us all.

"Good tae see you lads tae, aye. And eh'll be seein' more a' ye tae, or at least Deewok will."

A murmur of excitement swept round the room.

"Eh'll be here next week fur training wearing this suit so Boaby McCracken disnae catch wind o' it. Me and Walzo here will hae ye winning this league nae fuckin' bather next Saturday. Eh Walzo?"

Wally wrapped an arm round him and looked as happy as anyone.

"Damn right. The Dees are going up!"

Another cheer went up. Ever the voice of reason, Wally's expression became altogether more serious as he remembered that a significant obstacle remained in our way.

"Jock, what about Wullie?"

Bang on cue the door burst open and Willie Dawes bounced in on a Space Hopper. He stopped, gasped and yelled, "JOCKY! WILLIE LIKES FUTBA!"

The gaffer burst out laughing.

"Hiya Wullie! Hiya pal! A'right wee man!"

Willie leaped off his latest mode of transportation and into the gaffer's arms.

"Eh see ye, Wullie. Jocky sees ye. Did auld Boaby gie you a joab? Fuckin' right he did!"

Willie had his legs wrapped round the gaffer's waist and looked joyfully at him.

"Willie likes futba."

The gaffer gave him a tender little kiss on the forehead and laughed, "Me tae, pal. Futba's fuckin' teckle!"

He pulled his little friend's head to his shoulder, looked over at us and winked, whispering, "He says that a' the time, likes. Boy's fucked in the heid. Funny as fuck, but a wee bit o' a shame tae. Fuckin' yassss!"

He paced the room burping Willie as if he'd never been away. It was the perfect morale boost ahead of the final game of the season.

* * *

On Monday morning we got down to the business of training for the league decider. Dundee sat two points clear of Partick Thstle, who'd mounted a strong run since we last met and were waiting in the wings should we fail to beat Livingston at home. The title was ours to lose.

The dressing room was in high spirits as we changed into our training kit and took turns pretending we'd stolen Willie's nose. The mood plunged when Wally Gordon entered; the colour had drained from his face and he looked shaky on his feet.

"Wally, are you alright?"

Harry was quick to get up and lend his big physical frame to the assistant manager, who looked incapable of standing on his own two feet much longer.

"You look like you've seen a ghost."

Wally let Harry guide him down to a seat on the bench and accepted a bottle of water.

"Not a ghost... Fong Du. He's out there on the pitch with Jocky."

My stomach knotted in an instant. He was going ahead with his plan. The bad dream was a reality. The rest of the lads were understandably confused about the state Wally was in over Fong Du's not-unexpected return from his homeland. After making sure Wally was okay we made our way out onto the pitch.

The gaffer, dressed in the Deewok outfit, was playing head tennis with "Fong Du". When he spotted the rest of the squad making their way out the tunnel he controlled the ball and let Monster Jocky know they had company before yelling over at us.

"Look wha's back, a'body! Fong Du in the hoose!"

The monster raised his right hand and moved it side-to-side in a glacial-paced wave. Good grief.

As the group of players drew closer they slowed down before coming to a complete stop.

"That's... that's not Fong Du..."

"What the fuck..."

"Who... what is it?"

When Monster Jocky barked, "HIYA LADS! HIYA PALS!" everyone started creeping back the way we came.

"Lads, it's just Fong Du! Look at his pus! Say hiya Fong Du, hiya pal!"

Monster Jocky misunderstood and parroted, "Hiya Fong Du! Hiya pal!"

"No' you ya big ride, them!"

At that point Monster Jocky started lurching forward toward us, and the cautious back-stepping gave way to a full-blown turn and run.

"GET BACK HERE YA CUNTS! WE'VE GOT A BOUNCE GEMME AGAINST THE HIRED MIDGETS IN 10 MINUTES! DUNDEE V AN OOMPA-LOOMPA XI!"

But it was to no avail. We ran back inside and hid in the dressing room.

Everyone spoke at once, 15 different versions of "What the fuck is going on??"

Davo was back on the bong, and between hits opined, "It's trippy as fuck is what it is, man. Freaky. I can't say I'm entirely against it."

Monster Jocky came through the door shoulder first. The entire first team squad, screaming like little girls, cowered together in the farthest corner of the room. The creature smiled, its shoulders shaking up and down and its eyes rolling back in its head. The gaffer entered and stood by its side as he tried to calm us.

"Lads, what's the problem wi' big Fong a' o' a sudden? Ye fuckin' racists."

"Gaffer, it clearly isn't Fong Du. The face looks like his, aye, but the rest of him's a big white guy. What in the name of fuck?"

Exasperated, the gaffer looked at the champions-elect shitting themselves in the corner and let out a slow exhalation of breath.

"Fuck sake. A'right, eh'll tell ye the score. Any cunt breathes a word o' it ootside these four walls and it's punch in the pus time on the hour, every hour until meh hands fa' aff."

And so the gob-smacking truth came out. It elicited the same initial reactions I'd experienced: horror, general disbelief and a few bouts of vomiting. Within 10 minutes the lads had passed through the Kubler-Ross scale and arrived at acceptance.

"Gaffer, you'll never get away with it! McCracken's going to know the minute he sees this thing."

"Ow! Some manners, Rafferty – his name's Jocky."

"Sorry. But McCracken's going to react just the same as we did."

Jocky was clearly still formulating his plan on the hoof.

"It'll be fine. The first time McCracken's gonnae see him is when he's on the pitch on Saturday and, by that time, it's too late. We'll win the league, and then eh'll deal wi' this moving tae St Andrews business."

I chimed in, "Mind if I ask how you intend on approaching that particular subject with him?"

He flexed his biceps and kissed them in turn.

"Eh've telt him tae meet iz fur a square-go."

There were a few laughs as well as cries of "yaasssss!"

"I really can't see him taking you up on the offer, gaffer."

A sly look came over his face as he raised an index finger.

"He'll be there, pal. Eh've telt him if he wins eh'll bullshit the polis and tell them that eh wiz match fixing. Eh'd end up in the jail nae bather. If eh win, he shelves the St Andrews plan and fucks off back tae Land o' Boaby or wherever he's fae. He's kens eh'm an honourable cunt; he kens eh'd keep meh end o' the bargain."

It sounded suspect.

"If he did agree to it and you did win, would you trust him to keep his end of the bargain?"

He put an arm round my shoulder, gave me a kiss on the cheek and whispered, "Lloyd, cunts wha square-go me end up in a place whaur they're likely tae hae their foot chopped aff and used tae build teckle Frankenstein futba players, if ye ken what eh mean."

He slapped me on the cheek playfully and walked away chuckling to himself.

Just then the door burst open and a little fellow dressed as an Oompa-Loompa came in.

"Here, are you cunts fuckin' playin' or what? We've got a boy needin' to get tae Forfar for a Willow convention at half two."

The gaffer clapped his hands to rouse the troops.

"Right, a'body oot on the pitch! Ye need tae gel wi' Jocky here beh Saturday, 'cause eh didnae rob a' they graves no' tae play the cunt fae the start!"

The Oompa-Loompa poked his finger in his ear to check if there was some kind of blockage in there before asking, "Did you just say you've been graverobbing?"

The gaffer ushered him out the door.

"Nane o' your business ya chocolate-making wee bastard. Tell iz, wha's the better gaffer – Gene Wilder or Johnny Depp? Eh wouldnae mind daein' a bit o' overtime wi' Depp, if ye ken what eh mean. Handsome man so he is."

Monster Jocky followed his creator out the door. We gave them a good head start before following suit.

* * *

I felt my heart pounding in my chest as we waited for the ref's signal to move out on to the pitch. The last day of the season had arrived. Win and we would be promoted to the Premiership as champions. Lose and the consequences didn't bear thinking about.

'Let the proud Rangers sing of the records they hold...'

I could barely hear Up wi' the Bonnets play as the capacity crowd created an atmosphere worthy of the occasion. Such was the demand that queues had snaked halfway down the Hulltoon when tickets were released earlier in the week.

'And Celtic acclaim all their heroes of old...'

The gaffer had spent the week preparing us in as sensible a fashion as I'd seen in my time at the club. There were no ludicrous training sessions, no shoplifting, games of manhunt or giant catapults hurling faeces at our rivals. It may have been due to his resignation and subsequent realisation of what he was missing or perhaps he'd planned on cooling his red-hot jets when it came to the crunch all along.

'We will follow and follow o'er land and o'er sea...'

It was the second time the song had been played that day. After finalising his instructions on how he wanted us to play, the gaffer switched on the dressing room TV. The screen showed a team photo he'd taken of us during the week. He asked us to keep our eyes on it as *Up wi' the Bonnets* had played through the speakers. They were words we not only knew off by heart, but also felt in our hearts. We didn't even notice that the gaffer had slipped out without saying another word.

'For the brave boys who wear the dark blue of Dundee...'

We took to the pitch as proud to wear the colours as any team in the club's history.

"Are you OK there, Jocky pal?"

3pm in the centre circle, and Dens was a maelstrom of noise that made me concerned for the strike partner I was about to kick-off with. He'd loosened off a fair bit over the course of the week, his lurching gait becoming smoother and his ability to communicate without scaring the piss out of you improving. He'd developed a close bond with Willie Dawes, who'd surprised us all by taking Monster Jocky to heart immediately. Our official manager spent most of his time on his back, amusing himself with the Henry Smith hair and whispering that he loved futba in the ears of the delighted-to-have-a-little-friend former dead man.

Perhaps most surprisingly of all, Monster Jocky was exactly what his creator intended him to be: a hell of a good football player. He really was the classic Scottish player. After a shaky start which saw the Forfar Willow convention lose its star guest because a large chunk of his skull had been bitten off, he'd quickly developed into the big, bustling, skilful and deadly striker the gaffer envisaged as the embodiment of all that was good about game in this country.

"JOCKY LIKES FUTBA!"

He'd also taken to shouting Willie's often-repeated phrase of choice in response to questions coming his way.

"Ok big stuff, I love futba too. Let's win the league, eh?"

He growled and went to give me a kiss, which I managed to dodge when the ref's whistle signalled the start of play. I tapped the ball to him and ran off as quickly as possible.

After a nervous opening period, we eventually settled down and started playing like we knew we could. The defence comfortably dealt with any Livi attacks, the midfield began winning every ball, and Jocky and I linked up well.

The dugout was a bizarre sight, with the trio of Wally Gordon in his usual tracksuit, the gaffer as Deewok, and Willie dressed in the rainbow-coloured spandex bottoms, tasselled leather jacket, Stetson and sunglasses of Macho Man Randy Savage. As Deewok prowled the technical area and berated the nearest linesman for no good reason, our interim manager sat on his tricycle shouting "OHHHHHHH YEEEEEEAH, DIG IT!" through the gaffer's megaphone. The three of them and Soapy were the only inhabitants of the dugout, as the only way my presence on the park could be justified to the CEO was for every outfield member of the playing squad to feign injury. We had to hope karma wouldn't catch up with us.

I wondered what Bob McCracken was making of it all. Although I couldn't make him out I knew he was in the director's box, no doubt as baffled by the "Fong Du" situation as everyone else in the ground and surely noticing the dramatic changes in Deewok's behaviour.

We were well into the second half before the deadlock was finally broken. Monster Jocky picked the ball up on the halfway line and decided it was time for his first goal for the club. He weaved past four players, sent another two sprawling when they tried to body-check him, and drilled the ball low past the 'keeper. Dens erupted.

"KEEP IT UP, LADS. ONE MAIR GOAL WILL KILL IT."

The gaffer had commandeered his megaphone. Again I looked to the director's box and wondered how McCracken would react.

I expected to see a posse of stewards heading toward the dugout but they were making no obvious moves and remained stationed at various points around the ground. With just minutes left in the season, it was as if he'd resigned himself to the inevitable and decided now was not the time for confrontation. That moment would come soon enough.

I desperately wanted a goal to seal the championship and end the season on a personal high. With the entire ground whistling and imploring the ref to blow his, Harry burst through midfield and knocked the ball through to Eddie. He beat an opponent and launched a high ball into the box and on to Monster Jocky's head. As his knockdown bounced in front of me I checked my stride and put the laces of my right boot through the ball. It was in the top left-hand corner of the net before the 'keeper even thought about stopping it.

I wheeled away with an outstretched hand pointing a finger into the heart of the Derry's wild celebrations. Just before my teammates buried me under their mass I took the Dundee badge in my hand and pulled it to my mouth to kiss it. You're never gonna believe us, we're gonna win the league.

No sooner had the game restarted than the full-time whistle went. Each and every Dundee players' arms reached up to the sky in celebration. Monster Jocky let off a growl that would have attracted a Wookie mate had there been any in the area. On the touchline the management trio held each other tight in an emotional embrace.

When I turned to hail the fans in the Derry I realised most of them were leaving it and charging toward us. A wave of ecstatic supporters washed over us, scooping us up in their arms and carrying us as they broke upon the pitch.

"Lloyd! Fucking yaasssssssssssss!"

Mikey and Hendo from the Hulltoon were in among the throng and I was hoisted up on to someone's shoulders. I took the hands they offered and screamed "Yasssss!" right back at them.

Each player found himself amid similar scenes. Well, apart from Monster Jocky, who the fans had got to within five feet of before fleeing in the opposite direction. Not that he was fussed; his new pal Willie was already on his back twirling his pointed finger in the air and shouting "DIG IT!" at no one in particular.

As the fans receded back into the stands I met the gaffer. He had removed the head from his costume and was looking up into the director's box where Bob McCracken was glaring right back down at him.

"Gaffer, you better get out of here."

He turned and wrapped both arms round me, giving me a hug that near enough squeezed the life out me.

"Congratulations, pal. Champions! That's what eh'm talkin' aboot!"

As I returned the hug and patted him on the back I saw half-a-dozen stewards coming out the tunnel and making their way on our direction.

"Gaffer, you need to get out of here. They're coming for you."

He broke off the hug and stared back up at McCracken.

"Fair doos, pal. Enjoy getting the trophy, it's a moment yer gonnae remember fur a long time tae come."

The tears in his eyes suggested he would have liked to have shared the moment with us.

"I will do. When's the square-go? Do you need someone to watch your back?"

He fought a little harder to keep the tears from spilling down his cheeks.

"It's right here, pal. Midnight on the centre circle."

He embraced me once again before heading off in the direction of the Bobby Cox Stand.

"Gaffer!" I shouted after him. "I'm not much of a fighter by the way."

He grinned and shouted back, "Dinnae worry aboot it, ye'll be fine."

He jogged off into the departing crowd and made his escape.

A showdown on the centre circle at midnight. I whistled

apprehensively to myself then went to join my jubilant team-mates as we prepared to receive the championship trophy that was helicoptering its way to Dens Park as we danced.

* * *

Under a sky filled with stars and the benevolent face of a bright full moon I shimmied over the outer wall of Dens and jogged over to the pitch. There was ample celestial illumination to let me see that the gaffer was already in the centre circle. He had company.

"Mr Lloyd George, so pleased to see you again. Congratulations on winning football championship."

Dong Chu was dressed in a white karate outfit and a head band.

"Pleased to see you too, Dong Chu. And thank you."

The gaffer offered a hand and I shook it.

"Cheers fur comin' up, Lloyd. How wiz the perty?"

After sinking several bottles of champagne in the dressing room the team had headed to Frews in order to keep the celebrations going. Most of them were still there.

"It was grand, gaffer. We raised a few glasses to you."

Our Tartan Special tributes were as heart-felt and fitting as any homage could be.

"How's Jocky getting on?"

The monster had been downing pints with the thirst of a man discovering an oasis in the middle of the Sahara.

"He's having a great time. I think he was on pint number 26 when I left."

The gaffer looked as proud as punch.

"That's meh boy."

The ground was deserted, a stark contrast to the scenes that had taken place earlier. I could still hear a faint trace of the roar that went up when Harry had lifted the trophy aloft.

"Any sign of McCracken yet?"

As if catching a scent on the wind his nostrils twitched as he tilted his head to the side and narrowed his eyes.

"That's him here now."

Right on cue a yell came from the direction of the tunnel.

"What have we here, Jocky? Too scared to come on your own were you?"

The sound of the gaffer cracking his knuckles could probably have been heard in the tipi. Bob McCracken strolled over as casually as he would when negotiating the fairway of the Old Course. He sneered at Jocky before turning to me and chuckling to himself.

"And I suppose it's only fitting that the fool who had no idea how big a role he played in his old friend's downfall is here to suffer alongside him."

The gaffer and I exchanged quizzical looks.

"You never did figure it out, did you, Lloyd? Did you think it was mere coincidence that 'Charmaine' was your masturbatory fantasies come to life? It's almost as if someone was monitoring your internet usage, don't you think?"

What the fuck?

"And didn't it strike you as odd that the Dundee United support were aware of your extra-curricular activities with ancient hags from god-forsaken working men's clubs? It's almost as if someone was reading your text messages and was given enough evidence to go digging a little deeper. The East Angus Arabs supporters club were overjoyed to be made aware of your affairs prior to the derby."

I took my phone out my pocket. The phone McCracken had given me the day I signed for the club. Realisation dawned. He'd had it tapped from the start.

"I must say Lloyd, most entertaining of all were the pathetic, pleading texts you sent what you thought to be your girlfriend in the wake of her departure. I haven't been so amused since Baroness Thatcher wiped out the mining community. Not many calls from family or friends though, eh? No wonder you were so desperate to latch on to this pathetic Neanderthal."

The dirty fucking bastard. I dropped the phone and made a move for him. The gaffer held me firmly in place with the grip of one strong hand on my arm.

"Hiya Boaby! Hiya pal! Question fur ye, cunto: wha's in cherge here? You ken the score. Square-go; if eh win you get tae fuck, if you win eh get tae fuck."

McCracken extended his hand. Jocky accepted it. A gentleman's agreement was struck.

"You must understand, Jocky, that I'm not one for physical confrontation. It's a tad brutish for my tastes, a little unseemly for a gentleman of my calibre. As such I'll be represented in this "square go" by some affiliates more used to the rough and tumble of violence."

I spotted the first stewards emerge from the Shankley end of the ground. Around a dozen of them appeared through the vomitories leading to the stand's concourse. Another dozen came through the gaps in the corrugated iron wall at the top of the Derry and made their way down the stairs. More still came from the Main Stand and, when I turned round, another dozen of their hi-viz colleagues were clambering out of the Bobby Cox. A noose of yellow jackets tightened around us; it was a trap from which there was no escape.

"Outsourcing, gentlemen. A truly beautiful concept."

The gaffer seemed nonplussed by this highly threatening development, and in fact appeared to be rather pleased.

"Good. These cunts huv been needin' telt fur months now. The mair the merrier."

I was less enthused, and tried my level best to keep the fear that was rising like bile from my stomach from accenting my words as I spoke my mind.

"Gaffer, we've got absolutely no chance here. There must be 50 of them."

He turned to me, and without a care in the world said, "It's nae bather, pal. Ain't no thang but a Dee thang. Check this oot."

He plucked his mobile phone from the pocket of his tracksuit bottoms, tapped his fingers on the touch screen and held it at arm's length. A powerful beam of light emitted from the screen and projected an image onto the night sky. It was a circle within which lay the silhouette of a woman preparing to throw a dart.

"Gaffer, what in the name of fuck is that meant to be?"

He looked at me like I was daft.

"Ken Batman? Ken the bat signal? This is the Frews ladies' darts team version."

"It's what?"

"It's the Frews ladies' darts team signal! They'll see it and come runnin' doon the road tae help oot, aye."

"Are they expecting to see this? Have you spoken to them about it?"

The look of confusion that fell upon him told me everything I needed to know. After giving the matter due consideration he switched the light off and mumbled, "Shite."

McCracken enjoyed the moment immensely.

"You're a buffoon, Jocky. This franchise is so much better off without you. It'll be so much better off without this God-forsaken stadium and city, too. With you and your lapdog here out of the picture it'll be relegated and St Andrews-bound by Christmas. The delay is regrettable and will certainly cost us some traction in the Korean market, but the pleasure of watching the two of you suffer a lingering, painful end will act as some form of compensation."

The impenetrable ring of stewards now stood but 10 feet away.

"Given that you've surprisingly turned out to be a reasonably valuable commodity it's perhaps slightly unfortunate that you're destined to suffer the same fate as your friend here, Lloyd. But you shall be judged by the company you keep. You won't be missed; Scottish football is littered with young talents whose foolish lifestyle choices saw them vanish off the radar."

The fear gave way to a surge of anger. All of a sudden, and despite having never thrown a punch since Primary Seven, I was ready to fight.

As was Dong Chu. He suddenly burst into life by grabbing

a set of nunchucks from a hidden pocket in his outfit and performed a brief but highly energetic demonstration that suggested he was more than capable of using them.

"Fuckin' Dong Chu in the hoose, check you oot ya wee cunt! Eh didnae ken ye were a ninja, pal."

Dong Chu swung the nunchucks round his head and finally came to rest in a defensive stance.

"Indeed Mr Jocky. Interpreter, scrotum washer, toilet attendant and ninja. I am also a skilled tailor should you ever require made-to-measure clothing."

"Could dae wi' a new pair o' trackie bottoms actually, pal, that'd be fuckin' teckle."

He let off a burst of high-pitched laughter as he slapped the nunchucks over each shoulder before returning to his static-but-ready stance.

We formed a "circle the wagons" three-man position, back-to-back and facing our enemy. The stewards were big, tough men and looked bloodthirsty. I cocked my fists knowing I'd take at least one of them out before they swamped us.

I feared it was the end. There was no way of winning, and no way out. I looked up into the night for what I thought would be the last time and saw a meteorite streak across the sky. A shooting star. I closed my eyes and made a wish.

The faint buzz in the distance signalled that it would come true almost immediately.

* * *

There was a small object hovering in the sky above the Bobby Cox, forming a black speck against the pale light of the full moon. The whirring of what sounded like a small engine grew louder as the object drew nearer. It triggered a memory from months back, from the morning after my first night in the tipi. I'd heard this before. Whatever it was, it had delivered me bacon rolls that morning.

"Here comes the cavalry," said the gaffer, smiling as he relaxed from his defensive stance.

McCracken and the stewards could hear it too, and they stopped and looked round to see what was happening.

Music started playing, and appeared to be coming from whatever it was that was approaching from above. After a few bars I recognised it, and Bob McCracken did too.

"Is that... is that Ride of the Valkyries? What the hell is going on here?"

There are few pieces of music so dramatic. The small object was above the main stand roof now, descending on a flight path that would see it land right by us. The stewards were shifting nervously, the fear I'd felt the first time this thing had approached very much apparent in them.

My eyes strained to make out what the incoming object was. It was white... it looked very much like a cat...

It was Wee Jocky.

It was Wee Jocky flying a fucking jetpack.

"Boaby, if you're a religious cunt it's time tae say some fuckin' prayers, because you're aboot tae say "hiya pal!" tae whichever sky fairy ye believe in."

McCracken was rubbing his eyes and mumbling, "A cat? A flying cat? In the name of all that is holy..."

All eyes were upon the flying feline. The stewards were backing away, leaving Bob McCracken standing alone, dumbstruck by the sight before him.

It would be the last thing he would ever see.

Wee Jocky accelerated and came hurtling in on McCracken like a bolt of white lightning. His little hind legs kicked back and forth until one of them connected with McCracken's head and took it clean off his shoulders. It rolled back and landed at the gaffer's feet. He scooped it up with his right foot and started playing keepie-up.

"Any cunt fancy a gemme o' fehve n' a boot? Lloyd, you're in goal."

He volleyed the head at me and, in a marked improvement on the last time I'd played, I caught it. Bob McCracken's severed head looked up at me with horror in the eyes that saw no more. I screamed and threw it over my head. As McCracken's body slumped to the turf his head rolled toward the stewards, who to a man screamed, turned and fled. They ran right into the Frews ladies' darts team.

"Yasssssss! Lloyd, eh fuckin' telt ye that signal would work! They lads ken the score. Eh'm haein' a fuckin' teckle night here."

As the ladies, along with Dong Chu, started beating the living hell out the stewards the gaffer grabbed McCracken's head and put it atop his own.

"Lloyd, check meh new hat – it's auld Boaby's heid!"

The gaffer swaggered over as happy as a Texan who'd just bought the Stetson JR was shot in off eBay.

"Let's see now. We're on the pitch at Dens under a full moon wi' the Karate Kid, a corpse, six lesbian darts players knocking fuck oot fifty stewards and eh'm wearin' some cunt's heid as a hat."

He looked wistfully to the sky.

"And so Vince Mennie's prophecy has finally come to pass."

The ladies had taken out more than half the stewards before the gaffer intervened.

"A'right lads, that'll dae. Any mair knockin' fowk oot and ye'll be using it as an excuse next time eh win at arm wrestling."

"Next time? Ye huvnae won a match yet ya auld spazzy."

He turned to me and twirled his finger at his temple.

Walking through the bodies writhing in pain on the turf he made a speech to the yellow-jacketed scourge of fans' enjoyment at Dens.

"Stewards of Dens Park, hear this: you are free. McCracken's reign of terror is over. No longer must you act like a savage for cash-in-hand payments nae cunt declares to the broo. No longer must you let the beast within you free because fowk are drunk and haein' a maist teckle time watchin' the match."

Wee Jocky flew alongside me at head height and offered me a nod in greeting.

"The futba fan is not the enemy. Welcome him to oor ground.

Respect him. Let him hae a fly smoke in the bog at halftime and dinnae gie a fuck if he stands in the back row when there's nae cunt unable tae see behind him anyway. Ensure he enjoys himself and returns next time his team play here. Go home, stewards. You are free."

Just when things couldn't have gotten any more outrageous or surreal, the cat started talking.

"See if any cunt mentions what happened tae nae-heid here? Big Jocky here will be adding tae his hat collection."

"Get them telt, wee aine."

"Fuckin' right, big aine."

Good fucking grief.

The ladies escorted the limping, injured stewards out the ground. I looked round at McCracken's body.

"So, what's the plan for the corpse then?"

Talk about words I'd never expected to hear myself say.

"We'll just ditch it in the wilderness at the back o' the Derry. Nae cunt'll ever find it."

Wee Jocky chimed in, "The Marrs used tae dae it a' the time, it's nae bather."

"But what will we say when people realise McCracken's missing?"

The gaffer adjusted his "hat" to sit at a jaunty angle as he insisted I shouldn't worry about it.

"We'll no' say fuck all. Nae cunt'll miss him anyway."

I had my doubts, but I was in no mood to let sense prevail whilst speaking to a man wearing a human head as a hat and a flying, talking cat who'd killed a man a couple of minutes ago.

The four of us took an arm and a leg each and hauled McCracken up through the Derry and out the back of it. As we did so, the gaffer rummaged through his pockets. I thought he might have been trying to remove personal details to prevent identification of the body but, typically, Jocky had more important things on his mind.

"Fuckin' kent it!" he cried as he dropped the leg he was carrying and triumphantly waved a small bottle of white correction fluid. "Fuckin' kent he hud meh Tippex!" The gaffer stepped back and volleyed the remains of Bob McCracken square in the nuts as we held him in place. His suspicions confirmed and revenge extracted, the gaffer took up his leg again.

A "high birdie fly" later and Bob McCracken's headless corpse was left to return to the earth.

"Any cunt fancy headin' doon the toon?" asked Wee Jocky. "Dong Chu and m'self are awa' tae fire in aboot the poontang in the Vu, aye. No' sure you'll get in dressed like that right enough, Dong Chu, but eh'll hae a word wi' the boy on the door."

"Ach nah, eh'm done in. You lads fire on though, eh'll see ye back at the hoose."

With a polite bow and a "See ye efter, cunto" respectively Dong Chu and Wee Jocky made haste for the city centre and the Deja Vu nightclub. I feared for the female clientele.

"Well Lloyd, all's well that ends well."

I spluttered, "Gaffer, you're wearing Bob McCracken's head as a hat. His headless corpse in in a bush down that hill somewhere."

He looked to the stars and gave a content sigh.

"Like eh said, Lloyd: all's well that ends well."

We went back into the Derry and took a seat.

* * *

"Good view, eh pal?"

It was indeed. It was nice to see the pitch we'd won the league on from the vantage point of the supporters who had roared us on to the end.

"Aye, it's not bad, gaffer."

He turned to me and said, "It's Jocky, Lloyd. Eh'm no' yer gaffer any mair. Meh mates call iz Jocky."

Though delighted by the fact he considered me a friend, the realisation that he was right about not being manager hit me hard.

It didn't seem right somehow. He was as much part of things here as the goalposts, floodlights or dugouts. But it went beyond being part of the furniture – Jocky lived and breathed Dundee. He had fought for its very existence, for its soul. He was its soul.

"What are your plans, Jocky?"

He seemed pleased to hear me call him by his first name, but shrugged before responding.

"No' sure, pal. Gonnae miss this place, that's fur sure."

He leaned forward, balancing his elbows on his thighs and running his fingers through his moustache. As he cast his eye around the ground they misted over as the memories of days gone by flooded his head.

"Eh'll miss it mair than eh can tell ye, Lloyd."

He sniffed and wiped his eyes. I put an arm round his shoulder and gave him a little squeeze. He turned and smiled in gratitude.

"You never know, Jocky. With McCracken gone things will have to change over the summer. Maybe your time here isn't over. Never say never, cunto."

He spluttered, "Cunto? What sehze are yer futba baits, Lloyd?"

"Size 9."

"Dinnae get too fuckin' big fur them ya cheeky cunt."

We laughed together then fell into a comfortable silence.

"Lloyd, eh'm affy proud o' ye, son. Ye became a great player and a great pal. Thank you."

It was my turn to well up.

"I'm the one who should be thanking you. You've taught me more than you know."

He looked like he knew exactly what he'd taught me, which he probably did.

"Meh pleasure, pal." He patted me on the knee. "That's what eh wiz there fur, ken?"

He'd done a fine job on all fronts. I couldn't have asked for a better manager or friend. We sat for a while longer thinking our thoughts.

"Lloyd, as a matter o' interest, what team is it you support again?"

I got the 'M' of 'Manchester United' out before I stopped myself. The answer I'd given him on my first visit to the Fairmuir was no longer correct. I hadn't thought about them for ages and didn't even know where they were in the league. I hadn't realised it until then but my allegiances had switched from a team I liked watching on TV to one I fucking loved. When I'd kissed the badge less than 12 hours earlier it was no empty gesture to appease the supporters. I had meant it.

"I live in Dundee, I play for Dundee and I just had the time of my life lifting a trophy with Dundee. Who do you think I support?"

He stroked his chin and replied, "United?"

A broad grin broke across both our faces.

"Funny cunt."

He got up to leave, so I joined him in standing.

"Second and final question, Lloyd, and one eh want ye tae think aboot before ye answer, is this: wha's in cherge here?"

It was a question there had only ever been one answer to. Or so I thought. Given everything that had happened, given everything that he'd done for me, I now realised I had been wrong all along. Using the instincts of the promising young striker I'd become under his tutelage I responded with conviction "I'm in cherge here, Jocky."

He puffed out his chest, jutted his chin out and tapped his fist against his heart. I mirrored his movements exactly, and we embraced like the supporters who'd stood in this very spot earlier in the day. A couple of guys who love their team and love proper futba.

Without another word he slipped on his jetpack, hit the ignition and flew out the Derry. After a quick lap of honour round the pitch he flew off over the roof of the Main Stand and out of sight.

See ye Jocky, see ye pal.

ACKNOWLEDGEMENTS

Huge thanks and big love to Grant Hill, Sean Hamilton, Chris Brookmyre, Dave MacDonald and everyone at Pie and Bovril, Calum and Fraser Brownlee, Ryan Law, Ross Cargill, Bob McDevitt, Mum and Dad, Anna Day, Chris Collins, Linda Isles, Vicki Birmingham, Fraser MacDonald, Catrin Jeans, the Tin Roof Arts Collective, Gordon Craig, and last, but certainly not least, Fiona Morrison.

ACKNOWLEDGMENTS

DVD EXTRAS

JOCKY'S PERFECT STOVIES RECIPE

MIND BUMPIN' INTAE Gordon Ramsey aine time at the Fairmuir. He wiz like that, "How do you make those incredible fucking stovies, Jocky?" Eh says, "Watch yer fuckin' mooth you ya chef cunt, there's wummin present." Eh didnae tell him how tae dae it, 'cos he's a prick, but eh'll tell youse. It's nae bather.

Tae mak' the auld Jon Bons Jocky-style ye need the followin' ingredients:

- *Corned doag.*
- *Tatties.*
- *Ingins.*
- *Special.*
- *Me.*

Now ye'll be thinkin', "Fuck sake, Jock, eh kin git the corned doag and a' that nae bather, but you? What dae ye mean beh that?" Hud yer fuckin' hoarses and eh'll tell ye, aye.

Right, head doon the butchers and say, "Hola, cunto. Gies a' yer corned doag." When the boy says "all of it?" say, "fuckin' right ya cunt." Yer aimin' tae leave wi' a block the size o' a small car. Teckle!

Right, fire intae the greengrocers and say, "You ya wee cunt, three sacks o' tatties and 50 ingins, pronto." Dinnae tak' any shite aff greengrocers. Or electricians. Or any cunt, really.

Anyway, next stop is the kerry oot shop fur a case or twa o' the Special. That's the gemme.

Right, get back tae the hoose and get the cauldron oot. Ye kin use a pot, aye, but tae dae it Jocky-style ye need the kind o' cauldron cannibal tribes cook uppity honky God-boys in. Fill it up wi' water and crank up the heat – yase petrol if necessary.

Get the chainsaw oot. You fuckin' heard iz – the chainsaw. Start that bad boy up and get battered intae the corned doag, tatties and ingins. If ye hae bairns mibbe gie them a wee shot; they hae tae learn sometime, ken?

Right, hurl a'hin in the pot. No' the bairns ya daft cunt, the chopped-up grub. Get an oar and start stirring like fuck.

Get the Special oot. Open mibbee a dozen or so cans and chuck them in the pot. Dinnae pour it in, just throw the entire can in there. Get back on that oar and stir some mair.

Right, here's whaur shit gets real. When eh mak' stovies, eh get in the pot and hae a wee bath. Fuckin' strip aff, stick the goggles on, stick the rubber arm bands on (safety is paramount, cunto) and get in the cauldron. If it's big enough hae a wee sweem. Big Jock's a backstroke man, but each tae their aine.

Right, get oot the pot before ye boil yersel' alehve.

Beh the time ye tan the rest o' the Special it's pure ready, aye.

Bon appétit, cunto.

JOCKY'S TAP FEHVE TAPS-AFF TUNES

Beastie Boys – So Watch 'cha Want

Yassssssssssss! The B-Boys are fuckin' teckle! Mind bein' oot meh nut at MCA's funeral and sayin', "Here Mike D, wha's in cherge here? Ye needin' Big Jocky tae step up and replace the deid aine? Eh kin manage the Dees and be a Beastie Boy tae like, it's nae bather. Pure ken a' the words n' ahin, aye." Boy didnae appreciate it, which is fair doos. Probably shouldnae o' asked when they were still lowerin' the body intae the grave.

Kylie & Jason – Especially For You

Maist cunts think they twa are singin' aboot each other in this aine, but they're baith singin' aboot me. Met them at a perty in Lochee aine time. Crazy night. The details o' what happened are mair shocking than Jim Robinson's death scene in Neighbours, so eh'll say nae mair aboot it.

Rhythm is Rhythm – Strings Of Life

Derrick May's an auld pal o' mine. Boy yased tae play dominoes at the Fairmuir. Him, Kevin Saunderson and Juan Atkins would fly ower fae Detroit every Tuesday tae play league matches. Good cunts. Eh introduced them tae Tam McGinty and aboot 20 minutes later techno wiz invented. Tam wiz dodgin' the TV licence cunts at the time and didnae want any publicity, so the Fairmuir Four became the Belleville Three.

NWA – Straight Outta Compton

These cunts ripped me right aff wi' this. Eh wiz oot the back o' the Fairmuir smokin' doobs wi' Jeanie McKay when this black boy asks if he could hae a puff. Eh says, "Nae bather pal. What brings ye tae the clubbie?" Boy says, "Muthafuckin' bingo, yo." So anyway, we got bletherin' and he says he wiz a rapper. Eh says, "Me tae! Check this oot," and started bustin' oot a tune me and Jeanie were workin' on called

Straight Oot o' Dundee. The boy said it wiz fuckin' teckle then disappeared again. A week later NWA hit the headlines wi' a tune that wiz AFFY fuckin' familiar. If yer readin' this, Ice Cube, it's punch in the fuckin' pus time if ye ever show face at the Fairmuir bingo night again.

Hector Nicol – Up Wi' The Bonnets

End o' the night classic. Mind bein' in Ibiza at thon Space wi' auld Walzo. Sasha wiz playin' and every cunt wiz haein a rare time. It wiz just aboot the end o' the night so eh went up tae the DJ booth and goes, "Here Sasha, John Digweed's gettin' a hiding in the bogs aye." He went chargin' aff tae save his pal, leavin' me and Walzo tae close the set. Walzo put on some progressive hoose pish fae Sasha's record box, and eh finished it aff beh drappin' Up Wi' the Bonnets. Place went mental. Eh've been banned fae the island ever since. Teckle!

JOCKY EMBRACES THE INTERNET

The following is a first-person piece that appeared on the Pie and Bovril website after Jocky was drafted in as official "cunt in cherge".

"Hiya Peh & Bovril! Hiya pal!

Yer probably thinkin', "Fuck sake, man, here's Big Jocky; what's this teckle cunt daein here?" The answer is: Runnin' the fuckin' show, cunto.

Eh wiz in the Fairmuir waitin' meh turn at the gloryhole when Tam McGinty piles in the bog and goes, "Here Jock, three Paisley cunts just turned up askin' tae see ye." Eh wiz gonnae tell him tae get the bats and futba socks filled wi' snooker ba's oot, cuz last time eh wiz in Paisley me and Archie Knox got in a bit o' bather.

The pair o' us ended up in a tag team championship wrestlin' match wi' Tony Fitzpatrick and Campbell Money in the centre circle o' Love Street at half fehve in the moarnin efter a wee post-match swally got oot o' hand. The match ended in slightly controversial fashion when Archie DDT'd Tony, got the three-count then shat on his mouser.

Eh didnae see much wrang wi' it, but they cunts swore revenge. But then eh remembered the 1987 Cup Final, thought fuckin' hud that McLean ya cannae-win-at-Hampden cunt, and decided tae throw caution tae the wind and let them in.

It wiz three weird-lookin' cunts, which, given they were fae Paisley, wisnae particularly surprisin'.

The first aine wiz a right wide-o. Reynard somethin' or other. Called iz a "buckled leftie cunt". Eh pulled meh toby oot and says, "Eh'll buckle your fuckin' arse ye miserable Weegie bastard." That wiz him oot the door and in aine o' they white taxis wi' the flashin' lights that drap ye aff at Ninewells, aye.

The next aine wiz a'right. Quiet fella wha went beh the name o' Captain Sensible. Didnae get much oot him, he wiz too busy knittin' a jumper he wiz gonnae send Daniel O'Donnell fur his Christmas. Apparently he does aine every year.

The leader o' the squad wiz called Div. Baldy fella wi' a *Bring Back Bergerac* t-shirt on. He says, "Ye mibbe ken meh website, big aine." Eh says, "www.blackdudespumpingfatwhiteburds.com? www.jimmcleanisbiblejohn.org?" He says it was this Peh & Bovril kerry on, and he wiz needin' some cunt tae come in and spice it up a bit.

Now, eh'm an auld cunt wha minds the days before this futba forum pish. It used tae be aboot the fanzines, ken? *The Absolute Gemme* wiz a good aine. So wiz that aine Danny McGrain did called *Check ma Beard by the way Big Man*. As a matter o' fact Big Jocky here did aine tae, the short-lived *Get United Telt*. It wiz just a list o' a' the United players, their full addresses and a list o' suggestions as tae how they could get telt if ye fancied payin' them a wee visit. Fur example, eh mentioned some cunt might want tae hunt Davie Dodds wi' a blunderbuss, or try and burn the cheating Arab bastard right oot o' Paul Hegarty. The polis turned up at the door and says, "Fuck sake Jock, ye cannae dae that, ken? It'll take mair than fire tae change Heggie's ways."

But it's a' different now, eh? Every cunt's got an opinion and a forum tae mak' it heard. Given the nick o' some o' the monglords contributing tae this place eh'm no' entirely convinced it's such a good idea, ken?

Anyway, that's me runnin' the show here. Expect changes, like a dedicated '*Dundee Fuckin' Rules*' forum and that wee shite fae Greenock tae end up gettin' a maist appropriate full Viking funeral on the Clyde beh the end o' the week. Eh'll be back again next week tae tell ye a wee story or twa aboot yer new gaffer.

Until then, question fur ye, internet cunto: Wha's in cherge here?"

COMING IN 2014

CLUBBED TO DEATH
Grant Hill

TWO MEN. ONE DREAM. NO CLUE...

Andy Brennan feels fate dealt him a bad hand. Trapped in a job he hates, he can pinpoint exactly where things began to go wrong. It was when Melody Maker closed down.

When Andy's father suddenly dies of a lifelong Scottish diet, his grieving son decides it's time to make his mark on the world and create his own musical utopia.

So he and his brother-in-law Cornelius, an eternal opponent of common sense, buy a nightclub. But not just any nightclub. One in a small post-industrial Scottish city. With a highly suspect safety record. That has never made a profit. And keeps shutting down and re-opening under a new name. And during the worst economic downturn since the 1930s.

But Cornelius has somehow discovered the world's greatest undiscovered disc spinner – the soon-to-be-famous DJ Quantum – and identified that structural investment, refurbishment etc all play second fiddle to buying the world's biggest mirrorball.

If you build it, they will come. Provided by "they" you mean organised crime syndicates, an adverse local press, injury-prone DJs, narcoleptic ticket collectors, pseudo-intellectual bouncers and borderline-sex-pest barmen, that is.

Welcome to Club Quantum, where mind-melting music expands horizons every night like a demented cross between the Hacienda and Haight-Ashbury. But round the corner from the bus station in Dundee.

A new publishing firm dedicated to producing comedy books written by witty authors for readers not afraid to laugh out loud wherever they happen to be.

We're not trying to reinvent the wheel – we just want to make people laugh.

Literature doesn't need to be serious and pretentious to be enjoyable and we firmly believe there is a need for comic fiction.

Yeah, books can make us cry, think and question the world as well, but comedy is an art form in itself and we want to discover and nurture writers with the ability to leave readers doubled over with laughter.

An important point of principle is that neither the reader nor the writer should be ripped off. None of our publications will ever appear in prohibitively expensive hardback format just to wring a few more quid out of loyal customers (should we ever get any) and all our books will be priced to ensure inclusivity while properly rewarding authors for their hard work and creativity.

For more info visit:
www.tecklebooks.co.uk

Or contact:
grant@tecklebooks.co.uk